Saving Her Highland Traitor

Time to Love a Highlander Series
Book Five

by Maeve Greyson

Text by Maeve Greyson
Cover by Dar Albert

Dragonblade Publishing, Inc. is an imprint of Kathryn Le Veque Novels, Inc.
P.O. Box 23
Moreno Valley, CA 92556
ceo@dragonbladepublishing.com

Produced in the United States of America

First Edition November 2022
Trade Paperback Edition

The characters and events portrayed in this book are fictitious. Any similarity to real persons, living or dead, is purely coincidental and not intended by the author.

ARE YOU SIGNED UP FOR DRAGONBLADE'S BLOG?

You'll get the latest news and information on exclusive giveaways, exclusive excerpts, coming releases, sales, free books, cover reveals and more.

Check out our complete list of authors, too!

No spam, no junk. That's a promise!

Sign Up Here

www.dragonbladepublishing.com

Dearest Reader;

Thank you for your support of a small press. At Dragonblade Publishing, we strive to bring you the highest quality Historical Romance from some of the best authors in the business. Without your support, there is no 'us', so we sincerely hope you adore these stories and find some new favorite authors along the way.

Happy Reading!

CEO, Dragonblade Publishing

Additional Dragonblade books by Author Maeve Greyson

Once Upon a Scot Series
A Scot of Her Own (Book 1)
A Scot to Have and to Hold (Book 2)
A Scot To Love and Protect (Book 3)

Time to Love a Highlander Series
Loving Her Highland Thief
Taming Her Highland Legend
Winning Her Highland Warrior
Capturing Her Highland Keeper
Saving Her Highland Traitor

Highland Heroes Series
The Guardian
The Warrior
The Judge
The Dreamer
The Bard
The Ghost
A Yuletide Yearning (Novella)
Love's Charity (Novella)

Also from Maeve Greyson
Guardian of Midnight Manor

Chapter One

Edinburgh, Scotland
May 2022

It made her heart hurt. Mila Carthson turned away and busied herself with the cardboard box of snacks and extra brochures, trying her best to honor her godson's wishes. Robbie hated being watched whenever he struggled with something an average fifteen-year-old boy should be able to do. The poor lad was so small for his age. Skinny as a stick. Barely four feet tall, and that was when wearing his dress shoes with inch-thick heels. Bless him. When bullies weren't teasing him for being awkward and brainy, they taunted him by saying he belonged in nursery school.

"Do ye want the cooler for the waters filled to the top?" he called out.

"Aye." She added a knowing wink. "But leave room for a bit of ice. Ye know how Americans like their drinks cold."

"Aww, feck!"

She ducked her head to hide a smile and struggled to assume a stern tone. "Language, young man."

"Sorry," he said, not sounding sorry at all. "But I already jammed both ice bags into the food coolers. Under the egg and cress sandwiches. Ye know how fast they turn when it's a warm day."

He made a fair point, but the last time she'd provided unchilled drinks to an American group, they left her a string of nasty reviews on every tourism site listing her as a guide. "The water must be cooled as well. Either unload and reload it or run and fetch more ice. The choice is yers."

Robbie's snorting huff made his druthers clear, but he didn't argue. Instead, he stormed down the lane in the direction of the corner market. Apparently, he had chosen not to unload and start fresh. Just as well. That would give her time to stow their backpacks and other necessities in the overhead rack. That chore always frustrated him because he couldn't reach it without standing on a seat.

The cell phone in the back pocket of her jeans dinged. She hurried to check the text. It couldn't be the market. She still had credit on their books. More than enough to cover another bag or two of ice. Or had he crossed paths with those boys again? Her jaw involuntarily tightened. She would skin those young brutes alive if they didn't leave her Robbie alone.

The contact name across the screen put her at ease. Cari. From the hotel where today's group lodged. Then she noticed the emojis. The text contained their agreed-upon signal for intel on tourists before she and Robbie picked them up. Red faces with a black band of curse-word symbols across the mouth. Ten times.

"All of them?" Still frowning at the screen, Mila typed ten question marks and sent it.

The phone dinged three times in rapid succession with the words *ALL OF THEM*, followed by endless exclamation points.

She blew out a heavy sigh. "Lovely." According to Cari, every member of today's group was an intolerable arse. "Robbie will charm them," she lied to herself while stuffing the phone back into her pocket. However, Cari was never wrong about ill-natured customers, and that message flagged this group as a high alert. It was doubtful even Robbie's sweetness could overcome the snarling of ten cursey-faces. All she could do was hope.

"Got the ice," the charmer in question said as he thumped it into the drink chest. While adding bottles of water, he glanced up and pulled a face. "And Gunner asked about ye. Again." He rolled his eyes, then faked a gag.

"Gunner is a nice man," she chided while inwardly celebrating she hadn't been the one to go for the ice.

"The bloke needs a bath, and I heard he killed all three of his wives." He forced the overfilled cooler lid shut, sat on it, and bounced for good measure. "Poisoned'm and keeps their bodies in the meat locker in the basement."

She had heard the same and was still amazed at the ridiculous gossip some folks repeated. "He does smell a bit, but do ye not think it would be discovered if he kept their bodies at the market? The butcher's lad would surely see them when he delivered the day's meat."

Robbie shrugged, bounced again, then frowned down at the cooler. "Going to have to take a few bottles out. Reckon twenty will be enough? Long day on the road, and ye said there's ten of them. Twelve counting us."

"I put thermoses of tea as well as canisters of water in our packs along with our lunch. That leaves two waters for each guest." She helped him gather the excess bottles and carried them back inside. "If we run short, we can always get more at Stirling. Ranald owes me."

"Better step lively, then," he warned. "Or we'll be late for pickup. Cari sent anything about this lot yet?"

She decided to show him the text and let him draw his own conclusions.

"Bloody hell."

"Robbie!" Even though she agreed, every time the boy swore, his mother's disapproving spirit nudged her conscience. Dearest Tana, best friend and taken from this world much too soon, never tolerated coarse language from anyone. "What is with ye today? Did ye have another row with those mean boys?"

"I may not look like it, but I am fifteen now." He puffed out his narrow chest to stress the point. "That is how teenagers talk, ye ken?"

"Take these and get on the bus, aye? We will discuss it later." She handed him two more bundles of brochures and shooed him onward. She understood the intent of his bravado but wasn't sure how to handle it. One way or another, there had to be a way to help him manage the hand life had dealt him and come out on top. She understood his struggles. Introverted to the point of dreaming of a life on a deserted island, she still fought against skittering away from situations that made her uncomfortable. She did much better now than she used to do. He had to learn to press on and manage his insecurities, just as she had.

She locked up and hurried after him, taking an appreciative sniff of the new-vehicle aroma that permeated the bus. This first tour of the season would chase away that clean, never-sat-upon upholstery fragrance. A shame, really. She loved that new-auto fragrance. As she buckled in, she adjusted the mirror that enabled her to keep an eye on her passengers. "All set?"

Robbie gave her a thumbs-up from the seat directly behind her where he minded the coolers and snacks. "*Ad astra per aspera.*"

She arched a brow and waited, knowing a translation was forthcoming. The scamp knew she didn't understand a word of Latin.

With the wisdom of an old soul glinting in his dark eyes, he lifted both hands and smiled. "To the stars through difficulties."

"Well said, my dearest brat." She started the engine and turned into the back street that led to the hotel. "Maybe we'll get yer results in the post today. Think so?"

"I told ye they are fine. Ye are a much better teacher than the ones at school." His tone went cold and flat. Like always whenever he spoke of his education. "And even if they are not—which I doubt—I willna go back there. Not for nothing."

"I wouldna make ye," she promised. As his godmother and legal guardian since the car accident that took his parents, she had done her best to protect and defend him. But the school had sided with the parents of the bullies who made Robbie's life miserable. Never again. Nonetheless, even though she considered herself a well-educated, intelligent woman, homeschooling this advanced lad was a challenge. Half the time, he taught her the material rather than the other way around. Except for history. On that subject, she always bested him.

The rhythmic swish of the windshield wipers turned to a squeaky drag as the rain lessened. Thank goodness. With the visitors already grumpy, they needed at least a wee bit of sunshine to make the day better. She spotted a group milling about at the back of the place as she waited for oncoming traffic to pass.

"They're already outside." She turned the minibus into the hotel's large parking lot. "Remember Cari's text, lad. Turn on yer charm, aye?"

"I dinna think I have that much," he said while stretching to eye their guests. "Ye sure about this bunch?"

"They have already paid."

"Into the breach, then."

Ten ladies, all exhibiting varying levels of grumpiness, waited beneath the canopy at the rear of the Old Town Hostelry.

"They look pure, dead miserable," Robbie said as Mila brought the minibus to a halt.

"That they do." She put on her best smile and nodded for him to do the same. "But we shall make their day better, aye?"

His dubious scowl mirrored her doubts.

She opened the door and hopped out to greet them. "Good morning, ladies. Are ye ready to enjoy Scotland's many wonders?"

"I am ready for the rain to stop," said the one with the hood of her bright pink raincoat pulled so low that all that showed was her wrinkly frown.

"Och now, it's already faded to a wee mizzle. Sure to stop soon." Mila motioned them forward. "Think of it as future whisky and fresh water to sate yer thirst." Her cheeks ached with the forced smile as, one by one, they grumbled their way onto the bus. "I am Mila Carthson, and in the seat behind mine is my assistant, Robbie Abernathy. It is our pleasure to meet each of ye."

None of the ladies bothered to respond with a smile, a nod, or their names.

"If I don't sit in the front, I will vomit. You know that, Mildred." The scowling lady in the hot-pink raincoat bared her teeth at a purple-haired woman cloaked in a crinkly black poncho. While the fuchsia rain-slicker woman appeared petite and fragile, she stubbornly straddled both front seats on the right side of the bus.

Each time the poncho-clad Mildred tried to shove her way into the aisle seat, Ms. Pink pushed back and refused to let her sit.

"There are two seats, Winona. Since when does hogging two seats cure motion sickness?" Mildred pushed closer so the last pair of the group could squeeze past her, then she angled back into the center of the aisle, glaring down at her travel mate.

Unable to get past Mildred and into the driver's seat, Mila stood on the steps. "We usually rotate seats at every stop so everyone gets an opportunity to sit in front." She cast a gently shaming frown at Winona. "And everyone gets one seat. Not two."

"I have to stay in the front the whole trip or you'll be cleaning up barf." Winona shoved back her hood and jutted her powdered chin higher.

"If ye would be so kind as to scoot over so yer friend can sit, we will be on our way." Mila noticed the rest of the group seemed enthralled by the standoff, as though it was their favorite form of entertainment.

"She is not my friend, and I got here first." The woman jerked a nod and resettled her outstretched position. Tittering laughter rippled through the bus.

"Kindly shove over, Ms. Winona, or I shall have to ask ye to get off the bus and make other arrangements for a tour." Mila stared the woman down. This was not the way to start the day. While she didn't want bad reviews, she refused to tolerate such unreasonable behavior. And she also refused to be bullied. Gasps and mutterings rippled through the seniors.

"You can't talk to her like that." Mildred squared off her cloaked girth like a great black crow guarding a bit of roadkill.

"That's right," shouted someone from the back. "Customers are always right, you know!"

For the first time that morning, snarling pink lady Winona gleamed a broad smile and scooted over. "Thank you, Mildred." She twisted in the seat and waved at her supporter in the back. "Thank you, Doreen."

"You are quite welcome." After a smug, snorting huff, Mildred seated herself with a haughty flounce of her crackling black wrap.

It was going to be a very long day. Mila composed herself with a slow, deep breath, climbed into her seat, and buckled in. She flipped on her mic and announced, "We shall take a brief turn around Edinburgh and then head to Stirling."

"Turn on the air!" The barking demand came from the one called Doreen. The individual who had supported Winona earlier.

"No way! We are soaked to the skin, and it will be too cold." Mildred swiveled around and shook a finger at Doreen, who wore rhinestone-tipped glasses that made her look like an oversized beetle.

"I don't care. I am boiling back here!" Doreen rose and lumbered into the aisle as if ready to brawl.

Mila stopped the vehicle, unbuckled, and stood to face them. "I would ask that everyone remain seated while we are in motion. For safety reasons, ye ken?"

"What is that supposed to mean? *Ye ken?*" Doreen waggled her head back and forth like a cobra preparing to strike. She wrinkled her bulbous nose, making her sneer even more pronounced.

"*Ye ken* means *do ye understand?*" Mila stood her ground. "I want no one injured on our outing today."

"Afraid we might sue you?" The woman snapped her head with every word, making her sparkly glasses bounce to the end of her nose. "Because we could, you know. Rita's son is a lawyer."

The more Doreen talked, the more it confirmed that hauling this group of belligerent women back to the boarding area and refunding their money was the best choice for all concerned. "Today is entirely up to yerselves, ladies." Mila paused, struggling to keep a professional tone. "Shall we all settle in and enjoy Scotland with a bit of civility or return to the hotel? The front desk keeps several guide cards on hand. I feel certain ye could find another tour that would be more to yer liking."

Doreen's mouth twitched as though she were holding back a torrent of ill-mannered replies. But instead of spouting off, she plopped back down into her seat. Several of the others peered out the window, while a few stared down at their laps. No one made eye contact nor offered a response.

Mila refused to take this sudden shift to meekness as an answer, knowing full well the snarling beasties could return at any moment. "What do ye wish to do, ladies? Continue this tour or return to the hotel?"

Mildred waved her toward the driver's seat. "Let's go. And you can turn on the air for Doreen. We've already burned through all the other guides. You're our last resort."

"Well, isn't that lovely," Mila muttered.

Robbie unbuckled, climbed up onto the seat, and pulled two lightweight blankets down from the overhead rack. He offered them to Mildred and Winona, adding the sweetest smile as he held them out. "If ye get chilled, these will knock the air off ye." He turned and addressed the rest of the women. "If anyone else would like one, we've got one for each of ye."

"I would like one, young man," said a lady in the middle of the bus.

He pulled free another plastic-wrapped blanket, hopped down from the seat, and took it to her. "We have them cleaned after each trip and sealed like this, so ye know nothing is lurking in the cloth."

"I am sure they're quite clean." The silvery-haired woman offered a genuine smile as she opened the blanket and wrapped it around her shoulders.

Mila released the breath she held. Perhaps they could salvage the day and make it enjoyable after all. She settled in, fastened her seatbelt, and waited for Robbie to do the same. As they headed through Edinburgh, she pointed out the Royal Mile, Princes Street Gardens, the castle, and several other sites. "Our lovely Edinburgh is best enjoyed on foot," she said. "For days and days, if yer itinerary permits it."

"You try walking days and days with arthritis and a hip that needs replacing."

A glance in the mirror failed to show her the commenter, so she ignored it. But it did make her wonder why they had chosen Scotland as their vacation destination. After all, so many of the sites were best enjoyed with sturdy walking shoes and the determination to soldier on and explore.

Stirling Castle proved to be somewhat of a struggle, since the mobility car was not in service. Ramps helped in some areas, but the ladies still found fault with everything. The cobbled courtyard was too rough, the grassy areas too wet. The adapted toilets failed to suit them. Every room was too cold, too damp, overcrowded, or hot. The concessions and souvenirs were overpriced and dared to require British pounds rather than U.S. dollars. When Mila suggested they pay by credit card whenever possible because the exchange rate was usually more favorable, they stared at her as if she had sprouted a second head.

After enduring all she could stand, she ended the tour of the castle earlier than scheduled. The promise of a picnic lunch while viewing the beauty of Glencoe appeared to put a bit of spryness into the ladies.

One thing she had discovered early on was that these ten women ate more than a dozen good-sized men. Both snack boxes on the bus were emptied in the first hour. She had to send Robbie for more while she led the group around Stirling. It was about a two-hour drive to Glencoe. She prayed they had enough to keep the group pacified until lunch.

"Are there any more cookies?" Winona shook an empty wrapper at Robbie as they bounced along.

"Aye. I've got shortbreads, parlies, and some empire biscuits. Which would ye like?"

"Just pass over some of all three. Mildred will help me eat them." The woman drained her water bottle, then tossed it at him. "And more water, too."

Robbie kicked the back of Mila's seat.

She made eye contact with him in the mirror and slightly nodded for him to do as the lady asked. After all, if Ms. Winona had a mouthful of biscuits, she was less likely to complain. Mila only hoped the woman's tendency toward motion sickness had been an empty threat.

She drove along in silence, having given up on her usual informative commentary about the countryside. Sharing the history of the area had turned out to be like poking an ill-tempered bear. The seniors took it upon themselves to dispute everything she said. Never had she led such a self-proclaimed group of experts on Scottish history. So she went silent. After all, who was she to argue with Hollywood's depictions of her native country?

"Our lovely lunch setting is just up ahead, ladies." Mila sent up a prayer of thanks and made a mental note to give Robbie half the take of today's tour. The lad had saved the day and held his tongue admirably.

"I see no restaurant, no tables, or benches," Doreen said.

"There is a fine area to pull off where we can eat our lunches and admire the beauty of the Three Sisters: *Aonach Dubh*, *Beinn Fhada*, and *Gearr Aonach*." Mila gauged the murkiness of the sky.

It looked to be lightening nicely, with the sun peeking through more and more. With their blankets on the large, flat boulders overlooking the glen, surely the women would be content or at least quiet for a wee bit.

"Speak English!"

Mila clenched her teeth and forced a smile. "*Aonach Dubh* means Dark Ridge. *Beinn Fhada* is for Long Hill, and *Gearr Aonach* means Short Ridge. These peaks radiate from *Bidean nam Bian*'s ridges. But the Gaelic is more romantic. Do ye not think so?"

"No," Rita said from her seat in front of Doreen's. "I think it's confusing. Everything should be in English."

Robbie kicked the back of her seat again, but she ignored it. There was no way out of this. They were both trapped with these grumblers until Fort William. There the ladies would spend the night, then take the train back to Edinburgh.

"And here we are." Mila halted the minibus alongside the stones intended to serve as their lunch tables and seats. If the rain returned, they could easily reload everything back inside. But if there was an ounce of mercy anywhere in the universe, the rain would hold off so she and Robbie could climb to their usual perch and have a few moments of peace while the others bickered and complained over their meal.

"Here? On those rocks?" Mildred bobbed her head up and down while squinting out the rain-spattered window.

"Aye." Mila hopped up from her seat and smiled at them all. "Everyone grab yer blankets to spread across the stones. Ye will find them the perfect height for sitting. Robbie and I will bring out the sandwiches, fruit, and chips." She knew better than to call the chips *crisps*. It would only resurrect the ladies' conversation of why Scots called so many things by stupid names.

Each of the grumbly grannies shot her a withering look as they ambled past. They hitched their way down the steps, then stood scowling at the boulders.

"Why did they even come to Scotland?" Robbie whispered while helping her slide the coolers of food and drink off the bus.

"I dinna ken, but mind yer tongue." She shot a glance over her shoulder and quickly scanned the group. "They claim they canna hear, but I would lay odds they can pick up a mouse's fart clear back in the States."

Robbie laughed and nearly dropped the drink chest. "But we can still eat on our ledge, aye?"

"Definitely." With his help, she placed the food coolers on top of the largest rock and opened the lids. "I shall leave ye to it, ladies. There are egg and cress sandwiches. Corned beef and pickle. Treacle. Even some ham, cheese, and ketchup pieces, too." She grinned. "Sorry. Pieces are what we Scots call sandwiches. I am sure ye think that's silly, too." She pointed at the rest of the feast. "Fruit, chips, and wee fairy cakes in this box and nice, cool waters in the drink cooler."

All of them stared at her with upturned noses and lips quirked into snarls.

"Disgusting," came from somewhere in the back.

Mila didn't catch which one said it. And it didn't matter. She threw up her hands, unable to believe their level of ingratitude and rudeness. "This is all there is, ladies. If ye canna choose something, then ye will have to wait till we reach Fort William." She couldn't resist a bit of smugness as she added, "And ye have eaten all the snacks. So there will be nothing to nibble on during that wee jaunt of roughly thirty minutes."

That spurred a few of them forward. The rest soon joined in, halfheartedly pawing through the food. Mila fully expected a brawl to break out at any moment, like dogs scuffling for a bone.

She turned to ask Robbie to fetch their packs, only to discover he had already done it. With a big grin, he handed over hers then slung his to his shoulder.

"Are ye that hungry?" she asked, already knowing the answer.

"Nah." He took the lead. "Ready for a wee stretch of my legs and some quiet."

"Ye have done well, my fine brat. I am proud of ye."

He ducked his head. "I feel a mite sorry for them. They must be verra unhappy to be so sour all the time."

"That they must," she agreed.

"Where are you going?" Mildred shouted while shouldering her way deeper into the food chest.

Mila pointed up the ridge. "Higher ground to watch the weather. That way, we can warn ye before it hits. Dinna worry. We willna go far."

"Watch the weather?" Robbie repeated with a snort.

"Hush it or ye can eat with the ladies, ye ken?"

He grinned and continued climbing.

They forged even higher than their usual spot, putting more space between themselves and the car park below. The trying day warranted it.

"This should be good enough." Mila turned and made sure she still had a clear view of the minibus and the ladies. A prick of uneasiness made her pause and reconsider. As irritating as they were, they were seniors. What if a medical emergency occurred while she and Robbie were perched halfway up the mountain? Of course, even though she had training for minor issues, anything severe would be beyond her skills. And the ladies had survived the trip from their beloved Cobeak, Illinois, to Edinburgh, Scotland. Surely, they would be all right.

"What's wrong?" Robbie plopped his backpack onto the ground, then sat beside it.

"Nothing." She joined him and unzipped her pack. "Just checking to see if they've started brawling yet."

"I think that's how they communicate with each other," he said around a bite of sandwich. "Like when animals growl, but dinna mean anything by it."

"Ye are a wise lad." She unwrapped her egg and cress sandwich, frowning at its mangled condition. "Look at this. The ice pack smashed it flat as a griddle cake."

"It'll still eat just the same." He grinned. "Least ye can lick the squished egg off the paper."

"True enough." She poured them both a cup of tea. As she

handed him his cup, she noticed him frowning at something and turned to see. A thick bank of dark clouds, its swirls and billows flickering with lightning, was bearing down on them. The speed of it was impressive. She unleashed a frustrated groan. "Bloody hell. Look at that storm coming."

"Aye." He shoved the rest of his sandwich in his mouth and started repacking his bag. "Be here in a flash."

She did the same, squinting as the wind whipped her ponytail into a wild frenzy. She cupped her hands around her mouth and bellowed at the tour group below, "Take cover!"

With all the debris spinning about, she could hardly make out anything past an arm's length. She hoped the women heard her warning, or at least noticed the storm and got back into the bus. As she slung her pack to her shoulder, her stomach lurched as if some unseen force had punched her. A cold sweat peppered her upper lip. Wave after wave of nausea washed through her. She dropped to all fours and threw up, heaving so hard it felt like she was turning herself inside out.

Even though the wind had reached a deafening howl, she vaguely picked up on the sound of nearby retching. Robbie. Sick as well. Fighting the storm and blinding dizziness, she crawled over to him. "Robbie!"

He shook his head, then threw himself into her arms, convulsing and gagging.

She closed her eyes and held him tight. No way could they make it down the hillside. Wind and rain lashed against them, but the worst part was the awful falling sensation. The relentless storm swallowed them whole and sent them spinning down its dark gullet. At least if they died, they died together.

A terrible, high-pitched keening screamed and whistled all around. She covered Robbie's ears while tucking her head against his. Never in her twenty-eight years had she ever experienced such a raging tempest.

Once the roaring squall died, it took her a while to realize it. Nature's attack had numbed her, made her feel fuzzy-headed and not sure of anything. Rain still peppered down, but nothing like before. The sky had softened to a murky blanket of grayness. The lightning-filled blackness of the angry cloud bank had passed. She straightened but kept a tight hold on Robbie. Thankfully, both nausea and dizziness had left her.

After swiping her soaked hair out of her face, she gently patted the lad on the back. "The worst is gone. I think so, anyway. Are ye feeling any better?"

He slowly uncurled and lifted his head, squinting up into the rain. Water streamed down his face, plastering his short, dark hair to his skull. While he was still somewhat pale, she took heart at the two faint patches of pink highlighting his cheeks.

"I dinna feel sick anymore," he said. "My eggs didna taste as if they had turned. Did yers?"

"No." She pushed herself up and helped him stand. "Mine tasted fine, and if it had been food poisoning, I think it wouldha lasted longer."

"It wouldha," he said. "Mama got it once after some bad clams. She was sick for a few days."

That was the first time he had spoken about either of his parents since the auto accident, but Mila didn't draw attention to it. She merely took heart, hoping that meant he was slowly healing from their loss. She waved him forward. "We best go check on our ladies, aye?"

He made a face. "Ye know they're going to be madder than wet hens?"

"I know. But there is no avoiding it."

"Ye go first." He adjusted his pack across his shoulders and grinned. "In case they start throwing shite."

She started to correct his language, then found herself unable to speak. Even through the rising fog and mizzling rain, she could tell something was very wrong. Their surroundings were entirely too quiet. "Robbie." She swallowed hard and pointed. "The bus is gone."

He stepped up beside her, his thumbs looped through the

straps of his pack. “Uhm—so is the road. And the grumpy hens.” He stared up at her, his voice cracking with the same panic strangling her. “Where is everything?”

“I dinna ken,” she whispered, hugging him close. “I dinna ken what has happened.”

CHAPTER TWO

MILA TURNED IN a slow circle, but it did no good. No matter how long she stared at the muddy path that had replaced the paved highway, nothing made sense. Everything was gone. Tourists. Vehicles. Even the man-made boulders placed along the overlook for visitors to perch on and take photographs. Nothing remained but the glen, the mountains, and a muddy trail creased with ruts, deep divots, and prints of hoofed animals.

"It canna be a hallucination," Robbie said. He edged closer to the drop-off and peered downward. "'Tis verra rare for two people to share the same imagery." His eyes narrowed as he surveyed the scenery, then a thoughtfulness took over his expression.

Mila braced herself. Something profound was about to come out of his mouth.

"Do ye know anything about quantum mechanics?" he asked as nonchalantly as if inquiring about the time.

She rubbed her forehead, massaging it to rid herself of this head-splitting confusion. "Now is not the time for complicated discussions. I am not up to it. Just tell me what ye are thinking."

"Mind ye, I have only read a few articles here and there." He frowned at the landscape, then jabbed his thumb at the crude road. "Basically, one theory I studied proposed if we can mathematically express particulate activity in one direction, then we can mathematically express it in a diametric one as well."

She hated it when he talked over her head. "Layman's terms, please."

He shrugged. "Time travel makes sense through a quantum lens. Whatever goes forward must also be able to go backward."

What he suggested could not be true. It just could not. "Ye think we traveled through time? Backward, even?"

"That would explain everything being gone." He gave her shoulder a sympathetic pat. "Why else would the turnaround park, the road, our braw minibus, and those lovely Americans disappear like they were never here? And it sure doesna appear as though we advanced into the future."

"I canna bear the thought of such a thing. I need to sit." The sudden wobbliness in her knees threatened imminent collapse. She leaned on the lad as he helped her to a nearby boulder. Several shaky, deep breaths didn't help either. All she felt for certain was that she wished he hadn't said what she feared aloud. Never call the demon by name. If you did, it always appeared.

She sagged forward and propped her aching head between her hands. What would they do? How would they survive?

"Give me yer pack." He tugged on one of the straps. "It's about to tip ye over."

She numbly relinquished it while staring at the muddy patch of ground between her feet. A sense of shame wormed its way through the numbness of her confusion. She was the adult here, and yet Robbie was taking care of her.

"How ye can ye be so bloody calm about this?" She swallowed hard, trying to control the rising bile burning at the back of her throat. Another round of vomiting would help nothing.

He made a clumsy yet sweet attempt at rubbing her shoulder again. "I think it exciting, Mi. Think about it. A real adventure."

Mi. The endearment made her heart swell and feel even worse about falling apart in front of him. The precious bratling had always called her *Mi* ever since learning to talk.

He bent and peered up into her face. "And no feckin' eejits are here trying to make me feel guilty about being smarter than I should be or teasing me about my height."

She lifted her head and managed a quivering smile. "Ye make a convincing argument." A shiver stole across her as she looked around again. "But I am afraid, Robbie. What shall become of us?" She was thankful for the rain still showering down. It helped hide her tears. "I am so ill-equipped to take care of ye here." She paused, then shook her head. "Wherever or whenever *here* is."

"And I am glad of that too," he said quietly. "Maybe now ye will stop treating me like I am nothing more than a wee babe. I can do stuff for myself, ye know? I'm most nigh grown."

His gently accusing tone made her sit straighter. "I dinna treat ye like a baby."

"Aye. Ye do. Coddle and overprotect me because of my size and cause Mama and Da are gone." A very mature sternness settled across his soft, babyish features. "I just turned fifteen and am cursed with remembering everything I read, see, or hear. I know I am small for my age, but that doesna mean I need to be treated like a bairn."

He was right. She bowed her head. "I am sorry. Ye realize it's only because I love ye."

He grinned. "Aye. I know." After granting her a rare hug, he gave her a teasing shake. "I reckon I love ye too."

"Brat." With a determination she didn't feel, she pushed up from her rocky seat and studied the area again. If Robbie could be so brave, she had to be brave too. "'Tis definitely the Three Sisters. At least we know where we are."

He pointed at the rutted path. "Whatever this era, they travel with wagons. If we follow this road, could be we'll be lucky enough to come upon a settlement or something."

"I dinna ken if that will be lucky or not. We must be cautious." She glanced down at her soaked clothing, then pointed at him. "We are dressed for our time. Not the past." A glance up at the murky sky gave her an idea. "We should stay here, ye think? Go back up where we were and hope another storm passes through and returns us home."

Robbie's dubious squint upward didn't give her any hope. "We can try. But my guess is that storm was a fluke of nature, some unnatural fluctuation triggered by an ionic imbalance somewhere. 'Tis doubtful it will happen again this soon. Whatever it was built up a lot of energy before it went off. Remember all the lightning and how sick it made us? I dinna ken what created it, but I am more than a little certain we dinna have the means to re-create it."

"Ye are supposed to humor a woman when she's feeling hopeless." The thought of never returning to the life she knew was terrifying. "I think we should at least go up there and wait for a bit. Just to be sure." Determined to make the anomaly happen again even if it meant wishing it into being, she started climbing.

"Did ye leave the keys in the minibus?"

She glanced back at him. "What?"

"Did ye leave the keys with those ladies?"

She checked the deep front pocket of her canvas jacket and pulled them out. "No."

He caught up with her and took them, then pressed the alarm button on the key fob. Nothing happened, but his grin grew even wider.

"What are ye doing?" Bless her soul; she couldn't bear it if this craziness had pushed the lad over the edge.

"If there is even the smallest bit of the time wrinkle still open, the signal will get through and set off the panic alarms." The impishness dancing in his eyes made her smile. "I thought it a nice way to bid those kind ladies farewell, ye ken?"

She needed the levity, and he knew it. "Ye are rotten!"

"Aye. But ye love me for it."

"That I do." She took the keys and shoved them back into her pocket. Silly thing to do, really. But she wasn't quite ready to let go of anything from the time where they belonged. "Come on.

Humor me. Let's sit up there a bit. What harm can come from it?" He needed to realize how badly she needed for them to at least try to get back.

He rolled his eyes, but waved her onward and dutifully followed.

She looked all around to ensure she was in the exact spot as before, then sat back down. They faced the same direction. She pointed for Robbie to sit on her right just as before. With her pack still on her back, she drew up her knees and hugged them. Now to wait. And pray. And wish. Maybe even plead with every power in the universe.

Robbie plopped down beside her and did the same. After a few moments of staring up at the clouds, he started whistling.

"Must ye?" He knew she hated when he whistled off-key.

"What? Afraid I'll scare it away?"

"Robbie."

He immediately won her forgiveness with another impish grin. "It will not work, Mi. If we dinna have a way to create that much energy, another natural occurrence could take millions of years to build. Think of it like a volcano. Dormant for years until enough pressure builds to make it erupt. There was once volcanic activity in Scotland, ye ken? Last eruption was some fifty-five million years ago. Whatever that storm was could be the same."

"Ye are making my head hurt worse." She frowned up at the sky that was growing lighter rather than darker. "We could pray?"

His jaw tightened, and he looked away. "I dinna pray anymore. Not since Mama and Da got killed."

"Sorry." She should have known better than to say that. A defeated sigh escaped her as she pushed to her feet. "Come on. Ye were right. It's not coming back. At least, not by the looks of the sky."

He hopped up and took the lead, bounding down the slope back to the road. She followed at a more sedate pace, terrified at what lay ahead. After walking to the middle of the rutted path, she checked both directions. "Should we head to Fort William?

Or, at least, where it might be? Or back toward Stirling?"

"I dinna remember reading when wagons were invented. Do ye know?" He squatted down and frowned at the ruts.

"It could be anytime. The wheel was invented in the fourth millennium BC, and wagons as early as the first century BC." She crouched down beside him. "Looks like the horses are shod. Manufacturing horseshoes became widespread during the thirteenth and fourteenth century."

"Well done you on remembering historical dates and such." His admiration made her smile.

"I am a font of useless information." She straightened and looked in both directions again. "King David I created Stirling as a royal burgh in 1130. Fort William wasna built until 1654. Since Stirling is older, shall we head there first?"

"Makes sense to me." He looped his arm through hers and tugged. "And dinna fash yerself. We're going to be finer than fine. I know math and science backward and forward, and ye know history inside and out. Between the two of us, we can manage anything."

"I admire yer confidence." She wished she felt the same.

They plodded along at a leisurely pace, stopping occasionally for sips of water and to remove their jackets when the sun broke through the clouds. Robbie's high spirits and ready acceptance of their predicament worried her even more. The lad didn't realize the dangers. They had no coin of the day—whatever the day was. No shelter. A scant amount of food. No weapons and wouldn't know how to use them if they did. And her close-fitting jeans, their backpacks, and his t-shirt with its glow-in-the-dark scientific symbols could get them arrested, hanged, or burned at the stake for witchcraft.

She kept a sharp eye for any sign of other travelers. As they walked, she constantly noted where they might run and hide if need be. She didn't intend to approach anyone until she had watched them for a bit and determined if they were safe. Descended from a long line of Wiccans, she'd never had to study the history of witch trials. Her grandmother had shared enough horrifying stories of what some of her ancestors had suffered. She and Robbie needed to take the utmost care with everything they said and did.

"This is a dangerous time, ye understand? No matter what century it might be?"

He frowned up at her. "I know we canna let them know we're from the future. Is that what ye mean?"

"Aye. That is exactly what I mean. Mind every word ye say." Best leave it at that for now. The lad was smart. He understood.

"What is that sound?"

A steady pounding got louder by the moment. It could only be one thing.

"Horses." She grabbed his arm and struggled to climb the rise on the right side of the road. "We must hide." She clawed the backpack off her shoulders and shoved it into a deep, stony fissure for retrieval later. "Give me yer pack. We canna be found with them." He handed it over. She crammed it inside and scraped some loose rocks and sticks over the opening. "Now, run!"

"But what if they're friendly?" He scrambled beside her, sliding in the mud and patches of wet grass.

"We canna take that chance. Not yet." She floundered and fell, slipping a short way back and losing precious ground. The other side of the road would be no better. Not with the sheer drop-off on that edge. They had to get higher and find cover.

Robbie slid back to her, grabbed her by the shirt, and pulled.

"Ho there! Halt yerselves!"

"Bloody hell. We are found." Mila pushed him away. "Run and dinna look back. No matter what." The lad's compact size would serve him well on the rain-soaked mountainside. She turned, ready to fight bare-handed to keep her Robbie safe and give him time to get away.

"I willna leave ye, Mi." He grabbed her arm and yanked. "Come on."

She clawed at the loose ground, fighting to keep up. "It is so feckin' steep!"

"Dinna kill them," one man said in a booming voice so deep and rumbling she would hear it in her nightmares. "Hie yerselves, though. Those bloody Campbells will gnaw through their ropes and give us chase soon enough."

Something snagged her belt and yanked her backward. She screamed, making what could be her last words to Robbie ricochet across the glen. "Run! Dinna look back!"

"Ye best come back here, boy, or I'll be cutting yer mam's throat for her."

Her captor yanked her back against his hard chest. She couldn't see the devil, but the coolness of his metal pressed to her gullet gave her the will to fight harder rather than cower. She had to protect Robbie.

Ignoring the blade against her flesh, she flailed and kicked, but the man's hold on her only tightened. "Dinna listen to him!" she yelled. "Keep climbing!"

Much to her anguish, the lad half slid, half stumbled back down to her. "Not a chance, Mi. Wherever ye go, I go."

"Good lad to stick with yer mam like that," the captor said. "Get on down by the wagons now, and be quick about it. The chieftain wants to give ye both a good look over and have a word." He took the blade away from her throat and, with surprising gentleness, helped her maneuver over the slope back down to the road.

A striking man with long black hair rode over to them and halted. "And who might the two of ye be?" He was the hulking brute with a voice like thunder.

She hugged Robbie close and squeezed his shoulder to keep him quiet. "We are nobody. Let us go."

With a charming grin that hitched one side of his dark mustache higher, he tipped his hat and walked his horse another step closer. "A pleasure to meet ye, Mistress Nobody." He scratched his chin through his short, neatly trimmed beard. A dark tattoo of what appeared to be crossed daggers covered the back of his left hand. He studied her, tilting his head first one way, then the other. "Ye dinna have the look of a Campbell about ye. Yer clan's name, if ye please?"

She remained silent. Clan Campbell had many enemies. Who this man was depended on the year.

"We should be getting along," called one of the blokes perched on the wagon's seat. "We're still over a day from the keep. Maybe two."

The darkly handsome leader agreed with a thoughtful nod. "Aye. Put them in the wagon. We must leave no one to show the Campbells the turns."

"The ruts will show'm the turns," Robbie called out.

"Robbie!"

The leader's grin stretched into a wide smile. "Robbie, is it? Well then, Master Robbie, how do ye suggest we throw our enemies off our trail?"

The lad lifted his chin and stepped out from the protection of her hug. She tried to snatch him back, but he skittered aside and dodged her. "Make so many ruts they canna tell what's what."

"That we shall," the deep-voiced brute agreed with a regal nod. "Chieftain Teague MacDonald at yer service, sir. What be yer last name, lad?"

"Abernathy."

Mila closed her eyes, wishing they had eaten with those snippy Americans rather than climb to that ledge for their fatal, time-traveling lunch. She clenched her teeth, forcing her words through them. "Robbie. Come. Here."

"I willna harm yer son, Mistress Abernathy." Teague's deep voice sobered. "Into the wagon now, if ye please. We must be on our way." He turned his horse northward, then cast a glance back at her. "And ye best be thanking God Almighty that Clan MacDonald found ye rather than those murderous Campbells."

Hatred between Clan MacDonald and Clan Campbell. That helped narrow down the possible year. Especially this close to Glencoe. The two clans had feuded for decades, but the bad blood between them reached a boiling point during the Glencoe Massacre on February 13, 1692. Archibald Campbell, the tenth Earl of Argyll, had led the treacherous slaughter of the MacDonalds ordered by King William, even though Lord Dalrymple ended up taking the blame for the heinous act.

The attack was particularly cowardly. After enjoying the MacDonalds' hospitality and shelter from the brutal Highland winter for two weeks, Campbell's troops struck while everyone slept, killing the MacDonald chief in his bed. Thirty-three men, two women, and two children were also slaughtered. Many more died from exposure after their homes were burned, and they found themselves ousted into the deep snow with no shelter.

Mila eyed the seven men making up their group of captors. Two with the wagon, the rest on horseback. Belted kilts, all the same color and pattern. Wide bands of muted greens and reds crossed with narrow bands of blue. The MacDonald tartan, she assumed. Some wore waistcoats with the first few buttons undone at the top to reveal their linen tunics or léines. Others didn't bother with the waistcoat or neckcloth at all. They simply wore the tunic alone. Chieftain MacDonald wore his waistcoat buttoned, a knotted neckcloth, and a black leather coat, long and impressive, with wide cuffs and brass buttons. The date had to be sometime in the eighteenth century.

The pair of good-sized Highlanders on the wagon's seat hopped down. They weren't as large as their chief, but were brawny enough in their own right. The one with dirty blonde hair held out a hand to help her up into the back of the wagon. He smiled and dipped a mock bow. "Yer chariot awaits, Mistress Abernathy."

She didn't comment. Instead, she backed up to the wagon and vaulted herself upward with a hearty push.

"Ha! Reckon she showed you, Bhric!" The other brute crouched, laced his fingers together, then nodded for Robbie to step into his hands. "Come on, lad. Up there with yer mam." This one wore a drab gray tam that sagged over his right ear. Tufts of curly brown hair cascaded down well past his shoulders. "I be Calder MacDonald. Brother to the chief. Take care where ye sit lest those barrels shift, ye ken? We dinna want ye crushed."

Mila shot a tight-jawed frown at the boy, then nodded at the spot beside her as she slid back against them. Robbie wrinkled his nose, receiving the unspoken message that she was not pleased with his behavior. He dropped beside her and propped his arms on his knees.

The wagon took off with a hard lurch. Two of their captors followed on horseback, to guard their goods, watch for Campbells, or make sure she and Robbie didn't jump. Mila didn't know which and really didn't care. Under the cover of the loud, creaking rattle of the rough trip, it was time to have a stern discussion with her godson.

"Why on earth would ye give these men yer name? And play up to them as if ye wish to be their friend?"

"What better way to get us some protection?" He shot her a disbelieving frown. "When Mr. Teague told his men not to kill us, I took that as a good sign. Did ye not?"

"And now we are captives."

"We wouldha been captives either way, Mi." His hurt tone jabbed at her. "Sorry if I didna do as ye wished."

The lad was right, and taking out her fears on him was not fair. She wrapped an arm around his shoulders and hugged him hard. "No, my sweet brat. I am the one who is sorry. Forgive me for being ratty."

"I know ye are scairt." He twitched a halfhearted shrug while easing free of her motherly hold. "I am too. But at least they dinna seem all that bad." He held up his wrists. "They didna bind us or get rough. It couldha been worse."

"True. Things could be worse."

The rain came down harder, as if the Highlands themselves were determined to add to her misery. Even though it was May, or had been in the year they left, Mila felt chilled to the bone.

"Lend me some warmth." She scooted closer to Robbie, and

this time, he didn't move away. "Thank ye." She balled up tighter, closing her eyes and ducking her head against the downpour.

"Hold!"

Chieftain MacDonald's bellow caused her to straighten with a snap. She skittered sideways and pulled Robbie with her as the man brought his mount closer to the wagon.

He scowled down at her in silence, looking almost insulted. "I mean ye no harm, Mistress Abernathy." He twisted around and untied the blanket roll from behind his saddle. With a nod to the man in the gray tam, he held it up. "Calder. Yer blanket for the lad, aye?"

"Aye." Calder removed his blanket roll and tossed it to the chief.

The dark-eyed leader smiled as he held them both out. "They are a mite damp, but they'll keep the worst of the weather off ye."

"Thank ye, sir." Robbie grabbed them, draping one around her shoulders before wrapping up in his. He offered the MacDonald an appreciative nod. "She's been shivering something fierce."

The man reached inside his coat and pulled out a silver flask. Even though he handed it to Robbie, he directed his focus to her. "Whisky. For the cold, aye?"

Trembling deeper into the folds of the wool blanket, she shook her head. "No thank ye. I will be fine with just the blanket."

"Mi, come on. He's just trying to be nice." Robbie pushed the flask closer. "It'll do ye good."

"Listen to the boy, mistress. He makes good sense." With a curt nod, the surprisingly thoughtful chief waved for the trip to continue and spurred his mount forward.

Robbie shoved it into her hands and hooded his blanket over his head. "What is that old saying ye always nag me with? Something about cutting off yer own nose to spite yer face?"

"Dinna sass me. I am not in the mood." She unscrewed the cap, sniffed the contents, then hazarded a swig. It burned all the way down, then settled into a cozy pool of warmth in her stomach. She screwed the lid back on. One sip was enough for now.

They rode for what felt like forever, especially since every bump bounced her hard against the boards of the wagon. As they slowed to a stop, she pulled herself to her feet and rubbed her sore arse. "This is it?"

"There is nothing here but a bit of flat ground between the hills," Robbie said.

Calder unchained the wooden gate of the wagon, lowered it, then waved them forward. "Horses are spent. We willna get to the keep till tomorrow." He glanced around, then made a face. "Or mayhap the day after that. 'Tis a full load they pull."

"Spend the night," she repeated, panic rising again. "Here?"

"Aye, mistress," Chieftain MacDonald said, joining Calder at the back of the wagon. "Here." He held out a hand to help her down. "Where did ye shelter last night?"

"That is none of yer business."

"Mi!" Robbie fixed her with an incredulous stare.

She shot back a narrow-eyed glare. "Dinna go there, Robbie. Ye are not too old for a smack on the bum."

He arched a brow and grinned, knowing she wouldn't follow through with the threat.

"Yerself and Master Robbie can make yer pallets under the wagon," the chief said, his hand still extended. "Out of the weather some, that way."

With Calder's help, Robbie hopped out of the wagon. "Can I help with anything?"

Calder grinned and clapped him on the shoulder. "Aye, lad. Gather what ye can for a fire."

The youngling offered her a wink and scampered away.

"Traitor," she said louder than she intended.

"Children and dogs always sense good folk, mistress." Chieftain MacDonald leaned against the wagon, his hand still extended. "Are ye going to have me stand here verra much longer? I must see to my horse."

She shooed him away. "See to yer horse, then. I dinna need yer help." After gathering her blanket out of the way, she took a running jump and stuck the landing on the ground right beside him. She couldn't resist a victorious tip of her head.

The infuriating man dared to laugh. Not a smirk. Not an amused snort. But a loud, rumbling laugh that sounded as if it rose from the depths of his belly. "Well done, Mistress Abernathy. Well done, indeed." With a wave of his hand, he directed her attention to a particularly large thicket. "If ye need some privacy, I give ye my word. My men and I will stay here beside the wagon." He offered a smug grin. "And, of course, Master Robbie shall stay here with us."

She needed to pee in the worst way and was also cold, tired, and hungry. A lethal combination for anyone who dared to speak with her. This man needed to realize she wasn't stupid. "Holding him hostage, so I willna run?"

"Wise as ye are beautiful, I see." He granted her a charming bow that made her itch to smack him. He sauntered away. "On wi' ye now," he tossed back without looking. "Soon as we get a fire built in this dreich weather, we will share a dram and an oatcake or two whilst we warm ourselves." Then he turned and winked while walking backward. "Ye can tell me yer story, then. I love a good story around the fire."

"My story is my own, ye ken!" She stormed off to the thicket, clenching her teeth as his laughter followed her.

Gran and Mother would say she had angered the goddess to end up in such a predicament. Her Christian friends would tell her to trust God's will, that everything happened for a reason. All she knew for certain was she needed answers, but had to be careful about getting them. One revealing word or question could cost her life and endanger Robbie. She needed to choose her words carefully, no matter how much he goaded her. The less she told Chieftain MacDonald, the better.

She emerged from her privacy bushes to discover Calder and

the one called Bhric showing Robbie how to start a fire. The rain had finally ceased, but with everything soaked, she couldn't imagine how they would accomplish it. The lad hopped up with excitement when Bhric's handful of dry tinder started smoking from the spark he struck.

"Look, Mi! I did it!" He waved her over. "Come see!"

"Well done." She patted him on the back.

"How is it the lad doesna know how to start a fire?" Teague asked. Her irritating captor studied her, his charismatic smile failing to hide the suspicion glinting in his eyes.

She returned his flask and changed the subject. "Here is yer whisky. Thank ye for sharing it, Chieftain MacDonald."

"Ye are quite welcome." After a slight tip of his head, he added, "And please, call me Teague."

He fit the name, or it fit him, she decided. It was the embodiment of dark, daring deliciousness.

Or so she assumed. She swatted away the ridiculous assessment, treating it like an annoying midge. A nervous shudder stole across her. She rubbed her arms to stoke her courage. Weakness was not an option.

"Would ye like another blanket, mistress?" Teague eased a step closer. "At least till the fire gets good and started?"

"No." It appeared the man missed nothing. Either that or he believed being thoughtful would wear down her defenses. "But thank ye," she hurried to add.

He gave her back the flask with a kindly look. "Keep it, aye? For the warmth."

It didn't escape her that the container was dear to him, since its sheen revealed it to be silver rather than pewter. "Ye trust me with something so costly?" In her time, it would cost a bloody fortune. It couldn't be cheap in his.

"Are ye a thief?"

"Of course not!" she snapped before picking up on his teasing tone. "Forgive me. It has been a verra long day."

He directed her attention to the wagon. "Fix yer pallet, mistress, and rest. Calder laid out extra blankets for yerself and young Robbie. Even that far from the fire, ye should be warm enough. I shall have the lad bring ye an oatcake or two to fill yer wame till morning, aye?"

"That is verra kind of ye," she said, and meant it this time. "Thank ye."

He gifted her with a smile that made her feel as if she were the only person in the world deserving of his attention. "Ye will find I am a verra kind and generous man, Mistress Abernathy."

She didn't respond, just hurried to the wagon, unable to decide if his kindness and generosity were good or bad.

CHAPTER THREE

"SHE ATE NAUGHT but half an oatcake last night." Teague stirred the fire while watching the lovely Mistress Abernathy sleeping beneath a pile of blankets. He kept his voice low. Not only to keep from disturbing the lady, but also to shield his words from her son. Young Master Robbie sat on the other side of the fire talking nonstop to Bhric.

"She slept well, though." Calder snorted with an amused huff. "Snored so loud I thought a rutting boar had found us."

Teague chuckled and turned his attention to the boy. "Good lad, that one."

"Robbie! Robbie!"

The boy jumped up and ran to the wagon. "It's all right, Mi. I am here."

Her quiet sobs of relief interspersed with harried whispers tore at Teague's heart. What tragedies had these two endured? Perhaps she would warm to him a bit more today and finally share her story.

He ladled the last of the morning broth into a cup and ambled over. "Something to help warm ye, Mistress Abernathy. A bit of soup to break yer fast."

She peered up at him. Her dark curls, tempting in their loose messiness, tumbled around her shoulders. Her strange tunic, a faded blue material that buttoned up the front, had come undone down to her breasts. A tempting expanse of flesh and a peek of her stays' lacy edging made it impossible for him to look away.

As she moved to accept the cup, he forced himself to lift his gaze to her eyes.

"Thank ye," she said quietly.

With a hand propped on the wagon, he crouched to join her at her level. He itched to know more about this fetching woman and her son. "Did ye rest at all?"

She realized her shirt sagged open and disappointed him by hurrying to button it. "I rested fine, thank ye."

"Camping turned out to be all right, eh, Mi?" Robbie squatted next to them, fidgeting with a chain hanging off the side of the wagon. "Bhric said I can help with the team, so I am off to do that, aye?"

Worry filled her face. "Dinna get stepped on. By the horses or anything else, ye ken?"

The lad rolled his eyes, waved away her warning, and scampered off.

"I mean it," she called after him, only to be ignored. "I hate how he dives in headfirst into everything with no caution or fear."

"The young think themselves immortal." Teague rose to his feet as she crawled out from under the wagon and stood beside him.

She kept her focus locked on the lad.

"Dinna fash yerself, mistress. He will learn. Ye wouldna wish him to be cowardly and hold back."

"A wee bit of cowardice might keep him alive longer." She leaned to one side to improve her view and continued watching the boy.

"Children learn what they see," he said. "His mother doesna show the traits of a coward. Why should he?"

That tore her gaze from the boy, and she leveled it on him.

She studied him with a leery, feral look for the span of a heartbeat. "Will we arrive at yer destination today?"

Sly woman. She avoided answering anything that might pull the conversation deeper.

"Depends on the horses." He tipped a nod at the heavily laden wagon. "Full barrels make for a heavy load. Especially through *Bidean nam Bian.*" He couldn't resist testing the waters just to see what she might say. "Back of the wagon canna be comfortable. Ye are more than welcome to ride with me."

She cut another feral look his way. "That willna be necessary, thank ye. The wagon is fine." Her eyes took on a calculating glint, warning him more was coming. "Ye could go on without us." With a noncommittal shrug, she added, "Less weight in the wagon. Easier workload for yer horses."

"And where would ye go, Mistress Abernathy?" He delighted in this jousting with words.

Before she composed herself, he picked up on her unsettledness. "Robbie and I would be fine. Dinna worry about that."

"I think ye safer with us, mistress."

"Prisoners are never safe," she said, with a quietness lined in steel.

"I never said ye were prisoners." He offered a smile. "It would be most unmannerly of me to ignore a woman and her child in need." He winked. "No matter how stubborn and secretive that woman might be."

Her jaw flexed, then hardened with what was surely the clenching of her teeth. "If ye will excuse me, Chieftain MacDonald, I must attend to my morning ablutions so we can be on our way."

"Call me Teague, mistress."

She didn't comment, merely shot a stern glare back at him as she marched off toward her privy bushes.

"There is a fine burn running a few paces beyond yer wee hedge," he called after her. "In case ye wish to splash a bit of water on yer lovely face."

She threw up a hand as though demanding silence.

He couldn't resist chuckling to himself. What was it that made nettling this lass so pleasurable? Perhaps because she sometimes rose to the challenge and gave back in kind? Or maybe because, when she forgot to be afraid, he glimpsed a passionate warrior within her. He knew she would fight to the death to defend her son.

Calder joined him at the wagon. "Are we nearly ready, then?"

"A bit longer." Teague folded his arms across his chest and leaned back against the load. "Give the lady a chance to take care of her morning needs."

Calder squinted at him, disbelief filling his face. "Ye know a lot about a woman's morning needs, do ye?"

With a smugness befitting his pride about the knowledge of such things, Teague cast a sly look at his friend. "Ye would know about them too if ye stayed awake after a good tumble." He thumped the man's shoulder. "Or at least that's what Lucy told me."

Calder snorted and headed toward the horses. "I shall see we are packed and ready when the lady is, aye?"

Since his men and the lad had everything well in hand, Teague meandered closer to Mistress Abernathy's privy. It had been a while since she disappeared behind it. He tipped his head closer and listened, growing mildly concerned. Then the sound of splashing water came to him—along with soft weeping.

A heavy sigh escaped him, and he bowed his head. He could bear no one's suffering. Especially not a woman's. He was born amid the Glencoe Massacre and survived when many in his clan did not. He and the throes of suffering were well acquainted.

Silent as a breath, he eased around the screen of bushes and made his way to the stream. There, he found her, kneeling at the water's edge, face in her hands. Her shoulders trembled in rhythm with every new wave of tears. Just as he was about to go to her, she lifted her eyes to the sky as though pleading with the Almighty. Sunlight flooded her face, setting her misery aglow.

Her beauty struck him hard. If he was God, he would grant her anything she asked.

"How can I fix this?" she softly cried to the clouds. "Tell me how."

Even though he knew she wouldn't wish it, he could stay back no longer. He went to her and knelt at her side. "Let me help ye," he said with tender quietness. "Please."

She stared at him with such a woeful expression that he ached to gather her into his arms. But he stopped himself, sensing she would not wish it.

"Ye canna help me," she whispered. "No one can."

"How can ye know that, lass?" He risked taking her hand and gently cradling it between both of his. "How can ye know if ye dinna share yer troubles?" He offered a gentle smile. "I am a MacDonald chief, powerful, connected, and sly when I need to be. I can protect ye and yer son both. Avenge ye, if need be. Tell me what causes ye such sorrow. Let me aid ye."

With a tearful smile, she eased her hand free and hugged it to her middle. "Ye are verra kind." She leaned forward, splashed water on her face, then dried it with her shirttail. After several sniffs, she gave him a steadier smile. "I will be fine. Robbie and I both will. But thank ye, anyway."

He rubbed his knuckles across his brow, frustrated beyond measure. "I dinna understand why ye feel ye must carry this burden alone."

"Because it is my burden to carry. No one else's."

"I willna rest until ye tell me, so I might help ye. Ye understand that, aye?"

She sniffed, wiped her eyes again, then gifted him another sad smile. "Then ye shall grow verra weary." She rose to her feet and vainly attempted to brush away more of the dried mud encrusting her trews. "I am sure yer men are ready to be on their way. We best join them."

He didn't want to join them. He wanted to stay here and keep her all to himself until he convinced her she could trust him.

But the vexing woman was right. They needed to get moving. "Verra well, then." He gallantly offered his arm.

She spared it a glance, then took off at a rapid pace. "It isna rocky or difficult walking here," she said without looking back. "I can manage quite well, thank ye."

"Mistress Abernathy." He hurried to catch up with her. "The offer of my arm was an act of politeness. Respect. I didna think ye incapable of crossing a few rocks."

Without slowing, she tossed him a dismissive shrug. "I said *thank ye*. Was that not a gesture of politeness too?"

"Fine. On wi' ye, then." He waved her toward the wagon.

As she marched away, he forgot his wounded pride while taking in the tempting sway of her hips. Those trews left nothing to the imagination. Or more aptly, they fanned the fires of many heated imaginings. Why the devil would she dress in such a tempting way? If she and her son were on the run, such clothing only created more risk for them. Did she not realize that?

He caught back up with her just as she hoisted herself up into the wagon. "Wrap a blanket around yer waist, aye?"

"Not necessary," she said. "I am quite warm enough now that I have dried out."

With an easy lunge, he joined her up in the wagon, grabbed a blanket, and slung it around her waist. As he knotted it, he leaned in close and locked eyes with her. "Every man who sees yer fine arse in those trews will be quite warm enough, if ye ken my meaning." He yanked the knot tighter. "Show a bit o' sense and heed my words for yer own protection, aye?"

Her eyes widened. The fears he longed to free her of filled them once again. She looked down at the makeshift skirt, then blinked rapidly as though waking from a dream. "Ye make a good point." She squared her shoulders, donned her jacket, and buttoned it up to her throat. "Thank ye, Chieftain MacDonald."

"Teague, mistress. Call me Teague, aye?" He allowed himself an irritated growl, jumped down from the wagon, and strode to his horse. Once seated on his mount, he threw up a hand. "Arses in the saddle! Now! The day burns." He took the lead, not looking back to make sure they followed. It was better that he rode alone for a while to ponder the puzzle of the most frustrating woman God Almighty ever created.

"WHAT DID YE say to give him such a case of the red arse?"

Mila started to correct the lad then decided not to bother. "When I call him Chieftain MacDonald, it irritates him."

Robbie eyed her like he didn't understand. "What does he want ye to call him?"

"Teague."

"Well then, call him that." The boy scowled at her. "Ye've used first names with lots of men." He wrinkled his nose. "Even smelly old Gunner from the shops."

"This is a different time." She had neither the inclination nor the energy to explain it. The only bright spot that gave her the strength to get through this was that Robbie appeared to be adapting quickly. "Did any of them mention the date?"

"Nah." He drew up his leg and propped his arm on his knee. "And I didna ask. Figured they might think it odd."

"Probably." She pulled in a deep breath and blew out, dreading what the day would bring. "Ye chatted with them a lot. What about?"

He grinned. "They noticed yer prettiness and kept trying to get me to answer questions about ye. About us."

A surge of panic increased her heart rate. "And what did ye say?"

"Dinna worry. I can change the subject good as you can. Remember?" He flinched as the wagon lurched over a big bump, bouncing them hard against the boards. "I kept asking about knives, horses, anything I could come up with to wear out their ears." He shrugged. "I dinna think they are bad people. If they were, they wouldha already hurt us both." He turned to her. "Do ye not think so?"

"They seem kind enough." She didn't add *for now*. She feared the kindness would end if she or Robbie said or did anything out of the norm with whatever year this was. Their clothing endangered them enough. Even the chief said so, and he thought they belonged here.

They careened along in silence for a while, made a hard turn in a wide area, then retraced the route they had just traveled. "It appears the chieftain remembered yer advice about hiding their tracks." She cast a glance at the barrels behind them. "Wonder if he lifted all this cargo from the Campbells?"

"Speaking of lifting things, what do ye reckon will happen to our stuff back home?" Robbie swayed hard to the left as the wagon made another hard roundabout. "Ye think Auntie Loraine will come back to Edinburgh when we dinna answer her texts or emails?"

"Doubtful." Mila huffed out a pitiful laugh, filled with both sadness and amusement. Auntie Loraine. Her mother's eccentric, seventy-eight-year-old sister who ran off to the Caribbean with a lover half her age. "Auntie Loraine will consult her tarot deck and accept whatever they tell her." She massaged her temples. The lack of her regular dose of morning caffeine was bringing on a fearsome headache.

"Do ye believe in all that stuff? Tarot cards telling the future?" They both bounced hard as the wagon lurched around again, went a short way, then made a sharp turn. "I mean—really?" He shifted again, his narrow behind bouncing across the boards through a stretch of even rougher road.

His question gave her pause. She had seen Gran, her mother, and Auntie Loraine correctly predict, or at least hint at, many things that had come to pass. In fact, all three had proven themselves accurate roughly ninety percent of the time. Or so they claimed. All had been big believers in the mystical power of candles, colors, and crystals, too. But Gran had still died of cancer that the powers never warned her about, and her mother had committed suicide after her father's surprising death from a stroke.

"No. I dinna believe in such things." Mila gave him a teasing nudge with her elbow. "Gran and Auntie both said I would find my soul mate after traveling farther than humanly possible. And that he would be a pirate. How silly is that?"

He grinned as they lurched to a stop. "Maybe not so silly. Most dinna think time travel is humanly possible. Could be ye will find him here." He pushed himself up and stood on tiptoe to see over the barrels. "Ye got to see this, Mi."

She stiffly rose and turned, then leaned against the cargo to keep from collapsing. Éirich Castle. And it was not the crumbling remains from her time but a tall, forbidding structure of impressive limestone blocks tucked deep in the complex ridges and peaks of *Bidean nam Bian*, the mountainous region that included the Three Sisters of Glencoe. Brand new and shining in the sun. Some parts still under construction. The keep and smaller structures of the inner courtyard looked complete, but the protective outer wall encircling them still needed a few sections and the installation of the portcullis.

She dragged her gaze from what she had previously known as overgrown rubble and eyed Teague. Construction had started on Éirich Castle in 1712 under the new MacDonald chief, who was reportedly only twenty years old at the time. Considered somewhat young for the task, he prevailed because of his impressive pedigree. He was the nephew of Old Maclain, the highly respected MacDonald chieftain murdered in the Glencoe Massacre of 1692.

Éirich Castle. Rumored to be one of the slowest castle builds in Scotland. Historians said it took eleven years to complete, but the young chief did not live to see it. Arrested for treason at just thirty years of age, he was executed by hanging, drawing, and quartering. That realization puckered her brow with confusion. That poor man's name had been Drummond Maclain. Not

Teague MacDonald.

Perhaps Teague replaced Maclain the younger? That would put the current year at about 1722 or later. She eyed the castle. A good bit of work remained, but a year's worth? Perhaps. Getting materials to this remote area couldn't be easy. And none of these men appeared upset about a recent hanging or their clan's renewed oath of loyalty to King George I rather than the exiled King James VIII. Again, historians reported the oath was the only way they could keep their lands after Maclain's execution.

"Ye've gone all quiet." Robbie bumped against her. "Are ye feeling sick again?"

"No. Just thinking."

"Help Mistress Abernathy down," Teague said before dismounting. He cast a congenial wink at Robbie. "I am sure the lad can manage his own departure from the wagon."

"Ye wish to come and help us tend the cargo and horses?" Calder asked Robbie.

"Aye." Bhric coaxed the boy with a mischievous grin. "Lasses always watch from the wall. Ye can impress them."

Robbie looked at her and waited.

Mila clenched her fists until her nails dug into her palms. "Robbie—I would rather ye stay with me."

"They mean him no harm, mistress," Teague said. He swung down from the saddle and joined her. Apparently, the ride had rid him of his bad mood. He aimed a slight nod at the pair of men, then leaned in close and spoke soft and low. "They are trying to gain yer favor through yer son, ye ken?" One of his sleek, dark brows slanted higher. "Ye are widowed, aye?"

"Aye." Might as well go along with their perception of her. The less truth she shared, the safer. She sensed her luck at avoiding every question was quickly running out.

"Come on, Mi? Can I?" Robbie said. "Remember what ye promised about not babying me anymore?"

Bloody hell. What could she say to that? She took hold of his shoulder and squeezed. "Mind yerself," she warned with a stern look.

"I will." Then he took off, leaving her wondering if she had done the right thing.

"He will be safe, mistress." Teague offered his arm. "And it will give us time to talk and come to an accord."

She moved back a step, knowing if she refused his arm again, he would not be pleased. And even with her heightened anxiousness, it was difficult to remain aloof and untouched by the powerful man's subtle charm. In another time…another place.

She blinked away the ridiculous notion. "What accord might that be, Chieftain MacDonald?"

His dark eyes narrowed to watchful slits, and he came closer. "Ye may call me Teague, mistress. Remember?"

She veered a half step away. Her inner sense of survival demanded it. "And ye may call me Mila," she said, knowing that eventually, she would forget to answer to Mistress Abernathy.

"Mila," he repeated. The natural sensuality in his rumbling tone made it feel like a caress. "Miracle. Gracious. Dear one." The warmth in his smile embraced her like a lover. "It suits ye."

She cleared her throat, fighting his magnetic charisma. "What?"

"The meaning of yer name." The way he spoke made her feel as if they had known each other forever. He chatted like a close friend. "Depending on what part of the world ye are in, of course," he added as he nudged his arm closer and set his chin to a challenging angle.

"World traveler, are ye?" she said, ignoring his gesture.

He allowed his arm to drop and eyed her with an unreadable expression. "Ye might say that." Resettling his stance, he clasped his hands behind his back and assumed a cautious sternness she hadn't seen in him before. "Even though I canna fathom why ye would be on the run wearing such trappings, I offer ye protection." His dark-eyed stare drove deeper into her until it touched her soul. "But I demand much in return from those I keep safe."

She braced herself, expecting the worst. "Yer terms, sir?"

"Unquestionable loyalty and trust."

She blinked, waiting for the rest, but he remained silent. "That's it?"

His sternness shifted to befuddlement. "What do ye mean *is that it*? True, steadfast loyalty is everything."

"I agree," she hurried to say. "I feared yer terms would be less honorable." She offered a gracious nod. "Ye have my loyalty, and I am sure Robbie's as well."

"Ye willna be mistreated here, lass." With another tempered scowl brimming with challenge, he offered his arm yet again.

His form of a test. Of sealing the pact. And not even thinly veiled. She tried not to smile as she relented and took it. "Thank ye, Chieftain MacDonald. Robbie and I welcome and accept yer protection."

"It is Teague, ye ken?"

"Sorry—thank ye, Teague."

His charming, lopsided smile returned, eroding her resistance. "There now. That wasna so difficult, was it?"

She almost laughed, but stopped herself. Better not. At least, not just yet. Instead, she smiled while taking in the amazing surroundings. "No. It wasna difficult at all."

"Yer face lights up whenever ye let yer smile reach clear to yer eyes."

"Thank ye," she said, then ducked her head. Her cheeks warmed with the compliment. It triggered memories of uncomfortable years because of her introverted nature. She found it difficult to relax around new people and make friends. Still did, even though she had learned coping techniques. She was and always would be a loner at heart.

"Mistress?" Teague's expectant smile made her wonder what he had just said.

"Sorry. Woolgathering." The forced lightheartedness of her tone sounded fake, even to her.

"Woolgathering?" He looked even more amused.

"Forgive me," she said, and meant it. "I have a great deal on my mind." The man had no idea of all she had on her mind. "What were ye saying?"

"I forget now." The look in his eyes revealed that to be a lie.

Time to get the conversation back on track and pay closer attention. "So many working and scurrying about. Do many live here?"

"Enough do." He sounded evasive. "But there is always room for more."

While she appreciated the invitation, she still felt she and Robbie had a better chance of surviving in a town. Of course, it all depended on the year. So many opportunities to make the wrong choice threatened to paralyze her. "A growing clan is a powerful clan, aye?"

"Most definitely, mistress. Most definitely, indeed."

Mila managed a nervous smile at the suggestiveness in his tone. Teague MacDonald was too endearing for her own good.

CHAPTER FOUR

DAMNED IF HE had not done it again. Taken in more strays. And after swearing to break that dangerous habit. Especially after the last one tried to shackle him into marriage.

Teague shuddered, recalling that near miss. He stole a glance at the beguiling woman at his side. Ah, but this one was different. She fought to hold herself away from everyone, trusting no one. Not just a fine-looking lass, but temptation incarnate with that mix of stubbornness and beauty. Hair black and shining as an onyx jewel and eyes the rich amber of smoked whisky. He especially liked how her chin came almost level with his shoulder. Tall filly she was, since he stood well over six foot six. And those strange clothes of hers revealed curves enough to satisfy any man. Thank the saints, he had convinced her to cover herself with that makeshift skirt. He still wondered why she had dressed as she had. That and why she and the lad were trekking across the Highlands with naught but the clothes on their backs. A mystery to be solved, indeed.

But even wetter than a drowned rat and muddier than a peat cutter, she had captured the attention of his men as soon as they laid eyes on her. Himself too. But this one would take careful wooing, if she allowed wooing at all. Her leeriness bespoke of ill-treatment in her past. That thought made him clench his teeth in disgust.

As they maneuvered through stacks of building materials, she slipped her hand from his arm and fisted it against her middle. If the poor woman grew any tenser, she would pop like a bubble in a boiling cauldron. A worker tossed an armload of planks into a pile with a loud bang. She skittered aside with such an unsettled look that he fully expected her to hiss like a startled wildcat. She didn't. Which he found both surprising and mildly disappointing. He liked a bit of untamed wildness in a lass.

"If ye dinna mind my asking, how long have ye been widowed?" Her secrets tantalized him. He needed to know more about this mysterious lady.

She eyed him with something akin to fear.

He halted and gently pulled her to a stop. Bending to level with her gaze, he caught such an intoxicating whiff of her sweetness that he almost forgot what he intended to say. It took a shake of his head and a hard swallow to break her fragrance's spell. "I dinna ken what happened in yer past, and I can do nothing to change it. But I can promise ye are safe here. Understand?"

The dark centers of her brown eyes expanded to larger pools, revealing her fear held strong. He recognized the telltale sign from battle.

He took a step back and gave her more space. Perhaps that would grant her some ease.

"Ye are safe here," he promised again. "And if ye dinna wish to answer something, just refuse, aye? No ill will come to ye from yer refusing." He offered an understanding smile. "Many live here who dinna wish to revisit their past. Ye will find us a somewhat unusual gathering of folk, but we have made ourselves into a proud clan just the same."

Her tense smile still looked forced. "Mr. Abernathy has been gone a little over a year now," she said quietly.

So she referred to her husband as *Mr.* Interesting. It had been his experience that only elderly widows used that turn of phrase. He offered a polite bow. "My condolences, mistress."

"Thank ye."

He tried to take her arm again to guide her around a rough patch of cobblestones, and she jerked as though startled. "Mistress Abernathy. Please. Ye are making it appear as if I abused ye all the way here." Her apologetic cringe made him soften his usual booming voice to gentle the teasing. "I willna hear the end of it from Vivyanne if she thinks ye have suffered while under my protection. She will skin me alive."

At long last, she bloomed with a genuine smile that gleamed in her eyes. Her amusement lifted his heart. She held out her hand. "Here. I would hate for yer wife to be upset with ye."

"Oh, she is not my wife," he hurried to explain. "Vivyanne is just—here." There was no delicate way of describing the motherly madam of the clan's parlor of ill repute. He had brought her and several of her whores to Éirich when a rival brothel torched theirs and left the poor ladies homeless. "She is just an old friend who needed shelter."

"Like myself and Robbie?"

"Aye," he agreed, wondering if he would pay for that comparison at a later date.

"Éirich is a fine castle." She studied the thickness of the skirting wall as they entered the courtyard. "Not much left to finish at all."

"Just the arch and portcullis." He led her around another uneven stretch of ground. "But they canna seem to get the pavers settled properly in spots, so watch yer step."

"Probably the ground still settling where ye dug the root cellars and whisky dunnage." She shied away and clamped her mouth shut as if regretting the words.

He made no mention of her discomfort, hoping she would relax and reveal more about herself. He did find it interesting that she knew so much about the groundwork of the place. Perhaps her husband had been one of the earlier workers. That would be strange, though. For the life of him, he couldn't recall an Abernathy among them.

"Come back here, ye feckin' bird!"

The screeching bellow halted their progress halfway across the bailey. "We best wait here," he warned, wondering what had set Vivyanne's arse on fire this time.

The red-faced madam careened around the corner of the keep. Her scarlet curls, wild and frizzy, accentuated her abundance of bosoms about to jiggle free and spill over her neckline. She brandished a hatchet overhead while struggling to catch up with her prey. "No eggs in a month means the cook pot for ye, ye bloody layabout!"

The frightened chicken flapped and fluttered out of reach, leaving a cloud of feathers in its wake.

"Leave the thing be, woman," Teague ordered her. "Are ye that hungry for chicken?"

Vivyanne fumbled to a hard stop, chest heaving. Her eyes went wide as she noticed Mila. She swiped her forehead with the back of the hand holding the hatchet. Then used the same hand to wipe the sweat from her upper lip.

"Pardon me a moment." He gave Mila an apologetic glance, then marched over and yanked the small ax away from the flustered woman. "Bloody hell. Give me that afore ye cut yer own throat."

Vivyanne pointed at the chicken that was now contentedly pecking at a crack in the cobblestones. "I told Greta that one there's not laid a single egg in nigh on a month. She said if I fetch it, she will make us a fine soup to go with supper."

He refused to argue about the chicken's right to live when more important matters were on the horizon. "Come meet our newest guest. And behave yerself."

At least Mila appeared to be somewhat amused. Her eyes sparkled with mirth, and the corners of her mouth quivered with a smile trying to break free.

"Where did ye find that poor waif?" Vivyanne whispered loud

enough for half the keep to hear.

Teague ignored the question. Instead, he ushered her over at a faster pace. "Mistress Mila Abernathy, meet Mistress Vivyanne Allderdice." He shot a warning glare at the madam. "The *old friend* I was telling ye about."

"Hello." Mila's anxiousness thickened the air.

"Ye poor thing." Vivyanne sidled around, standing closer to her as she graced Mila with a sympathetic up-and-down look. "Did they drag ye behind the whisky wagon in all this rain? Ye're muddy as a pig and soaked to the bone. And where on earth did ye get those clothes, child?"

"Well, no…see. He, I mean, Chieftain MacDonald—"

Teague interrupted her with a loud clearing of his throat.

Her mouth tightened with a determined pucker. "*Teague* has been verra kind," she said. "Both to myself and Robbie. We are grateful for his hospitality." She shrugged. "And clothes are really just clothes, aren't they? I needed these. So, I wore them."

"I see." Vivyanne quirked a sparse brow. "And who is Robbie?"

"Her son," Teague said. "Fine lad. Bhric and Calder asked him to help with the load and team."

"Ahh." With a knowing lean closer, the madam winked at Mila. "They are trying to impress ye, lass. Both have decided they are ready to sow their seeds at home rather than in rented fields."

Mila parted her lips in surprise and eased back a step.

Teague groaned. "Vivyanne! Is there nowhere else ye need be?"

Unfazed by his scolding tone, the old harlot shrugged. "Ye willna let me kill that useless feckin' chicken. I have already rousted the girls, and they are nearly finished moving all our things into our grand new place." Her overly painted cheeks plumped even rounder as she aimed a proud smile at Mila. "'Tis finer than Moll's coffee house by Covent Garden. Wait till I write her."

"Moll *King*?" Mila repeated. Both her brows rose to her hairline. Her uncomfortably knowing gaze slid to him. "On Drury Lane?" Apparently, she knew Covent Garden to be the heart of London's prostitution trade. He heard it in her tone. Clear and loud, as if she had shouted it from the top of the keep.

"Aye, Moll King and Vivyanne are sisters," he said. "In a manner of speaking."

With a thoughtful tilt of her head, Mila remained silent for a long, tense moment. Then she offered a polite nod. "Congratulations on yer new establishment."

"Why thank ye, lass." Vivyanne aimed a smirk at Teague before turning back to Mila. "Come by anytime ye like. I'd be more than happy to show ye around."

"That willna be necessary," Teague interrupted. Again, he took hold of Mila's arm and steered her away. "Goodbye, Vivyanne. We shall speak later, ye ken?"

"Oh, I *ken*, all right." Vivyanne gathered her skirts in both hands and trudged off in the other direction. "Pleasure meeting ye, Mistress Abernathy," she called back. "I am looking forward to more chats."

"Thank ye, Mistress Vivyanne." Mila returned her attention to him with a stern narrowing of her lovely eyes. "I am not a prostitute, by the way." She lengthened her stride to keep up with his faster pace to escape Vivyanne.

"I never said ye were."

"Just wanted us to be on the same page." She pulled her arm free. "And Robbie and I will be moving on as soon as we figure things out for ourselves."

Figure things out for themselves? Interesting way to put it, but he daren't press her for more information. At least not yet. "Ye are both guests here, lass. Not prisoners. However, when ye choose to leave, ye will be escorted out in such a way that ye willna be able to reveal our whereabouts. Too many lives depend on it."

While he hadn't ordered them blindfolded on the way in, he sorely doubted she could retrace the route. As frightened as she was, and as worried about the boy, he would lay odds she didn't remember which turns had led them to the castle. And she also would not be allowed to leave until she explained how she knew so much about the ground preparation for his home. But he wouldn't tell her all that just yet.

He held out a hand to help her up the front steps. The builders had made them a mite steep.

She stared at him, then looked down at his hand as though weighing the consequences of accepting his help.

"Ye seem a bit wobbly in the knees, lass. If ye dinna wish to take my hand, I dinna mind throwing ye over my shoulder." He couldn't resist a teasing smirk. This fine lady needed to realize he meant her no harm. On the contrary, he would treat her very well indeed. If only she would allow it.

Her eyes narrowed to slits, and her jawline hardened. He fully expected a terse comment, but she surprised him and took his hand. "I dinna mind. I appreciate a *gentleman's* help."

That made him laugh as they climbed the steps. "Verra few have ever accused me of being a gentleman. As I am sure ye can imagine." He shouldered open the heavy oak door and waited for her to enter. "But I thank ye for the kindness of yer words."

Her steps slowed as she entered the great hall. It appeared she couldn't look in every direction fast enough to suit herself. She turned in a slow circle, taking in his life's work. Or, at least, one of his life's many accomplishments.

"Is it not grand?" he said, unable to contain his pride.

"It is indeed." She trailed a hand across the end of the nearest long table, one of the many arranged in an open-ended square around the room with their benches on the outside so diners could see each other whilst enjoying their food and drink. Her gaze lit on the MacDonald colors and crests flanking the wide hearth. Something made her smile.

"What is it, lass?"

"It is even more beautiful than I imagined," she said in a hushed tone as her focus rose to the gallery above them. Then she twitched as if shaken and stared at him. Her fearful expression had returned. "I mean—the finery and workmanship in everything. The grain of the wood gleaming with polish. The brass sconces, how they shine. And those mahogany cabinets are lovely. I have never seen such elegance firsthand."

What made her suddenly afraid? Rather than press her, he pretended not to notice. Instead, he accepted her praise with a slight bow. "Thank ye. We have worked verra hard here, and continue to do so to make our keep the finest."

"Ye better have knocked the mud from those boots afore stepping in here."

He turned to find Mrs. Cain doing her best to look threatening. "I assure ye I did, Mrs. Cain. Come meet Mistress Mila Abernathy, our newest guest." He took on a low, ominous tone while aiming a mischievous look at Mila. "Mrs. Cain is not only Éirich's housekeeper but also the fierce beastie to whom all troublemakers and layabouts are fed." He leaned closer and continued in a horrified whisper, "If ye listen close, ye can hear her crunching their bones in the wee hours afore dawn."

"Hmpf!" The plump matron, elderly yet still spry enough to strike fear into the surliest warrior, swept forward. She gave Mila a hard up-and-down squint. "Pleasure to meet ye, Mistress Abernathy."

"Please. Call me Mila."

"Good enough." The housekeeper planted her fists on her wide hips. "Ye may call me Mrs. Cain." She ambled closer and shook a finger at Teague. "What the devil did ye do to her? Drag her behind a horse?"

"I did not." Why did everyone keep accusing him of such? "When have ye ever known me to treat a woman in such a coarse way?"

Mrs. Cain hissed out a very prim huff. "A few have come here that ye shouldha dragged some sense into."

A faint noise that could almost pass for a giggle escaped Mila before she clapped a hand across her mouth.

"Already siding with Mrs. Cain?" He struggled to maintain a somber air, even though her reaction pleased him. "Just as well. She will be the one helping ye settle in." He turned back to the white-capped matron. Her critical scowl had returned as she eyed his boots and the floor behind him. "I didna track up the floor, ye worrisome old hen."

"Mallie and Dorrie worked all morning scrubbing it clean. I willna have their work undone in a flash of ill-consideration, ye ken?"

Mila ducked her head, but her twitching shoulders betrayed a struggle not to release her pent-up mirth.

Perhaps he should keep the banter going for a while. He loved it when this lady was happy.

He cleared his throat and turned back to Mrs. Cain. "Mistress Abernathy has a son. I reckon they will need the space and privacy such a wee family entails."

The housekeeper studied him. Her wrinkly face tightened. "A pair of bedchambers connected with a sitting room, aye?" The mischief in her eyes gave her away even though she maintained a terse tone. "Since there be no mistress of this keep, what say ye to her and the lad staying on yer floor? Not yer personal solar, of course, but the suite intended for yer wife whenever ye trick some poor lass into marrying ye?"

"Ye are a cold, hateful woman, Mrs. Cain." But he didn't mean it, and she knew it. "But aye, that will be suitable enough as long as Mistress Mila here doesna mind."

The lovely lass's fearful, doe-eyed look had returned. "Just Mila. Aye? And I am not too sure about such an arrangement."

"The door between my bedchamber and yers locks, mistress. From yer side, and Mrs. Cain shall see to it that ye possess the only key. Agreed?"

Her dubious expression shouted that she still didn't believe or trust either of them.

"There is naught but the one key, lass," Mrs. Cain said. "And if ye wish, I can show ye how to bar the door with a good, sturdy chair."

Mila squared her shoulders. "Thank ye, Mrs. Cain, but I already know well enough how to block a door." She held out a hand. "I would appreciate the assurance of the key, though."

The housekeeper removed a key from the large ring at her waist and placed it in Mila's hand. She tipped a nod at the lass's strange trappings. "Since I see no belongings with ye, I assume ye have no proper clothing?"

Mila swiped her palms on her strange trews. "These are all I have."

Mrs. Cain nodded, then turned back to him. "Grissa can make the rounds and see what can be gathered for her, aye?"

"Aye." Although he thought it prudent that Grissa avoid any donations from Vivyanne and her girls. "Have her choose appropriately, ye ken?"

"Well, of course," the housekeeper replied. "I shall have food and drink fetched for her as well. Anything else afore I take this shivering lamb to her rooms?"

"I dinna mean to be rude, but can ye not talk about me as if I am not standing right here in front of ye?" Mila tucked a muddy strand of hair behind her ear. "I am grateful for such generous hospitality, but afore I wash up a bit, I would like to see Robbie."

"He is fine, lass." Teague supposed it was natural for a mother to fret about her bairn, but her lack of trust grated on him. "Bhric and Calder willna let anything happen to him."

She squared off in front of him as though ready to battle. "Be that as it may, take me to him. Now. If ye please."

"Appears to me ye best do as yer told," Mrs. Cain said. "While ye are gone, I shall set the girls to airing out the rooms and making everything proper. All will be ready when ye return, Mistress Mila."

"Thank ye, Mrs. Cain."

"Have a bath readied for her as well," Teague said. Perhaps it would soften her refusal to believe Éirich Castle a sanctuary for all. Or at least for those with the loyalty to deserve it. He politely eased a slight bow in her direction. "With yer permission, of course."

"Thank ye," she said, but didn't smile. Just went flinty with determination. "That would be lovely. After I see my Robbie, of course."

"Of course." He made a grand show of offering his arm, knowing she wouldn't take it. "Allow me to escort ye, mistress."

She surprised him and clamped on to it as if trying to snap it in two. It made him nearly bite his tongue to keep from laughing. Rather than lead her back the way they came in, he decided to take her through the library and out through the gardens. Then she would see they weren't an uncivilized den of thieves, but well-educated, skillful procurers of goods, information, and properties.

"Where are we going?" Her grip tightened as her attentiveness switched to the hallway and every door they passed.

"'Tis a shortcut to the offloading ramp and stables. That is where yer Robbie is helping Bhric and Calder." He pushed open the library entrance and stepped back. "After ye, mistress."

A soft gasp escaped her as she entered and slowly circled the room, pausing behind his desk. "What a wonderful place."

The awe in her voice pleased him. He hurried to draw her attention to every overflowing shelf. Each wall, from ceiling to floor, was filled with maps, papers, and every book he had collected over the past twenty years. "My personal library."

"How many are there?" she whispered, walking her fingers along the titles and pausing here and there.

"I dinna ken. Never bothered to count them."

"Robbie would love this one." She tapped on a thick spine. "He speaks Latin quite well."

"He can come and enjoy these anytime he likes." He admired her backside as she bent to check a volume on a lower shelf. The opening in her blanket skirt revealed everything he had tried to hide from his men. Perhaps those trews of hers weren't such a bad thing after all. "Ye can come here as well, if ye wish it."

She straightened and gave him a smile that actually seemed relaxed. "Ye are verra kind."

"Aye, I am, and it is high time ye realized that." He directed her to the double doors on the far side of the large, high-ceilinged room. "Those lead to the garden. Looks as though the rain's kicked up again. Are ye certain ye dinna wish to wait inside for the wee one? It would give ye time to rest by the fire. Have a drink and a bit of bread."

Her smile disappeared. "Dinna call him that. Not ever, ye ken?"

Confusion filled him. "Beg pardon, mistress? Dinna call who what?"

She wet her lips as though struggling to choose her words carefully. "Dinna call Robbie a *wee one*. Not ever. He is fifteen and verra sensitive about his size. Many have bullied…treated him poorly because he is so small."

"I see." He bowed his head, regretting his unintended slight of the lad. "I beg yer forgiveness. I thought him much younger. As ye said, because of his size." He moved to the garden doors, opened them, and stared down at the rain bouncing off the flagstones. "It willna happen again, and I shall also have a word with Bhric and Calder, so they know as well."

"I fear Robbie doesna always realize his worth because of it," she said as if fearing Teague didn't understand. She joined him at the doors. Sadness and worry etched lines in her face as she watched the rain. "People can be so verra cruel. Like animals smelling fear or weakness. They attack and dinna let up until it is too late."

The more she spoke, the more he understood her need to check on the boy and do all she could to protect him. It wasn't because she feared himself or his men. It was because the lad had suffered what sounded like a terrible shunning in the past.

He studied her. "Ye do realize ye risk doing him more harm than good by trying to shield him from everyone and everything?"

Her gaze remained locked on the puddle just beyond the threshold. A soft, huffing laugh escaped her. "Ye sound like Robbie. He says I treat him like a baby and need to stop."

"There is a difference between protecting yer bairns and making them so vulnerable they canna survive without ye."

"I suppose that's true." A weary sigh underscored her words. "Perhaps I shouldna meddle with him while he is helping yer men." She gave a flinching shrug. "But it makes my heart tight with uneasiness when he is out from under my wing." She slid a glance his way, her sleek brow quirked to a plotting slant. "I dinna suppose there is a window or ledge where I might at least catch sight of him without his knowing?"

The windows of Teague's private chambers overlooked the area where Robbie would be, but he hesitated to tell her. She might think it his ploy to get her into his bed. Not that he wouldn't enjoy her company, but it was too soon to even hope for such. Skittish as a new colt, this lovely lady required careful planning. An artful tactic at which he excelled.

"Teague? Please?"

The pleading in her tone decided it. "My bedchamber window has a view of the yard where Robbie should be."

"I see." She studied him as though trying to weigh the goodness of his soul.

He lifted both hands in surrender. "The choice is yers, mistress. I can take ye there and leave or have Mrs. Cain or one of the maids escort ye. I leave it to ye."

She lifted her chin. "Ye can take me there. I dinna fear ye."

"Good enough, then." He directed her back to the hallway with a wave of his hand. "My chambers are on the third floor." As he closed the library door behind him, he turned to the right. "Of course, yers are there as well. I planned that floor for the family I might find myself having someday. A nursery connects to those rooms also."

"Sounds as if ye planned for everything."

They came to the narrow stairwell. He stepped back for her

to take the lead. "Planning is critical in everything."

"The best laid schemes o' mice an' men..." Her voice trailed off. She climbed faster, running her hands along the walls.

"The best laid schemes o' mice an' men...?" he repeated, encouraging her to finish.

She cast a nervous smile back at him. "Nothing. Just a silly saying I read somewhere. I can't remember it word for word."

"Tell me the gist of it, then." It behooved him to keep her talking. He might discover more about her.

"The best laid schemes o' mice an' men gang aft a-gley," she said so fast he almost didn't catch it. "Even the best of plans sometimes go verra wrong."

"Why mice?" The verse had a pleasing tempo, but why pair vermin with men? "Why not a woman—or an animal other than a wee mousie?"

"I have no idea. Ye would have to ask the poet." She increased her speed, almost running up the steps.

"Take care now. The way is steep and narrow." He took two at a time to keep close behind her in case she should stumble.

She came to a halt and stared upward with a frustrated scowl. "I have lost count of the landings."

"I dinna doubt it. Ye were running like someone set fire to yer skirts. What came over ye?" Only her profile was visible, then she turned away so he couldn't even see that. "Mistress Mila?"

"Just Mila—please? I am not yer elder to be respected." Her tone softened but still held a tenseness. "Did I miss the landing? How many floors are there? The keep looks quite tall from outside."

"Four." So she refused to answer his question and scolded him for addressing her properly. Such a complicated lass. That enticed him even more. He always loved solving an intricate mystery. "Ye havena missed our floor. 'Tis this one. Just a few more steps. Around that turn is the door."

Without a word, she resumed climbing but at a normal pace rather than the breakneck run of before. When she reached the landing, she waited with her head bowed, staring at the floor.

"Are ye all right, lass?" With his hand resting on the latch, he waited for her answer.

"Aye." Her soft curtness revealed it for the lie that it was.

"Mila." He fixed her with what he hoped was a stern but kind glare. "What ails ye? Ye lost yer fear and relaxed a bit back in the library. And now—"

She lifted her gaze to his. "I am overwhelmed by all that has come to pass." She shifted with a disheartened shrug. "A turn of phrase, a memory, or a feeling brings back my worries all over again. Makes them rush in and try to drown me. 'Tis hard to explain." She tried to smile, but failed. Her dark eyes glistened with unshed tears that her rapid blinking held at bay.

He pulled in a deep breath, then released it while offering a curt nod. "I will say it again for ye: ye are safe here. As is yer young one. Both of ye are welcome to stay as long as ye need." He left it at that, pushed open the door, and stepped aside so she could enter first.

CHAPTER FIVE

WHY ON EARTH would she be foolish enough to quote Robert Burns? The poet wasn't even born until 1759. She had to be more careful. The open journal on Teague's desk showed the year to be 1722. That was, if it was opened to the latest entry. Considering the amount of work left on the castle, that made sense. Historians reported the fortress was completed in 1723. But if this was 1722, that was also the year Chieftain Drummond Maclain of Éirich Castle died.

The English caught him in late November and executed him on December 12, 1722. If Teague was chieftain, where was Drummond? Or had Teague been left in charge while Drummond tended to business elsewhere? Perhaps Teague was the chieftain's trusted friend. After all, he looked to be about the same age as the historians reported the chieftain to be when he died.

Mila mulled the dates over and over as she followed him through his large solar. Maybe she had the years wrong. After all that had happened, she had a right to be confused.

She trailed her fingertips across the top of a chair upholstered in sumptuous leather. Definitely a masculine room. Dark furnishings. Swords, daggers, and axes hung beside the hearth. Piles of books cluttered the tables beside the chairs. The faint scent of tobacco and whisky lingered in the air.

"And here we are," he said as he opened a door and stepped back. He pointed inside the room. "The window over there beside the bed overlooks the ramps. Ye should be able to spy yer Robbie from that one."

His gallantry touched her heart, but she didn't dare reveal it. Such a handsome man. And everyone they had encountered so far appeared to think highly of him. His men respected him, and Mrs. Cain doted on him like a loving grandmother with all her grumpy fussing. A weary sigh escaped her. More's the pity that she and Robbie would move on soon and would probably never see him again.

A subtle shifting of his stance made her realize he had caught her staring. As she stepped across the threshold, she managed a polite smile. "Thank ye. I appreciate it."

She moved across the room very much aware that the space smelled of him. Oil of clove, sea air, and raw masculinity. She had noticed his striking yet not offensive scent the first time he offered his arm. The faint hint of the sea had confused her. At least, at first. Then she realized how he came by it. This braw, handsome man was a smuggler. She would bet her brand-new minibus on it. Well, she would if she still possessed it.

"Ye can tie the other curtain back if ye wish," he called from the door.

She took his advice and pushed back the heavy damask on the left and secured it with the braided rope meant for that purpose. Only the right side of the deep red curtains had been tied back earlier. Apparently, Teague didn't care for a room full of sunshine.

"If the window seat is dusty, wait a bit and I shall fetch one of the lasses to clean it for ye."

"It's fine." She knelt on the bench overflowing with pillows. "If ye intend to keep calling out from the doorway, ye might as well join me." He reminded her of a child told to stand in the hall while its parents decided its punishment. "But leave the door open," she added. She doubted if screaming or running would do her any good, but if he meant to do her any harm, surely he would have done it before now.

"Only if ye are certain." He remained in the doorway, leaning against the frame with one foot crossed over the other.

She turned back to the window, pressing her nose against the pane to see the area directly below. "If I wasna certain, I would not have said it." Her moist breath steamed up the glass, making her lean back and wipe it off with her sleeve.

"Here. Open it so ye can see better." He released the latch and pushed both tall sections of the broad window open wide.

She backed up. "Shh! I dinna want him to see me spying on him."

Teague leaned farther out, peered downward, and grinned. "He willna see ye. He's hard at work impressing those wee lassies lined up on yon wall."

Mila joined him on the windowsill. "I see him."

The men had assigned Robbie the task of unhooking the team and leading them into the open-sided feed shelter while they unloaded the wagon. There he was, standing on a stool, brushing the animals while they ate. At first, she wondered how he had known what to do, then scolded herself. The lad was pure dead brilliant. He could solve any challenge in a matter of minutes. And Teague was right: even in the drizzling rain, several young girls sat on the low stone fence, swinging their feet and sending shy smiles his way.

"Who are those girls?" They better be nice to her Robbie.

Teague directed her attention to a trio of women standing inside the gate and casting bold smiles at Calder and Bhric. "The eldest daughters of those three."

Mila couldn't help but notice the suggestive dip to the ladies' necklines, the brightly painted hue of their cheeks, or the heaviness of the bold lipstick smeared across their mouths. "They dinna happen to work for Vivyanne, do they?"

"Aye, they do." He pointed to the one on the left. "The one in yellow is Lucy, red is Scarlett, and blue is Fannie." He faced her then, his expression turning sober. "We dinna judge anyone here, Mila. Not for who they were, nor for who they are. All are welcome in this clan as long as they be loyal and true."

"I was not judging them."

"Aye. Ye were." His head took on a thoughtful tilt. "'Tis understandable enough. I know ye worry about the lad. But know this: I maintain the peace and prosperity of all—no matter the *level* at which society might deem them."

His smug lesson in acceptance soured her. Superior airs and uppity scoldings like that were the main reasons she had never married. She refused to be talked down to by anyone. She was not a bad person.

"Thank ye for showing me that Robbie is well and appears to be settling in nicely." She pushed off the bench and exited the room. Once he joined her, she pointed at the other two doors. Bookcases framed one. A pair of long, low cabinets flanked the other. "Which way to my chambers? I am ready to rest a bit if ye give me yer word Robbie will be sent up as soon as he finishes."

"It appears I have stepped on the wee wildcat's tail." He jerked a thumb back toward the bedroom. "The door connecting our chambers is in there to the right of the bed." As she moved to step past him, he stopped her. "Dinna be cross, aye? Ye needed to know how things are here. How folks are treated."

She pulled her arm free of his grasp. "What I need is to rest then speak with Robbie. And let me reassure ye, Chieftain MacDonald, we willna overstay our welcome here." She eyed him to see if the formal address caused the irritation she intended.

The muscles in his jaw flexed, signaling clenched teeth. Good. Her subtle message had been received.

He rendered a curt tip of his head. "As ye wish, Mistress Abernathy. If ye will excuse me now, I have much to attend to and have delayed it long enough. I shall see that Master Robbie receives word to report to ye as soon as he finishes his tasks." Without waiting for a response, he strode from the room and firmly clicked the hall door shut behind him.

A tinge of guilt tarnished her golden cloud of victory. The man and his people had been nothing but kind. She shouldn't be ratty with any of them. She hadn't been judging the women.

Well, perhaps just a little.

The admission didn't ease her guilt. It just made her angry at herself and even more irritated with Teague because he had read her so easily. Well, it didn't matter what he thought of her. The man knew nothing of all that Robbie had endured. Her best friend had entrusted her with the lad before the accident. Robbie was hers to protect now.

She tossed her head to rid herself of the turmoil. She had enough to worry about without adding more to it. After another glance out the window at Robbie, she fished the key out of her pocket and hurried to the door on the other side of the bed. After passing through it, she locked it, then turned to search for something to block the way, and immediately forgot her intent.

While Teague's room had been dark, cavelike, and manly, this bedchamber bloomed with gentleness, light, and comfort. Pale hues of yellows, pinks, and greens gave the room a feel of a hidden, ivy-covered grotto in the middle of a multicolored rose garden. Tapestries of florals covered the walls. A lush canopied bed. Delicate chairs, washstands, and wardrobes. A dividing screen of creamy silk painted with dainty trailing vines and lavender blossoms. Furnishings chosen with a woman in mind. Opulent curtains. An abundance of pillows on the bed, the chairs, and the couches. No expense had been spared.

She hated to touch anything. Especially since this room was not meant for her. This glorious space was for Teague's future wife. His thoughtfulness for every detail touched her. Had he selected everything himself? Surely not. Surely he had hired someone to finish out the room.

She slipped off her muddy sneakers and left them beside the door, not wanting to soil the fine, thick Turkish carpet. Moving carefully so as not to shake the drying mud from her clothes, she headed for the door she assumed led to the sitting room. She eased it open and peeped through just to make sure.

"Mistress Mila?" A young lass, maybe in her late teens, stood beside an enormous copper bathtub. A sheet was draped over its curved sides, and additional folds of linen were piled high on one end to provide a cushioned headrest. "Mistress?" the girl repeated. "Are ye unwell?"

"No." Mila blinked, trying to take in the scene of the small, private area that was most definitely not a sitting room. "I was…uhm…looking for the sitting room to find a plain wooden chair. I didna wish to sit on the bed and soil it."

The maid smiled and nodded at the tub. "This here's yer bath, mistress. Steaming hot. The lads just brought in the last kettle." She dipped a curtsy. "My name is Grissa. Mrs. Cain sent me to be yer lady's maid and help ye with anything ye need."

"A lady's maid?"

"Aye." Grissa leaned to one side, giving Mila's muddiness a hard up-and-down look. "Are ye dressed as a man to make running easier?"

The girl was definitely bold. Mila decided to reserve judgment about whether that was a good thing. "Ye are verra perceptive," she said, deciding to evade the question. She had enough lies to keep straight, what with everyone thinking her Robbie's widowed mother.

The lass gave an understanding shake of her head as she refolded a cloth. "Ye dinna have to answer anything ye dinna wish to answer. Mrs. Cain made that clear too, and I know well enough I can be a busybody at times."

Mila couldn't recall the last time she'd had this much difficulty with people seeing right through her and knowing her thoughts and intentions. "I shall bear that in mind."

The maid uncorked a small glass vial and poured a dollop of oil into the water. A light fragrance of fresh-cut roses filled the room. "Ye can pile yer things there by the door. I'll see that they're laundered, then returned to ye." She looked up from the small table near the tub, bubbling with excitement as she opened several jars. "I found the nicest petticoat and skirt for ye. All that goes with it too. And all in a shade sure to make ye shine with that dark hair of yers. Since they told me ye be a tall woman, I knew Mrs. Gillicutty would have something to spare. I dinna ken if the slippers she sent will fit. If not, we can have Duff make ye a pair in no time at all. Himself ordered ye to have anything ye needed." Grissa glanced up again and stopped preparing the bathing articles. "Is something wrong? Ye've not removed a stitch."

"Ye've not left yet." Mila tightened her grip on the blanket tied around her waist.

"Left?" Grissa seemed astonished, so much so that she backed up a step. "I have to help ye wash and comb out yer hair. 'Tis a pure muddy rat's nest. When Mrs. Cain told me to be yer lady's maid, she listed all that I should do. Wash ye. Dress ye. Mend yer things. Anything at all ye need."

Mila wondered if Mrs. Cain had also advised the kindly girl to babble nonstop. She closed her eyes and massaged her throbbing temples.

"Willow bark tea will help that. I can run and fetch it whilst ye soak. The bath might ease yer poor aching head too." The maid watched her as if waiting for a starter pistol to fire and launch her into her run. "Or I can wash ye first. Whichever ye like."

Mila blew out a deep, defeated huff. There was no escaping this girl. She felt sure the lass meant well, but bloody hell, she talked nonstop. "A cup of willow bark tea would be lovely if ye dinna mind fetching it while I soak."

Grissa responded with another beaming smile that made Mila think of happy, wiggly puppies. "I dinna mind at all, mistress. 'Tis my responsibility, and I am proud to do it." She flicked a hand at Mila's clothes. "Off with those now, so I can take them with me while ye rest in the water." Before Mila could answer, Grissa hurried to the hearth, poked the fire, and pushed two large black kettles closer to the flames. "If the water cools too quickly, these will heat it up again nicely."

"I best get busy, then, before it gets cold." Mila had never been overly modest, but stripping down in front of the maid was uncomfortable for a number of reasons. How would she explain her bra and panties? Zippers and snaps on her jacket and jeans? Labels that listed materials, washing instructions, and possibly the year manufactured? She eyed the fire, wondering what Grissa would think if she tossed everything into the flames.

"Mistress? Are ye feeling poorly?" The lass stepped around the tub and eased closer. Compassion shone in her kind eyes. "Ye've gone all faraway-eyed again. Pale, too. Do bad memories trouble ye?"

"Aye." Mila untied the blanket from around her waist and let it drop. "It is hard to forget the past." *Especially when it's the future.* The thought made her stomach gurgle.

"That it is, mistress." The maid gave a decisive nod. "Sounds as though ye need something for yer innards too. I will head down now and get yer tea. A wee dram or two might do ye some good as well. I can tend to yer clothes once I have ye dressed and resting proper after yer bath."

Mila agreed with a faint nod. At this point, as stressed as she was, she would agree to anything for a little quiet alone time to decompress.

Grissa bounced a happy curtsy and scurried from the room. As soon as the door clicked shut, Mila lowered herself to a short stool and held her head in her hands. "I have no choice," she muttered. Her favorite jeans, jacket, and t-shirt had to go into the fire. The backpacks and their contents had been dangerous enough. Her clothes were damning as well. But first, just to be safe, she had to ensure she was alone.

She yanked open the narrow door connecting the bathing area with the bedroom and looked around. No other maids or servants anywhere. Thank goodness. Much needed to be done before chatterbox Grissa returned. One more look around just to be on the safe side. A steady rattling deeper in the room worried her. It turned out to be something outside, the noise coming in through the open window.

With urgency making her rush, she loped back into the bathing closet, stripped down, and fed her clothing into the fire. She crammed too many things in at a time and nearly put it out. Crouching on the hearth, she gently blew on the coals until the blaze strengthened and took hold. The sound of approaching footsteps made her heart pound harder. She hurried to the tub, stepped in, and dropped into the water, clenching her teeth to keep from shouting. The hot liquid nearly scalded her. As the door slowly eased open, she pillowed her head on the linens and tried to look as if she had been in there a while.

"If I spill, I shall be verra cross with m'self." Grissa bumped the door open wider while scowling at the contents of the tray she carried. "Is the water still plenty warm, mistress?" She carefully lowered the tray to a table beside the hearth. "Merciful heavens, what has got into that fire?"

"My clothes, and yes, the water is perfect." Mila forced herself to act as if burning clothes was the most natural thing in the world.

"Ye burnt yer things?"

"Aye." She sank deeper into the water and kept her eyes closed to the barest slits. If she acted nonchalantly, maybe the maid would buy it.

"But why, mistress? I couldha washed them up proper for ye." Grissa brought a steaming cup over to the tub and held it out. "Of course, 'tis no never mind to me. Just seems a mite wasteful. Here is the willow bark for yer head."

"Those clothes are from a time I can never return to." Or, at least, as far as Mila knew, she and Robbie couldn't get back. "To wear them again would be folly." That truth was as bitter as the willow bark tea.

"Ahh...bad memories for ye. I understand." The lass patiently waited until Mila emptied the cup, then took it and set it aside.

She grabbed a pitcher from the floor, dipped it into the tub, and smiled. "Now we shall return yer hair to its loveliness, aye? That will make ye feel better. I gathered the best soaps and oils to make sure we rid ye of all those muddy tangles."

Mila opened her mouth to argue, then gave up and closed it. Grissa's determination would not be stopped. She leaned forward and bowed her head. "Dinna drown me, aye?"

The maid laughed. "I willna drown ye, mistress." Her voice took on a gossipy, excited lilt as she dumped the water over her. "I did find out the best thing whilst fetching yer tea."

Hidden in the curtain of wet hair, Mila covered her eyes while waiting for another dousing. "Did ye now? And what might that best thing be?"

"Himself sent for a seamstress and told the lad to have her bring her finest wares." Grissa soaked her with another deluge, then started scrubbing.

The soap made Mila's scalp tingle, but not in an unpleasant way. A floral scent spiked with the crispness of peppermint filled the air. She failed to see why Teague sending for a seamstress was so exciting to the girl. Perhaps she hoped to get a new dress? "That will be nice for the ladies here. Are many of them needing new things?" She flinched as the maid scrubbed her head with renewed vigor. "Ye are digging into my brain, Grissa. Let up a bit, ye ken?"

"Sorry. I get carried away sometimes. Time to rinse. Shut yer eyes tight. The oils in Mrs. Cain's soap can burn like a fiend."

Several pitchers of water sloshed over her in rapid succession. When the dousing finally ceased, Mila flipped her hair back out of her face and straightened. She held out a hand. "If ye will hand me the soap and a rag, I'll scrub myself, aye?"

Grissa's snort conveyed that she didn't agree, but she complied without argument. "Here ye be. Now back to yer question about the ladies here needing new things." Her beaming smile returned as she squatted by the tub and propped her arms on its side. "Himself sent the seamstress so ye willna have to wear borrowed things that dinna fit ye proper." She shrugged. "And even if they do fit, they still are borrowed. Ye need yer own things." Her expression became even more animated as she lowered her voice to an excited whisper. "I think himself fancies ye."

"Himself does not even know me." Mila lathered the rag and started scrubbing, realizing too late that once she washed away all her deodorant and body spray, that was the end of it. She sniffed the soap, wondering how the lather might react with her armpits if she let it dry to use as an antiperspirant. "And I am sure ye're mistaken. I gave him a case of the red arse right before he left me."

Grissa waved away the excuse, then snatched back the soapy rag. "Move yer hair so's I can scrub yer back. And himself never stays angry long. Leastwise, not over little things. Why, one of the stable lads let a horse run away. Most chiefs wouldha ordered him whipped for it. But not himself. All he did was make the boy scrub the garderobe sluices for a fortnight."

Mila only half listened. She was too hypnotized by the pleasant back scrubbing. "Himself probably stole the horse in the first place," she said, then clamped her mouth shut. She should not have said that, even though horse and cattle lifting were common practice in the Highlands.

Grissa laughed and paused the washing. "That is exactly why himself didna have the lad thrashed! He said so, even."

Water sluiced down Mila's back, reminding her she needed to pee. While she wouldn't mind learning more about Teague, the urge had become impossible to ignore. "Is the garderobe close by?"

"Oh no, mistress. Ye dinna want to go there. 'Tis on this floor but a good ways down the hall." She drew Mila's attention to a small cabinet next to the door leading back to the bedchamber. "Himself brought this fancy piece in from France." She flipped back the top, then pulled open the side door, revealing a seat with a hole and the porcelain chamber pot underneath. "Is it not fine?"

She tapped on the small drawers on the other side. "And in here are bits of wool and such for cleaning yer bum and lady parts." She snapped her fingers and her eyes went wide. "I must add some rags to the bottom drawer for when yer courses come. 'Tis not done yet, but will be. I swear it."

Her courses. Mila almost groaned aloud. No more decent feminine products. A despondent sigh escaped her as she mentally calculated when she would have to deal with that uncomfortable inconvenience. She stepped out of the tub and looked around for some sort of towel.

"Here, mistress." Grissa descended on her with an enormous length of linen, scrubbing her dry and squeezing the water from her hair.

Mila grabbed the cloth. "I've got this. Could ye get my clothes laid out? I will finish drying, use the facilities, then join ye."

"Facilities?" The lass fixed her with a befuddled frown.

"The chamber pot. I prefer to take care of such things in private." Mila willed the girl to leave while wrestling with the urge to shout at her. It wasn't Grissa's fault this time-traveling rabbit hole had swallowed her. "Ye can leave the door open and tell me more about himself while I—relieve myself, aye?"

"Oils for smelling pretty are in those bottles." Grissa pointed at a trio of dark vials lined up on the table beside the tub. She wrinkled her nose as she lightly patted her armpit then delicately pointed below her waist. "Keeps down the stench in yer oxters and such, ye ken?" After that sage advice, she twirled about and bounced out of the room.

Mila closed her eyes and pulled in a deep breath, reveling in the quiet. She had always been a loner. Never the sort to join in on chatty girl gatherings, pub crawls, or midnight gossip sessions. One close friend had been enough. Tana. Robbie's mum. Tana had helped her learn to cope and actually get out in the world. Even enjoy being a tour guide for busloads of people. Heaven help her, she missed Tana.

She shook away the attack of self-pity and availed herself of the chamber pot, knowing the quiet wouldn't last.

"What would ye like to know about himself?" Grissa called out from the bedroom.

Might as well solve the mystery of Drummond Maclain. Mila took her time drying off and selecting an oil that smelled of lilacs as her new deodorant. "How long has he been acting chief?"

The maid stuck her head through the doorway, looking confused. "What?"

Mila wrapped the linen around herself, tucking it under her arms. She hoped the flowery scented oil soaked in soon. The slimy feel was not pleasant. "I assumed Teague is watching over the clan while the chief is away."

Grissa fluttered her fingers, urging her through the doorway. "Himself has been chief since he was born." Her voice dropped, taking on a somber tone. "He was born the night of the massacre, ye ken?" She shook out a simple white shift, then slipped it over Mila's head. "His mam birthed him in a cave with no one to help but his grandmam and his mam's sister. The poor woman died bringing him into this world. Thank the Almighty his mam's sister had milk to feed him. Her poor wee one froze to death whilst they searched for shelter that awful night." As Grissa tugged the shift down in place, she continued, "His uncle, Old Maclain, died too. Bloody Campbells killed him in his bed. They murdered himself's father, too. 'Twas a wonder he survived that bitter winter as a new bairn." She held up the stays, waiting for Mila to lift her arms. "His grandmam named him after her son, Old Maclain, and raised him with a thirst for vengeance." She gave another sad shake of her head. "His poor auntie that nursed him died of the ague when he was barely weaned." She moved around and tightened the stays until Mila could hardly breathe. "Himself has lost so many. That is why he gathered all of us soon as he got old enough. Many MacDonalds were scattered the night of the massacre when their homes were burned. But now we are together and a clan again. With a purpose."

Grissa's long-winded tale made little sense. Unless...? "Ye said his grandmam named him after Old Maclain." Mila tugged on the overly tight bodice, fighting for air. "He told me his name was Teague MacDonald." The more the lass talked, the more Mila dreaded confirmation of what she suspected.

"Aye." The girl helped her don a petticoat and tugged it down in place. She walked over to the bed and held up what looked to be two small embroidered sacks with ribbons sewn around their opening. "Mrs. Gillicutty even sent ye some pockets."

"Grissa?"

"Aye?"

"What is Chieftain MacDonald's full Christian name? Do ye know it?"

"Aye. He is Chieftain Drummond Maclain Teague MacDonald." The maid shrugged as she placed the pockets against Mila's sides and secured them by tying their ribbons around her waist. "I once heard him say he goes by Teague because no man could fill the boots left behind by Old Maclain." She held out the outer skirt for Mila to slip on over her head. "But as the younger Maclain, we all think he has done more than a little right by us. We are more prosperous than most and know he is going to lead us to become even more so. But if he wishes to go by Teague, 'tis his right."

Mila closed her eyes, hating the revelation. The kind, generous, charming Teague would die in a matter of months in a very horrible way.

CHAPTER SIX

TEAGUE EYED THE lad, noticing how he didn't use his size as an excuse to avoid anything. The boy charged in and tackled every task with cleverness. He thought things through and overcame every obstacle with skill. A rare trait in one so young. The quick-witted pup was sharper than a freshly honed blade.

His gaze following the lad, he kept his voice low. "Has he said anything?"

"Aye. Talks nonstop," Calder answered with a wide grin.

"Ye know what I am asking."

Calder shook his head. "Nary a word about where they came from or were running to. Or how he made those strange marks on his shirt." Suspicion and wonder filled the man's voice. "Those odd runes shine like hot coals whenever he steps into the shadows. Damnedest thing I have ever seen."

Teague snorted. "Remarkable indeed, considering all we have witnessed." While Calder might not be blood, he was the closest thing to a brother as any man could want, and twice as trustworthy. Teague resettled his folded arms across his chest. "His mother is just as tight-lipped. All she shared was the lad is verra sensitive about his size. Never call attention to it or call him *wee*, ye ken? Our young Master Robbie there is fifteen, though ye would never think it to look at him."

"Talk to him much and ye know he is older than he looks." Calder dipped a nod in the boy's direction. "Wisdom of an old soul in that one. In his eyes, too. Shadows of many trials. No telling what that lad's been through." He sidled a step closer, ducked his chin, and lowered his voice. "He would make a fine son, and I be interested in his mother. She is a widow, aye?"

The question awakened a possessive inner stirring that caught Teague off guard. "Aye, Mistress Mila shared that much. Widowed a little more than a year, she said."

"Mila," Calder repeated in a way that gave Teague the unreasonable urge to punch him. "Lovely name for a lovely lady." He chuckled. "Even when she be covered in mud."

"I have settled her and the lad in the quarters next to mine." Teague took a long, slow look at his friend, waiting for the man to realize the unspoken intent of that statement.

"I see." Calder's jaw rippled. After a significant pause, he nodded. "As ye wish, brother." His easygoing demeanor quickly returned. With a sly wink, he added, "I will make a damn fine uncle, though."

Teague clapped him on the back. "That ye will, but let us not put the wagon ahead of the horse, aye? The lady might not give either of us a passing glance." Her announcing that she and her son's stay would not be long still troubled him. Where the devil could they be headed? "She is dead set on leaving here as soon as possible."

Calder shrugged. "Could be she was traveling to family after losing her man."

"Could be." Teague had no idea but was determined to find out. "But that doesna explain her clothing. Why was she dressed as a man? And with such odd clothes. I have never seen the like of those trews and that coat of hers."

"Safety, perhaps? And could be she fashioned them herself." Calder pondered the mystery with a frown. "Maybe she wore them for ease in traveling? Would skirts not be bothersome while traveling the Highlands on foot?"

"Teague!" The screeching shout pierced the air like the sharp keening of a gull.

A groan escaped him before he could catch it.

Calder snorted a laugh before cutting it off with a cough. "I thought ye spoke with her?"

"I tried." Teague adopted a smile he didn't feel as old Liam's daughter sashayed into view. "How is yer father, Lizzie? Duff tells me the forge turned on him."

"His burns are healing well. Mrs. Cain's poultice did wonders." The curvy lass, known to turn the head of every lad in the keep, gave a coy toss of her blonde curls. "But I didna come here to speak about Da." She fluttered her pale lashes. A tactic that left Teague cold. "I came to scold ye for being gone so verra long," she said. "I missed ye."

He ignored that part. "Duff also said yer da gave the two of ye permission to marry." He rocked back on his heels and added an approving nod. "When is the big day, or did I miss it?"

Her flirtatiousness melted into the sullen pout of a spoiled bairn. "I have not agreed to marry him, no matter what Da says."

"He is a good man, that Duff." Teague slanted a brow at Calder.

"Aye," Calder agreed. "Fine as they come, old Duff is. Talented with leather, too. Ye could do a far sight worse for a husband."

"Or I could do better." She pinned Teague with a bold stare.

"Ye could at that." Teague grabbed hold of Calder's shoulder and pulled him forward. "But ye understand Calder here travels as much as I do, so he wouldna be home a good deal of the time." He shrugged. "Of course, yer house would stay cleaner." He shook the scowling man. "This one never has been known to wipe his feet."

"Ye know good and well what I am speaking about, Teague MacDonald!" She stamped her foot so hard that her curls bounced.

"And ye know good and well we already talked about this,

and I have not changed my mind." He had tried to be kind, but the stubborn woman refused to listen. "Ye would do well to choose another, ye ken?" He pointed at her and then pointed at himself. "You and I will never wed, lass. Never."

She turned and flounced away, a fuming growl echoing in her wake.

"Ye realize her father is strong as an ox?" Calder's gaze followed the girl as she disappeared around the corner of the keep.

"I spoke with her father and made my druthers known. He respects my stance, since I never misled her or treated her coarsely." That had been his saving grace. Whenever Teague felt the need for female company, an entertaining evening with one of Vivyanne's girls cured that itch. He always made it a rule never to dally with any women of the clan. Not when Highland winters could be long and filled with enough snow to trap a man at home for weeks. Nay, he would not be snared into marriage until he found the woman who made such an entrapment irresistible.

Calder tipped his head. "I still say ye best watch yer back with that one. Ever seen her throw a blade?"

Teague had indeed, and preferred not to dwell on it. "Master Robbie!"

The lad paused in brushing the horse and looked his way. "Aye?"

"Ye have done well enough for now. Come. Yer mother worries after ye. 'Tis time to ease her mind by showing her yer grubby face." Teague grinned. If Mila was like most mothers, the poor boy would be scrubbed within an inch of his life before nightfall. He didn't miss Robbie's sullen eye roll but managed not to laugh.

"She knows I am well. I saw her spying down from that window up there."

"Dinna argue with yer chief, boy," Calder said, but softened the scolding with a smile. "When the man says go, ye go. Understand?"

The lad's mouth tightened, but he didn't argue further. Instead, he hopped down off his stool, gave the horse one last wistful rub, then plodded over and joined them. "Let's get this done with, then," he said, sounding defeated.

Teague took hold of the boy's shoulder and steered him toward the library's double doors. "Chin up. Her maid helped her with a bath, so maybe she willna be too fretful with ye."

"Mi does like a good, long soak in a hot bath. 'Tis one of her favorite things." Robbie perked up as they stepped across the threshold. "So many books." He hurried to the shelves, leaning his head to one side as he scanned the spines.

"I told yer mother ye could read them all if ye wish. Come in here anytime ye like." Perhaps tarrying in the library would get the lad talking. Teague sauntered over to his desk, leaned back against it, and crossed his feet at the ankles. "By the way, do ye always call her Mi?" 'Twas an odd name for a bairn to call their mother.

"Aye," Robbie said in a faraway voice. He sidled along, studying the titles, transfixed by the offerings. "Ever since I started talking. Leastwise, that's what Mama always said."

Interesting. The boy spoke as if Mila and his mother were two different people. Teague didn't point it out, fearing if he did, the lad might go quiet on him. "I keep my favorite books in my solar. Ye are welcome to those as well. But ye must take care with them, aye?" As the youngling moved to another shelf, he added, "Of course, I dinna ken how long ye will have to enjoy them. Ye might not have the time to read them all."

Robbie selected a book and plopped down on the floor, sitting right where he'd stood. With careful reverence, he opened it and slowly turned the pages. After a moment, he paused and looked up with a frown. "What do ye mean, ye dinna ken how long I will have to read them? Must ye return them to another library soon?"

The boy thought the books were borrowed. Teague shook his head. "Nay. Every book in this keep is mine, but yer mother says ye willna stay here long. 'Tis my understanding the two of ye will be continuing yer journey we interrupted."

"Oh." Robbie jerked his attention back down to the book in his lap.

"Are there family or friends expecting ye?" Teague gently wheedled. "We could send word that ye are well. Then ye could stay longer and read all the books ye like."

The lad twitched a nervous shrug without looking up from the pages. "No one expects us. It's only Mi and me in this world."

"Then where were ye headed, boy?"

Robbie closed the book, returned it to the shelf, then shoved his hands in his pockets. "I can read later. Best get to Mi now before she comes looking for me."

"As ye wish. Follow me." Teague had pressed the lad too hard, but at least now he knew a wee bit more than before. No one expected them. That meant they were on the run. "We are headed to the third floor," he said. "Once ye've scrubbed some, yer mother and yerself can join us in the hall. 'Tis nearly time to sup."

Robbie paused before entering the stairwell. "I prefer to be the one to tell Mi about what I told ye in the library, ye ken?"

Teague studied the lad, realizing Calder was right: this one had endured much. "I will never repeat anything ye ask me not to repeat," he said. Then he caught the boy's shoulder and stopped him from climbing the stairs. "Unless it endangers yerself or yer mother. Then I would have to share it. Understand?"

The youngling grinned. "Aye. Mi's the same. I know I can trust her to keep a secret unless I'm about to do something stupid."

"Good, then." Teague waved the boy on. "Third landing."

As the lad climbed the stairs, Teague noticed his shoes. He had never seen such footwear. Black cloth with bright yellow soles and matching yellow stripes up the sides. Even muddy and in the dimly lit stairwell, the colors stood out. Almost glowing, like Calder had described the runes on the lad's shirt. Which reminded him he wished to witness that as well. "Robbie?"

The lad halted and turned. The marks on his shirt, the strange dots and whirls, were lit as if on fire. Teague's amazed stare clearly gave him away, because the boy looked down and rubbed his hand across the symbols. "I dinna ken why this looks the way it does. I stole these clothes. But dinna tell anyone, aye?"

"Yer secret is safe, lad." Teague motioned for the boy to keep climbing. The more he discovered about these two, the more they puzzled him. A huff of amusement escaped him. He loved nothing better than a challenge.

"Here?" Robbie glanced back at him before pushing open the door.

"Go ahead, lad. It opens into the hallway, not a lion's den."

"Yeah, well, ye have never seen Mi with a case of the red arse," he said. "I would rather face a lion."

Teague laughed. "Fearsome, is she?"

"Ye have no idea, and if ye are wise, ye will do yer best to never find out."

"I shall bear that in mind." He led the way to a door farther down the hallway. "This leads to the suite of rooms the two of ye can use as long as ye like. A sitting room, a bathing chamber, and two bedchambers."

Robbie looked suitably impressed. "I didna realize castles had bathing chambers. I thought ye only washed in bowls or rivers." Then his eyes flared wider. "I mean…Mi and I never had a bathing chamber before. Just washed in bowls or rivers."

"Earlier ye said yer Mi loved nothing better than soaking in a hot bath." He eyed the boy, then tried to ease the youngling's worries with a wink. "Lying takes a good memory, lad. 'Tis much easier to tell the truth."

Robbie glanced at the door, then shook his head. His voice dropped to a whisper. "I canna say more. Sorry."

Teague bent and locked eyes with the worried young sir. He kept his voice low. "I can help. Both yerself and yer mother. If ye will let me." He waited a moment, letting the words sink in and settle. "There is safety here, Robbie. Ye have my word."

The boy gave another nervous shake of his head. "I canna," he whispered again. "Sorry."

"I understand." Teague straightened, stepped past him, and opened the door. "Come, lad. Time to face the lioness."

"Lioness?" Mila repeated.

"Wow! Ye are like that painting, Mi." Admiration rang in Robbie's voice. "Out of our favorite history book. Remember the one with the—"

"Robbie!" The comely mud hen found on the roadside had transformed into an even more breathtaking woman. She fixed the lad with a sharp stare as she stormed toward him. "Thank ye for the compliment, but that is enough, ye ken?"

Teague recognized immediate regret registering on the boy's face. Robbie looked the same as he had every time he accidentally said more than he should. "He is right, mistress. Ye are a fair sight to behold."

"Thank ye, sir." She cast an appreciative glance around the large sitting room. "And thank ye as well for allowing us to stay in such lodgings. 'Tis verra kind." Before he could respond, her focus slid back to the lad, and she pointed at the door leading to the bathing chamber. "The bathwater is still hot enough, I think. If not, there are kettles over the fire. Make good use of it, aye? And dinna forget to use soap and wash yer hair."

Robbie opened his mouth to argue, then snapped it shut, snorted an irritated huff, and shoved through the door.

Teague expected the lad to slam it and was surprised when he didn't. At least the boy possessed some sense of survival. "I take it he doesna like baths?"

She shook her head, still glaring at the door. "It is not that he doesna like them. He resents when they take him away from his reading or whatever else he has going on." Her glare softened to a look of affection. "Robbie is a very single-minded lad. If he is engrossed in a book or working out a difficult equation, he doesna like leaving it unfinished."

"A difficult equation?"

Her cautiousness returned, shuttering her features like a mask. "Aye. Equations. He is quite good at mathematics, the sciences, and astronomy."

"As well as Latin."

"Aye. As well as Latin."

In other words, the lad was brilliant and more educated than an average bairn of the Highlands.

Teague ambled over to the petite cabinet beneath a tapestry he had procured in the East because he thought a future wife might like it. "Have ye tried the port?" He held up a fancy decanter.

"No." She put more distance between them, eyeing him as though preparing for a challenge. "While I appreciate yer hospitality, I would welcome some rest, if ye dinna mind."

He poured two glasses, picked them up, and joined her. "How long have ye been on the run, Mila?"

She managed a calm exterior, but alarm flashed in her eyes. "On the run?" She eyed the glass he held out. "I dinna ken what ye mean."

"Aye, ye do." He moved closer, nudged the glass toward her, and whispered, "It is not poison, mistress. Watch." He drained his petite goblet in a single gulp.

Her chin ratcheted upward to a defiant slant. "I didna think it poison." She took the drink and sipped it, glaring at him over the rim.

"I take it his mother was a dear friend of yers. Did she bid ye get him to safety?"

She answered by choking, turning aside, and beating on her chest while coughing and wheezing.

Apparently, his suspicions were on point, as usual. That part of the puzzle had been easy enough to sort. Especially after everything the lad had said and the fact he looked nothing like her.

Teague strode back to the cabinet and poured another port and a glass of water. "Here, lass." He handed the water to her.

"Forgive me. I am not trying to kill ye. I swear it."

"Ye have a bloody strange way of showing it." She sipped the drink, glaring at him as if ready to throw it in his face. "Robbie is my son. How dare ye say such a thing!"

"Yer words dinna match yer actions, mistress." He studied her, wishing he could win her trust. "Have I not proven ye are safe here? Would it not be easier to tell me the truth?" He moved closer, trying to ignore the not-so-subtle rise and fall of her fine, firm breasts beneath the light kerchief modestly covering the low neckline of her fitted bodice. "Even when a lad is the spitting image of his father, ye can usually see his mother in his eyes." He offered a knowing look. "I dinna see ye there. Not anywhere."

"Maybe ye are not looking hard enough." She marched across the room, thumped her glass on the cabinet, then went to the hall door and yanked it open. "Good day to ye, Chieftain MacDonald."

He almost laughed at her attempt to run him off by vexing him again. Instead of leaving, he settled into the only chair sturdy enough to hold him. Perhaps he should have put more planning into choosing the furniture for this room. "I am not leaving until ye offer me some honest explanations, m'lady."

She had to be of high birth. He hadn't picked up on it before, but she reeked of it now. Those high cheekbones. That regal stance. Her mannerisms. She was someone of importance.

"Ye may start by telling me yer real name and who is after ye."

She held fast at the door, glaring at him with her teeth bared. "No one is after us. Now leave." Her eyes narrowed to match a sneer that only convinced him more of her noble blood. "Or were ye lying when ye said ye would do us no harm? That we were safe here?"

He sipped the port, wishing he had stocked the cabinet with whisky instead. He flicked his hand and shook his head. "How have I harmed ye? I merely intend to sit here until I get some answers." He uncrossed his legs, leaned forward, and propped his elbows on his knees. "In all seriousness, m'lady, if ye are at risk, then my clan is at risk as well." He shook his head. "That, I canna have. Do ye not agree?"

"Then Robbie and I will leave as soon as he finishes his bath." She slammed the hall door shut again, stomped back to the cabinet, and threw open all its doors. "And what poor excuse for a Scot cannot keep a decent bottle of whisky at the ready?" Her voice echoed with the sound of frustrated tears wanting to be shed. With her back to him, she bowed her head and leaned forward, gripping the cabinet until her knuckles went white.

"Damn and blast it all," he muttered. He couldn't abide a woman crying. Especially not because of him. "Ye will not leave," he said, louder. "Ye will share yer feckin' troubles so I can help ye. Understand?"

"Dinna bellow at her or I'll be coming out there to deal with ye!" Robbie shouted through the door.

"I am not bellowing," Teague retorted. "I happen to be a loud man. When I raise my voice, ye will know it." He resettled himself in the chair and jerked a thumb toward the bathing chamber door. "Ye see? Ye upset the lad. Is that what ye wish?"

"Dinna be turning this on me as if it was my fault. Ye started it." She descended on him, shaking a finger and thrilling him with her fire. So, here was the fearsome lioness young Robbie mentioned. "When I am ready to share our woes, I will share them, and not before. Did it ever occur to ye I am a mite cautious about pouring out my troubles to a man I have just met? What if yer kindness is naught but an act? What if all these folk only appear to respect ye when, in fact, they fear ye?" She stabbed the air again, accusation ringing in her voice. "And what happened to yer assurance that if I didna wish to answer anything, I didna have to?"

The lady made a fair point, but that didn't diminish the fact that if she was in danger, so was his clan.

He tempered his answer with a kindly look. "I understand what ye are saying. However, I have worked all my life to make this a safe place for my people after the bloodbath of Glencoe. The well-being of my clan outweighs my earlier promise to respect yer privacy. I fear I must now retract it." He slowly shook his head. "My charity and hospitality are great, but my protectiveness is even greater. Do ye understand what I am trying to say? Are ye familiar with what happened to the MacDonalds on that terrible day?"

She somehow softened, her tension melting away. One of her dark curls slipped free of its pinning and fell to her shoulder. She caught hold of it and nervously twisted it through her fingers. "I know of the massacre," she said quietly. "Terrible doesna begin to describe it." She lifted her gaze to his and studied him, her brow creasing with a most endearing frown. "I want to trust ye," she whispered.

While he wanted to rise from the chair and go to her, he forced himself to stay put. Nay, he did not wish to veer her from what he hoped was sharing more about herself and the boy. "Ye can trust me, m'lady. I swear it."

"M'lady again, is it?" One of her sleek, dark brows rose. "What happened to Mistress Mila or Mistress Abernathy?"

"Nay." He offered a sly grin. "Ye are most definitely a lady of noble birth." With a bold sweep of his gaze from the top of her head down to the hem of her skirt, he continued, "The way ye carry yerself. Delicate features. A long, lithe form Michelangelo himself would rise from the grave to sculpt. Silken locks as glossy black as the Earl of Hell's waistcoat and twice as tempting. Aye, m'lady. Ye are Mistress Mila no more. Yer title is most definitely *lady*."

She turned away and walked to the window, staring outside. Silent. Pensive.

He silently applauded himself. She was of noble birth. And on the run. With someone else's son.

"I canna tell ye everything," she finally said. "But ye are right about Robbie and me being on the run." She turned from the window and faced him. "And Robbie is my godson. But I love him like my own." Her expression became more intense, almost threatening. "And I will protect him like a son."

Teague lifted his glass. "He is a fine lad, m'lady." After draining the dredges left in the small goblet, he placed it on the table beside him.

"A vile group held us hostage. I canna say their names." She slowly walked toward him, wringing her hands while frowning down at the floor. "But we escaped them during a terrible storm and havena looked back since."

He rose from the chair, ready to order his men to ride out and thrash the fiends. "What *group*, m'lady?"

She shook her head and turned aside. "Please dinna ask," she said so softly he almost missed it. "I canna tell ye that or all that we endured. Not yet." Then she squared her shoulders and faced him again, her eyes glistening with unshed tears. "But I swear on my own life that they will not harm this clan. Nor will they harm you."

"How can ye be so certain they are not still after ye?"

"Because they are lazy bastards," Robbie said. He stood in the doorway of the bathing chamber, a wrap of linen clutched around his scrawny waist, water puddling around his feet. "The king paid them to take us to the port at Fort William and send us to the Colonies. They decided to save themselves the trouble and kill us here in the mountains. Figured nobody would find us. During the storm, we slipped away and hid. Clung to the side of a cliff." The lad gave a proud wink. "We tore a cloth and stuck it to a bush on the edge. Those fools laughed about us falling to our deaths and saving them even more time and trouble."

"So, they believe ye dead?" Teague wanted to trust the boy's story, but an uneasiness nagged at him.

"Aye," Mila said. "They thought us dead and headed on to Fort William."

"And why did the king exile ye to the Colonies?" That was the part that worried him most.

"Robbie's father was well favored at court. Jealousy and the fact that Robbie's mother would not cede to the Duke of Montfort's lecherous wishes ended that favor. The king ordered them exiled after a false accusation of treason. While fighting our captors, they were killed." She moved to Robbie's side and smoothed his dripping hair out of his face. "We escaped."

The story seemed valid enough—except for one thing. Teague gave her an encouraging nod. "That explains Master Robbie's presence here, but not yers. What is yer part in this travesty, m'lady?"

"I defended Robbie's parents and exposed the lies being told about them out of petty jealousy and wounded pride." Dark eyes flashing, she kept her gaze locked with his, daring him to call her a liar. "Since my house is not among the most powerful in the Lowlands, the court deemed me a traitor as well."

"I see." He really didn't see and hadn't decided if what the two said was the truth or not. Although he had to admit that what they described had a realness to it. They definitely appeared invested in the story. "And might I know yer real name, m'lady?"

"Lady Mila Loraine Carthson of Roxburghe. The duke is my brother."

"I dinna ken the name." A lie, of course. But only a harmless one to aid in discovering the actual truth this lady fought so hard to hide.

"As I said, my house is not among the most powerful in the Lowlands." She gave an embarrassed shrug. "The only time I ever attended court was to accompany Robbie's mother." Her expression hardened. "To lift my voice in defense of her."

Weariness painted shadows beneath her eyes. It tensed her voice to the point of hoarseness. The woman needed rest. She most definitely had not lied about that.

Teague offered a polite bow, gave Robbie a nod, then crossed to the door. He cast a look back before opening it. "Rest, m'lady, so I might enjoy yer company at supper." After a meaningful pause, he added, "Ye are safe here, Lady Mila. Ye need not run anymore."

CHAPTER SEVEN

"HOW ARE WE gonna remember all those names?" Robbie came to a standstill on the stairs. He angled sideways and frowned back at her. "What were they again?"

"Duke of Montfort is the bad guy. Roxburghe is my…whatever. Since I told him the house was minor, it'll need to be a low level of the peerage. More like an honorary something or other." Mila carefully lowered herself to sit on a step. All the yardage in this clothing would take some getting used to. She already hated the way the constrictive stays bit into her if she bent the wrong way.

"Will they not be waiting for us? Grissa said we are expected at the head table."

"I need a moment, aye?" She wasn't quite ready for whatever awaited them at supper.

Robbie followed her lead and sat too, propping his arms on his knees. "What if he tries to look up those names? What then?"

"At least he canna do an internet search." She had no suitable answer. "If he finds out I lied…" She couldn't finish that sentence because she didn't know what she would do. Lies did not come easy to her, but currently, anxiety did. There was so much to figure out. She massaged her temples. The pounding in her head had laughed at the willow bark tea.

A reassuring pat on her arm shamed her. She should be the strong one. Not Robbie. His sweet, trusting gaze made her eyes glaze over with tears.

"Aww now, dinna cry, Mi," he said softly. "Least we landed in a decent place, and Chieftain Teague seems kind enough. I like him. Do ye not?" He grinned. "I really think he fancies ye. Why else would he enjoy nettling ye or keep offering his help?"

"Robbie." The passage she had read about Teague's execution still made her sick. Worse than sick. It hurt her heart and battered her conscience because they had to ignore it. Why did the infernal man have to be so…so damn nice and caring? And big-hearted. Grissa's stories about those he had taken in and helped only made her feel worse. This good man would be dead in months. "Robbie."

The lad shook his head. "I dinna like it when my name gets stuck on repeat. Go on and say whatever it is that is so bad."

She had thought to spare the boy the truth, but he had the right to know. "Teague dies in December of this year. I remember reading about his execution while researching the history of Éirich for a tour. We have to leave here as soon as we can. I dinna ken if we will be safe after that."

Horror, then disgust, played across his features. "We canna leave here. We have to save him like he saved us." He rose to his feet and glowered at her. "How could ye be so heartless?"

"I am not being heartless." Aye, she was, and she hated herself for it. But Robbie's safety came first. "I dinna ken if it is even possible to change history."

His unforgiving glare hardened even more.

The lad needed to understand the risks. What chaos might they trigger if they tried to change what had already happened in the history books? Could they even change it?

She reached out to him, but he jerked away. "Robbie, dinna be that way. What if it is his destiny? What if his death must happen so something else, something good, will come of it?

Everything is connected. Ye know that."

"Since it is not a disease, we might could prevent it. Dinna ye dare say we canna even try. We traveled back in time, didn't we? Just our being here changes history. Think about that. We have to take the chance. His life is at stake. Maybe *that* is why we are here. To save him. Did ye even think of that?" He scowled at her, angrier than she had ever seen him. "Since when do ye turn yer back on someone in need? Since when do ye turn a blind eye to something ye could change for the better?"

"Since we landed in this godforsaken century, and I dinna ken how to protect ye!" A sob escaped her before she could stop it. "I love ye, Robbie. Ye are my precious family. The son I never had. Yet how can I keep ye safe here?"

"No matter the timeline, nothing is guaranteed, Mi. Not safety. Good health. Nothing." His bottom lip quivered. "Not even enough time with those we love with all our might is guaranteed." He sniffed and lifted his chin, revealing a battle against tears. "Mama and Da always told me if we live in fear, we dinna live at all."

She bowed her head and rubbed her tired, gritty eyes. How could she argue with any of that? A sad, huffing laugh escaped her. "How can ye be so wise at only fifteen?"

"I am pure dead brilliant. Remember?"

"I do at that." With the help of the wall, she pushed herself up to her feet. "The British catch him in late November. Near Stirling, I think."

"And kill him in December?" Robbie led the way, moving slowly as he took in everything she said.

"Aye. Hanged, drawn, and quartered on December twelfth. For aiding in trying to revive the Jacobite cause." The rumbling of conversations and people moving around the great hall filtered up into the stairwell. "We are nearly there. We shouldna speak of it anymore until we are alone in our rooms."

"I will think on it at supper." With a decisive nod, he stepped aside as they reached the main floor.

"I had begun to think the two of ye decided to stay in yer rooms," a familiar, deep voice said.

Mila clapped a hand to her chest and whirled to find Teague standing entirely too close to the stairwell archway. "Ye startled me!" Heaven help her and Robbie both if he'd overheard anything.

His teasing, lopsided smile eased her mind and made her heart flutter like it hadn't in a long while. "Why, Lady Mila. I believe that smacks of a guilty conscience."

"Not at all," she argued. "Merely a sense of self-preservation." She couldn't help but notice he had changed out of his dusty clothes into a long, dark fitted jacket that perfectly displayed the impressive width of his shoulders and the trimness of his waist. Belted kilt. Tall black boots cleaned of every speck of mud. Long, dark hair combed until it shone in the candlelight, secured at his nape. The chieftain cut quite a handsome figure, indeed.

Robbie cleared his throat and bumped against her. "Ye are staring, Mi."

Teague's rumbling laugh sent a rush of heat to her cheeks. "Ye will pay for that, lad," he said. "Never embarrass a lady."

"I am not embarrassed." She rested a hand on Robbie's shoulder and squeezed it hard while fanning herself with the other. "I am just a little over-warm."

"We have a bit of time yet before Greta sends out supper to the tables." Teague offered his arm. "We could step out to the garden and take some air if ye like. The rain has stopped."

"That would be nice." She managed a polite smile. Actually, that would be uncomfortably stressful, but how could she refuse? She took his arm, then turned to Robbie, counting on him to save her. "Ye will come too, aye?"

He wrinkled his nose. "I will not." He tipped his head toward Calder and Bhric idling beside a table with another amiable-looking man and young lad. "I think I'll go visit with them."

"Fine idea," Teague said. "Iagan, the man there beside Bhric, would like to introduce ye to his boy, Auley." He bent closer, as though wishing to keep their conversation private. In a low voice, he continued, "The lad struggles something fierce when it comes to speaking. 'Tis as though the words dinna wish to come out. He has endured a lion's share of cruelty and teasing because of it." He shook his head. "Before they swore fealty to our clan, he suffered greatly. They have had a better way of it since coming here. Auley can neither read nor write, nor do sums either. Even though many have tried to teach him." Teague eyed Robbie with a knowing smile. "Would ye be willing to help him? He doesna have any friends, and his da worries after him."

Robbie studied the boy across the way, then slid a dubious look back at Teague. "I know what ye are doing, aye?"

"I would never take ye for a fool, lad." Teague slanted a dark brow higher. "But the fact remains Auley needs yer help. Are ye willing?"

"I will help him. I never turn my back on someone in need." The boy fixed a hard glare on Mila that she immediately understood.

She glowered back at him, narrowing her eyes just enough to fire back. She had already agreed to try to save Teague, but it would take time and planning. Robbie needed to realize that.

Teague patted her hand as he turned them toward the hall leading to the library. "The two of ye spar like mother and son."

"Did ye spar often with yer grandmother?"

"I see Grissa has apprised ye of my beginnings and probably everyone else's as well." He opened the door and stepped back. "Amazing accuracy, that one. If Grissa tells ye something, ye can wager it to be the truth. I believe she somehow verifies everything she hears."

"That is good to know." But it also made her wonder if he or Mrs. Cain had planted Grissa in her rooms as a spy. As they stepped outside, she glanced back, noting he had closed the hallway door leading into the library. "How will they know where to find ye when yer food is ready? I dinna wish either yerself or yer people to have their meal delayed while I enjoy the fresh air."

He kept his gaze aimed straight ahead, revealing a strong, handsome profile worthy of immortalization on a coin of pure gold. "Have ye forgotten Master Robbie knows where to find us?"

There was that. "I have not forgotten. Well—not now, anyway." She blew out a despondent huff.

"What is it, m'lady?"

A deep breath of the cool, rain-washed air helped fight back her nervousness. "I have never done well at small talk or idle chitchat. And it has been a very eventful day." The slow stroll across the garden helped calm her, too. The winding patches of cobblestone led them toward an ivy enclosure. With the sun setting, she expected its interior to be dark, but instead, a light flickered out from the arched opening and the walls of thick green leaves. "Are there torches inside?"

"Aye." He halted them a yard or so from it. A somber, faraway look filled his face. "Torches are kept lit there. Tended by my cousin, Willie MacDonald, and his family. In memory of those lost at Glencoe. A spring feeds the pool at its center, symbolizing our determination to thrive and seek justice."

She bit her lip, remembering the overgrown rubble of the place in the twenty-first century. The shelter of ivy carefully trained here on trellises would someday become invasive vines overtaking everything. "It is verra lovely. A wonderful tribute." Such a bloody shame that wars, the clearances, and politics had prevented the descendants from preserving it.

"Would ye like to step inside and see it closer?" The quiet reverence in his tone touched her heart.

"I would be honored," she said, finding herself speaking just as reverently. The need to cry burned her eyes as she entered the lovingly tended area that time would eventually erase. A tear escaped before she could stop it.

Teague caught it on his finger and pressed it to his lips. "'Tis a precious thing for a woman to weep for tortured souls she never met."

She couldn't speak. To do so would betray the overwhelming emotions that would crack her voice. So, she managed a shy smile, tucked her chin, and turned away. There was no way to explain all she felt. To read about history was one thing. For it to come alive and embrace you was quite another.

"Ye are beguiling me, Lady Mila," he said in a voice soft as a breath.

This man tempted her. Not just physically, but in a much more dangerous manner. He tempted her to invite him into the sanctity of her inner circle, become one of the few she allowed to know her best. "Ye just met me," she argued rather than confess the beguiling went both ways.

"Nay, m'lady." He moved closer, stepping around to peer deeply into her eyes. "This may be our first meeting in this life, but I feel certain we knew each other well in another." He gently tipped up her chin and stroked her cheek with his thumb. "Do ye not feel the draw? Like the pull of the tides? Or the river's current?"

"Everything happens for a reason," she whispered. That had been her mother's, grandmother's, and great-grandmother's mantra.

"And everything is connected." His coaxing smile made her heart sigh. He eased closer, his gaze focused on her mouth, and hers on his.

She wet her lips, hungry for the taste of him even though she knew it would be a mistake.

"Teague MacDonald!"

His nostrils flared like he was a bull about to charge. Turning his head with a jerk, he let his hand drop away from her and stepped back. "What is it, Lizzie?" he said through clenched teeth.

"Supper awaits ye. All are hungry and ready to eat."

Mila offered the curvy blonde a smile. "Thank ye for fetching us. Lizzie, is it?"

"Aye," the young woman said without a hint of friendliness. "Lizzie Jamison. I know well enough who ye are." She spun about and flounced away.

"It appears I have made an enemy." Mila increased the space between them, both thankful and mildly disappointed about snarly Lizzie's interruption. It was for the best. As she had always been taught, everything happened for a reason.

"I shall be speaking to Mistress Lizzie about her rudeness. I grant ye that." Teague glared after the lass.

"Dinna trouble her." She dismissed it with a flip of a hand. "Perhaps she had been hunting for us for a long time. I get ratty too when I am hungry."

He gallantly offered his arm again. "Then let us get ye to yer supper, m'lady." He winked. "I dinna wish to see ye *ratty*. Master Robbie warned me about earning a poor opinion from ye."

"I am sure Robbie is full of warnings about my opinions. After all, he is a teenager." She almost flinched, praying he wouldn't glom on to her wording. "I realize he is small for his age, but he is still a young man." She needed to stop babbling like a fool. That helped nothing. Where was snarling Lizzie now that she needed another interruption?

"What was that word?" Puzzlement creased his brow as his steps slowed. "Teen-age-er?"

Of course, the man missed nothing. "Yes," she said, as if nothing was awry. "Since he is fifteen. His age is in the *teens*. So, he is a *teenager*." She offered what she hoped was a convincing smile. "I canna remember where I heard it the first time, but it made so much sense I decided to make it my own."

"It does make sense." He seemed impressed.

Mila breathed a sigh of relief while inwardly thrashing herself for the careless slip. She needed to be more careful. As they entered the great hall, most, if not all, eyes swiveled to them. She swallowed hard and tried to smile, but Robbie's wide-eyed expression told her she had failed.

Teague leaned in so close that she swore his lips brushed her ear like a lover's nibbling. Then again, maybe it was merely the warmth of his whisper sending shivers down her spine. "Relax, m'lady," he said softly. "They are curious because they have never seen ye before. That is all."

His nearness released a flash of heat and shut off her ability to breathe. She cleared her throat. "I am afraid I have never been verra good with crowds."

"'Tis a friendly crowd, though. Ye will see as ye get to know them." He pulled out her chair and helped her scoot up to the table. Still standing beside her, he held up a hand and waited for the quiet murmuring around the tables to stop. "Allow me to introduce Lady Mila Carthson of Roxburghe and her godson, Master Robbie Abernathy." He paused and cast a long, slow look at those gathered. "I have offered them safe haven here at Éirich. Make them welcome and treat them proper. Remember, for some of ye, it wasna so long ago that ye needed sanctuary as well, ye ken?"

Those seated agreed by banging their tankards on the table. Those standing agreed with hearty nods.

Teague took his seat beside her and motioned for their glasses to be filled. "See? All will take to ye. Just give them a bit a time."

She smiled and sipped the wine. Platters of roasted meats, bowls of boiled and baked root vegetables, and hampers of bannocks and torn chunks of bread made it to the table. Thankfully, everyone's focus shifted off her and to the food.

Except for one. Every time she looked up from her plate, Lizzie's glare burned into her. The lass was as jealous as a territorial feline. Mila would have to ask Grissa about her.

"M'lady?"

"Sorry. What?" She switched her focus back to Teague, realizing too late he had said something she missed.

"Do I bore ye, m'lady?" Once again, he teased her with that deadly, charming smile.

"Not a chance." She cast a glance around the large room filled with entirely too many people. "A feast this size is a lot to take in after today's adventures."

His teasing air faded, replaced with a troubled frown. "I

shouldha considered such. Forgive me." As he studied her, his worried expression became more pronounced. "Do ye wish to return to yer rooms? I can have Grissa or one of the lads bring ye anything ye like. Food. Drink." He nodded toward the cabinet behind them. "Ye wanted whisky before. I can send that too."

While she would have liked to accept that offer earlier, if she left now, she would surely look a coward to everyone watching. And she harbored no doubts that glowering Lizzie would do her level best to churn the waters against her. Instead, she rested a hand on his arm and smiled. A real smile from the heart. After all, this man had been nothing but kind and considerate. Or at least after he ordered them captured, he had been a generous host.

"I would be a rude guest indeed if I didna remain and enjoy this fine meal with such good company," she said. "Please forgive my poor manners."

His gaze dropped to her hand where it rested on his arm. That devilish smile of his returned. "Nothing to forgive, m'lady." He lifted his glass and waited for her to do the same.

While she didn't know what he intended to say, she couldn't very well decline a toast after apologizing for unmannerly behavior. She raised her glass and waited.

"To the finest company I have enjoyed in a while," he said in a voice meant for her alone. He touched his glass to hers, making them ting like a crystal bell.

"Aye," she said. "To the finest company." And she meant it even though she felt beyond a sliver of a doubt he was a smuggler, possibly a Jacobite, and most definitely a womanizer. She took a long, slow sip without taking her gaze from his. A rogue he might be, but he also possessed a lion's share of kindness, caring, and generosity. Robbie was right: they had to save Teague from his fate.

Movement inside the circle of tables pulled her from the depths of Teague's gaze and made her turn. The hairiest man she had ever seen ambled forward with a slow, unsteady gait. Wild hair pulled back in a ponytail fell past his shoulders. Tufts of coppery curls peeked through the untied throat of his tunic. His sleeves were rolled up past his elbows, revealing muscular arms thatched with hair so thick and ruddy it could pass for fur. A bright smile split his auburn beard as he lifted his tankard high, sloshing the contents on the floor. "Raise yer cups, ye ungrateful lot, and celebrate the return of our mighty chief!"

"We be more grateful than yerself, Duff, and not nearly as sotted!"

The burly man staggered in a slow circle with one eye squinted shut, searching through the diners. "Dugald! Get yer cowardly arse up here and say that to my face!"

"Are they going to fight?" While Mila hoped they didn't, at least the drunken scuffle would take the focus off her.

Teague chuckled as he settled more comfortably back in his chair. "Doubtful. Though sometimes they spar a bit. This is routine for them. Twins, ye see. Always trying to best the other. But while Dugald's talents make him an asset during our travels, Duff's skills serve the clan best here. Finest leatherworker the Almighty ever created."

While keeping her focus on the grinning brothers circling each other like a pair of wrestling bears, Mila leaned closer to Teague and kept her voice low. "And what are Dugald's talents?"

He gave a shake of his head. "Nothing I would discuss with a lady."

"Well, that isna fair." The words came out before she could catch them. Must be the wine and weariness loosing her tongue at both ends. Frustrated with herself, she decided to own it, since she couldn't un-ring the bell. "Just because I am a woman doesna mean I canna understand things, ye ken?"

"Ye misunderstand me, m'lady." Either seductiveness or admiration flashed in his eyes. Maybe both. "I have no doubt ye have the wit and wisdom to puzzle out anything ye wish. But, as ye already know for yerself, 'tis a cruel world at times, filled with many an unsavory character. I wouldna insult ye nor wish to upset ye by speaking of such sordid details that would make yer blood run cold." He gently took her hand and brushed the lightest of kisses across her knuckles. "I respect ye too much for that."

The brothers tumbled into the table, making every dish and glass rattle.

Teague gave a long-suffering roll of his eyes and bellowed, "Enough!"

The scuffle immediately halted. Both men bowed their apologies while backing away. Arms draped around each other's shoulders, they returned to their seats.

Mila swallowed hard, thankful once again for a well-timed interruption. Teague was a skilled charmer. Better than any she had dated in the twenty-first century. None held a candle to him.

She pulled in a deep breath and eased it out. She needed to be on her guard. If she caved and allowed him to get too close, her and Robbie's secrets might be discovered. That could be disastrous.

She tried to catch Robbie's eye and signal him they should go to their rooms. The boy ignored her, refusing to glance her way. But the longer she glared at him to get his attention, the more she realized he wasn't ignoring her on purpose. The lad was intent on teaching his new friend sign language. Or she assumed it was sign language. It looked very much like what she had seen interpreters use. What touched her most was Auley's father as he watched the boys. Even though he smiled at them, the man appeared ready to weep.

"What is he doing over there? With young Auley?" Teague leaned forward, studying the lads.

"Teaching him another way of communicating." She couldn't stop a proud, loving smile. "Robbie knows what it's like to be bullied. If Auley canna overcome his speech difficulty for whatever reason, he can always fall back on this." She huffed a frustrated groan as Robbie showed Auley an unmistakable hand signal from the future. Both the boys laughed loudly. "And it appears Auley will also be fluent in obscenities."

Teague gave an amused snort. "Ah, well—every lad needs to

have a coarse term or two ready. Comes in handy at times, ye ken?"

"Dinna encourage him. He already looks up to ye."

"Does he now?"

The man's pleased-with-himself air made her scold herself again for not better minding her words.

"I am glad to hear it," he said. Then all levity and smugness left him. He jumped to his feet, his focus locked on an arched doorway at the far end of the large room. "Excuse me, m'lady. I must beg yer leave." Before she could respond, he charged away, maneuvering around tables and people as if a beast chased after him.

Grissa appeared at her side as if she had waited in the shadows. "Be ye ready to retire, mistress?" The girl kept glancing in the direction Teague had gone.

"What just happened?" Curiosity piqued, Mila found herself not nearly as tired as before. Whatever made Teague rush off could be something she needed to know in order to save him.

The maid cast a hateful scowl down the tables to the right, pinning Lizzie with a glare that threatened to incinerate her. "'Tis best we speak of it once we reach the privacy of yer chambers."

"I understand." Mila slowly rose, spared Lizzie a dismissive glance, then motioned for Robbie.

At first, he shook his head, then hurried to her side. "What happened? Yer face looks like thunder."

"I am not sure yet." She turned them around so their backs were to those still at the tables. "I am going upstairs. If ye wish to stay down here, ye can, but stay away from that lass with the blonde hair that's almost white. She's at the table on the right in the light blue. Her name is Lizzie. I'll find out more about her once Grissa and I have a word." He started to turn to see the girl, but she stopped him. "Dinna be Mr. Obvious, ye ken?" After a quick hug that made him growl, she smiled. "Ye will never be too grown for my hugs, ye rascal."

He rolled his eyes, but she could tell he was pleased. As he started to walk away, she caught his arm again and locked eyes with him.

"Be careful, aye? We have not yet properly sorted friends from foes here."

"I'll be watchful and let ye know if I hear anything else." He winked as he backed away. "On wi' ye now, Mi. At yer age, ye need an early bedtime."

She shooed him away with a threatening shake of her finger.

"Should I fetch ye a stick, mistress?" Grissa glared after the lad. "And if that doesna thrash the disrespect out of his wee arse, I'll get one of himself's belts."

Mila laughed as they hurried to the stairwell. "He loves to tease. Always has. Dinna pay it any mind." As she climbed the steps, she tossed a glance back. "Now, what did Lizzie have to do with Teague rushing out of the room? Tell me everything ye know."

"I caught her whispering to Bethia."

"Who is Bethia?"

"Bethia looks after *the* Lady MacDonald." Grissa motioned for her to climb the stairs faster. "I daren't say anything more till we are in yer rooms. These stairwells carry whispers something fierce."

Mila caught up her skirts and scurried faster, dying to know more about the mysterious Lady MacDonald. She rushed into her sitting room and whirled about, waving for Grissa to hurry and close the door. "Who is the Lady MacDonald?"

The maid hurried across the room, caught her by the arm, and gently tugged her all the way to the farthest wall in the bedchamber. "Lady MacDonald is himself's grandmother," she whispered, as if the draperies hid spies. "No one sees her unless they go to her chambers because she is bedridden."

Disappointed as a child who had just received plain white socks for Christmas instead of a bicycle, Mila wasn't sure what to say. She stood there for a long moment, waiting for the rest of the story. It didn't come. "Why were ye so afraid to speak about her downstairs? Why all the secrecy?"

"She is a pagan." The maid cast another look around the room. "And some say she is well over two hundred years old because she honors the old religion."

"Rumors. Ye know how people love to make stories bigger than they are." Teague probably rushed from the room because someone signaled that his invalid grandmother needed him. Totally understandable.

Weariness and waning adrenaline triggered a yawn. Mila turned and pointed at her back. "Undo me, aye? I am ready to be done with this day."

"Ye dinna understand, mistress," Grissa insisted. "Folk only go to Lady MacDonald when they need a spell or an ill wish cast upon an enemy."

Mila had heard enough. She was tired, worried about surviving, and still none too sure that she and Robbie could change history and save Teague. Unintentional sharpness crept into her tone. "Whatever they send out shall come back to them thrice." She flexed as the bodice fell away and her stays loosened. "And if that doesna work, I'll light a black candle on Lizzie's arse. That'll fix her negativity for her."

Grissa gasped, making Mila realize what she had just said.

"Well, damn." Without looking at the girl, she climbed into bed. Might as well stare at the ceiling and figure a way to tell Robbie she would soon be burned at the stake for witchcraft. "Goodnight, Grissa."

"A good night to ye, mistress," the maid whispered, then ran from the room as if demons chased her.

"I am such a fool." Mila scrubbed her face with both hands, then let them fall away. "I hope Robbie fares better than I just did."

Chapter Eight

"I remember a time when ye hurried to see me first thing. Soon as ye entered the gate."

"I came to see ye earlier, and Bethia said ye were asleep and not to be bothered." Teague kissed his grandmother's cheek. "Dinna scold me, sly one. Not when yer maid just gave the signal and scared me white-headed."

She peered up at him from her throne of pillows and hissed like a boiling kettle. "Dinna lie to yer grandmother. Yer hair is still black as new soot." With a coy wrinkling of her nose, she patted a spot beside her. "Sit and tell me of this new guest yer jilted Lizzie spoke of to Bethia."

"Ye know good and well I did not jilt Lizzie."

"Whether ye did or did not matters to no one but Lizzie." She dismissed the subject with a flip of her arthritis-knotted hand. "Who is this lass who arrived dressed so strangely?" Her wizened face puckered with a thoughtful scowl. "And a boy. I believe Bethia mentioned a lad too? He belongs to her?"

"Her godson. Master Robbie Abernathy." Grandmother Cora might be aged and bedridden, but a sharper mind could not be found. She knew everything happening within the clan and guessed the rest with astounding accuracy. Her unknown sources were so thorough that he often consulted her with the sole purpose of learning all she ferreted out. She had even foretold the future a time or two. Many thought her to be a white lady with the sight. Teague neither knew nor cared. She was Grandmother. The woman who had forged him into the man he was today.

"Well? What about the woman? Tell me more."

"Lady Mila Carthson of Roxburghe." He maintained a neutral expression, knowing the family name for the Roxburghe peerage was Ker and not Carthson. He'd had a run-in with that Lowlander duke over a shipment of brandy.

"Mila Carthson," she repeated slowly. Her critical squint sharpened. She plucked at her covers and wiggled her narrow shoulders. "Fix my pillows, aye? I wish to sit higher."

He leaned forward so she could wrap her thin arms around his neck as she had done countless times before. She hated help of any kind. Hated asking for it even worse. But this way seemed to appease her, since it made her feel as if she still had a hand in her own care. "Hold tight now. Ye've wallowed one of them down under yer wee behind."

"I tire of riding this bed," she grumbled. She hugged him tighter, sniffing his hair in the process. "Ye bathed? This lass must be a beauty. Dare I hope to see a great-grandchild afore I die?"

"Dinna start." He plumped her pillows with one hand while supporting her with the other. "And I bathe regular. Ye know that."

"I know my idea of regular and yer idea of regular dinna always agree." She settled back in her freshly plumped nest and nodded. "I thank ye. Now, get on with it. This Mila Carthson—"

"Lady Mila," he corrected her, then dared to grin.

"We both know Carthson is not a name belonging to the Roxburghe peerage." She folded her hands in her lap and stared off into space. "Tell me where ye found her, how ye found her, and what she claims as her story."

The prospect of a fresh mystery to solve added color to his precious grandmother's cheeks. The sight made his heart glad.

Every time he'd traveled of late, he dreaded returning, fearing she would be gone. He could not bear the thought of her passing. She had helped birth him and raised him with a loving fierceness that had switched his wee arse red whenever he crossed her, and healed his skinned knees with kisses and fanciful stories. The world would be a darker place when she left it.

She poked him. "Well? Get on with it. I am not getting any younger, ye ken?"

"Found them on the road overlooking the Three Sisters. When they spotted us riding their way, they tried to hide." He gave her a look he knew she would read correctly. "We *invited* them to the keep, since they appeared quite worse off from whatever experiences they had endured. Drenched through, covered in mud, and lying. Badly."

Her eyes narrowed. She pursed her thin lips as though tempted to whistle. "And her lies?"

"Said the boy's parents fell out of favor at court. When she defended them, she fell out of favor as well. Supposedly, they all were convicted of treason and sentenced to deportation to the Colonies from the port at Fort William."

"Fort William?" She fixed him with an incredulous stare. "Why bring them all the way north to Fort William? Why Scotland, even? That makes no sense at all."

"I thought the same. I believe she wished us to think it all took place at Stirling."

"That fool Hanoverian king doesna have the desire nor the bollocks to hold court at Stirling. He keeps his arse in London when not traveling back to where he belongs."

Teague laughed as he pushed up from the bed, crossed the room, and poured them both a dram of the best whisky he had tasted to date. He handed her the drink then lifted his. "Here is to never mincing words, aye?"

She chortled like a wee hen pleased with extra feed. "Aye, to that." After taking a sip, she closed her eyes and smiled. "Ye always know what I need, laddie of mine."

"I try." He noticed her hand trembling as she lifted the glass to her mouth again. "I have wearied ye, and Bethia said ye ate even less supper than usual."

She snorted and downed the rest of the whisky. "I dinna need much supper to do nothing but lie abed."

He took her empty glass and set it on the bedside table. "Shall I read to ye awhile?"

Her thin brows drew together. She seemed distracted. Troubled. And that troubled him. "Not tonight. I am sure ye have much to do with this being yer first day back."

"I am never too busy for ye. Ye know that, aye?" He didn't like her sudden quietness.

She smiled and patted his hand. "I know that, laddie." She nudged him as though trying to push him off the bed. "Off wi' now to yer duties. Send Bethia in, aye?"

He rose, kissed her cheek, and gave her hand a gentle squeeze. "Dinna die on me, Grandmother. Ye are my only conscience."

She squeezed his hand back, her pale blue eyes suddenly watery. "I canna live forever," she whispered. "But dinna fash yerself, sweet laddie of mine. I will always be with ye. Whether in body or spirit, ye ken?"

He kissed her forehead and hurried to the door before she spotted the threat of tears in his own eyes. With his hand on the latch, he spoke without looking back. "Breakfast tomorrow? Eh, sly one?"

"Aye, laddie. Breakfast tomorrow. Now leave me be."

Without another word, he bowed his head, left the room, and closed the door softly behind him. He leaned back against it and released a despairing sigh. Her soul would free itself soon. While he understood her need for relief and freedom, he wanted her to stay. He was a selfish man and not too proud to admit it.

"Forgive me for scaring ye, my chieftain." Bethia gave him a sad smile. "She ordered it done just so, and I will never go against her wishes."

"And I thank ye for that." He read his own concerns in the kindly maid's face. "She is weaker."

"Aye." Bethia folded her hands in front of her apron as if waiting for further questions. Always quiet as a church mouse. He often wondered if she talked freely with Grandmother.

"Keep her comfortable. Anything she wants, ye ken? Absolutely anything." He doubted it needed saying, but the turmoil within him demanded he say something.

She nodded and stepped aside, obviously waiting to be dismissed to return to her duties.

"If she gets worse or anything happens..." He couldn't finish the sentence.

"Ye will be the first brought to her side, my chieftain."

He waved her away. "Go now. She waits for ye."

She dipped a modest bow and eased into the bedchamber.

Teague loped down the stairs but slowed before stepping back into the hall. He slipped into the shadows beneath the gallery and watched his people, studying those he hadn't seen for several weeks. Most, he trusted. Some, he knew held grudges against him for decisions he had made in the past. But all in all, he couldn't fathom being a part of any other clan. He would defend them with his life. And that was what worried him. Had he brought trouble into their midst? Was the lovely, yet lying, Lady Mila a danger?

"Why are ye creeping around inside yer own keep?"

Teague barely stopped himself from drawing his dagger and attacking. "Never sneak up on me, boy. Understand?"

"Sorry." Torchlight revealed Robbie's hurt expression as he retreated a step. "I thought ye heard me walk up."

Teague eyed the boy's feet. "Those feckin' shoes of yers are quiet. Where did ye come by them?" As the lad hesitated to answer, he shook a finger within inches of his nose. "And dinna lie. Ye nay stole them, as ye said about that otherworldly tunic ye wore when we found ye."

The youngling's gaze dropped to the borrowed clothing that

made him look like one of the clan. Worn, yellowed léine. Faded trews hitting him just below the knees. And then those feckin' black cloth shoes with the bright yellow stripes and soles.

He shrugged. "Mi got them for me. For my birthday. I been wanting a pair for a while."

Teague folded his arms across his chest and studied the youngling. He hadn't lied, but neither had he answered. "*Where* did she buy them?"

Eyes wide with obviously feigned innocence, Robbie shrugged again. "Some shop in Edinburgh. I dinna ken which one." He eased away, sidestepping to make his escape. "I best be going now. Mi's done gone up to bed. But I am sure she willna sleep till she knows I am safe in mine."

Teague found that believable but also disappointing. He had hoped to spend more time with the lovely lady before the day ended. "I shall escort ye to yer rooms, aye?"

"Uhm...okay."

"Okay?"

Robbie's eyes flared even wider. "Uhm...yes, sir?"

Teague scrubbed a hand across his eyes, then let it wearily drop. "That is not what I meant, boy. What is that word? *Okay?*"

The lad visibly relaxed. "It means agreement. Like *all right* or *aye*."

"Yerself and yer godmother come out with the strangest words." He clapped hold of the boy's shoulder and steered him to the stairwell, ignoring everyone they passed.

"Why are ye mad?" Robbie asked as they climbed the steps.

"I have not lost my mind. Yet. Although I am sure there are some who would argue the point."

"I mean *angry*. Not insane."

One of the boy's shoes emitted a strange squeak with every step. Teague found it mildly annoying. "I am not angry. I am travel-weary and also tired of sorting through lies."

"Oh."

"Oh is right," Teague said. "Would ye care to help me with

my sorting?"

"What do ye mean?"

"Ye know verra well what I mean. Dinna play the numpty with me."

Robbie came to a halt and stared at his feet. "I would rather ye asked Mi." He turned and made what felt like defiant eye contact. "Just remember the only reason either of us answers anything the way we do is 'cause we are afraid, ye ken?"

"How can I make ye understand I would never hurt either of ye?" Teague tried to understand the emotions playing across the boy's face and failed.

Robbie didn't respond. Just returned to climbing the steps. In silence.

They reached their floor without another word between them. As soon as Teague opened the door to their suite of rooms, Robbie bolted across the sitting room, charged into his bedchamber, and slammed the door behind him.

"What did ye do to him?" Cold, dark accusation dripped from Mila's tone. She charged forward, both hands fisted as though ready for battle. "Answer me!"

It was the first time he had ever been so insulted and aroused at the same time. "I did nothing to the lad." He jabbed a finger at the bedroom door. "Call him out here and ask."

Relentless, she took another step toward him. "If ye did nothing, then why is he upset? What happened downstairs?"

"Enough with yer games. Who are ye, Mila?" He closed the remaining distance between them, standing so close he felt the heat of her motherly outrage. "The truth this time, if ye please."

Her fists tightened, and her chin rose in defiance. "I already told ye. Are ye cursed with some ailment that makes ye forgetful?"

"Insults willna sway me from my course." He forced himself to keep his gaze locked with hers rather than allowing it to drift down and take in the revealing drape of her thin night rail. "Yer name, mistress."

"Mila Carthson." She glared at him, her jaw set.

"And where is yer home?"

"Edinburgh." She bit out the words, looking ready to spit in his face.

"And yer godson? If that be the truth. His name?" He struggled to remain cold and unyielding. The hatred building in her eyes pained him.

"Carthson Robert Abernathy," she said. "He prefers 'Robbie.'" She bared her teeth like a cornered animal. "He is my godson, and I would kill to protect him."

Of that, he had no doubt. "Ker is the family name of the Roxburghe peerage. Why did ye lie about that?"

Her expression cold and emotionless, she glared at him as though he hadn't spoken.

"Mistress? I would appreciate an answer," he said. "The truth this time."

She folded her arms and disarmed him with a chilling smile. "I didna lie. I am the duke's bastard sister, by his father's favorite mistress." With a toss of her tempting black mane, she strolled over to the cabinet and filled a single glass. A subtle yet obvious insult. "When several of the duke's *acquaintances* found me and Robbie's mother, my dearest friend, quite fetching…" She paused and drained the goblet, then slammed it back down on the cabinet. Slowly, she turned and shot another icy look his way. "Do ye understand the gist of *kill or be killed*?"

"More than ye realize, m'lady."

She huffed a bitter laugh and paired it with a sneer. "Oh, so we are back to *m'lady* now, are we?" She sashayed back to him. The tempting sway of her hips made him swallow hard. "I am a bastard, remember? Not a *lady*."

"Why did ye lie?"

"To protect myself and Robbie."

"That, in and of itself, is a lie. I offered ye sanctuary here. Did I not?"

"And as soon as ye discovered my lineage, ye wouldha made

me a fourth in Vivyanne's troop of whores." She bared her teeth again. "I know how men like ye think, but ye best understand, just because I am a bastard doesna mean I am a whore. At least, not yet. I consider selling my body the last resort to survival."

"Ye have no grounds for that accusation, woman. No grounds at all." Her unjust perception sent a renewed surge of frustration through him. He stabbed the air, aiming his finger at her. "I have been nothing but kind to ye and Robbie."

She glared at him, trembling with fury, her tempting curves silhouetted by the candelabra on the table behind her. "Ye dinna ken what grounds I have for anything. Ye have not lived my life or endured my troubles."

That he could not argue. He needed a drink before he said something he shouldn't. He strode to the cabinet, yanked open the doors, and searched for the strongest available spirit. "Why the blazes did I not stock this room with some feckin' whisky?"

"I believe I asked ye the same earlier," came her snide retort from the window.

He turned to find her perched on the wide sill, staring out into the night. The cooling breeze lifted her hair like the wings of a breathtaking, dark angel. He swallowed hard again, nearly choking on his hunger for her. Pure frustration incarnate or not, he wanted this woman with a fury.

He poured two goblets of port and marched over to her. "Here. It is the strongest there is. Tomorrow, I shall order whisky stocked in every room, I grant ye that."

"Thank ye."

He took her softer tone as a small victory, but saw her stilted coldness remained. His forcing of the truth had hurt her, shamed her even though she had nothing of which to be ashamed.

He bowed his head in her direction. "I apologize."

Without taking her gaze from the stars, she said, "Ye dinna have a clue what ye apologize for. I hear it in yer voice."

He downed his port, set down the glass, then took hers and set it down too. Turning her by the shoulders, he forced her to look him in the eyes. "Aye, I do know. And ye should understand this: I rarely apologize for anything."

The moonlight revealed the faint ticking of her heartbeat just below the angle of her jaw. He longed to run his lips across it, but didn't dare. At least, not yet.

"I truly regret upsetting ye," he said in a low, rasping whisper. "Please forgive me."

She stared up at him, eyes shining with tears that shamed him. But at least her hatred and scorn seemed to be gone. Thank the Almighty for that. "I am sorry too," she said.

Something about her tone, her expression, made him question what she really meant. He had no doubt she felt remorse. But for some odd reason, he didn't feel it had anything to do with him. Mila regretted something. But what?

"Ye are the most mysterious woman I have ever met."

Her sad smile made his heart clench. "Ye have no idea, sir."

The need to gently brush her hair back from her cheek overpowered him. His fingertips grazed thc softness of her skin as he slipped the silky strands behind her ear. She didn't flinch or slap him, just watched him with her fathomless gaze that had gone as dark and all-consuming as the night.

With his fingers still in her hair, he leaned in and brushed a kiss across her mouth. Her supple lips were even sweeter than he had imagined. He kissed her again, allowing himself to tarry longer, giving the kiss more urgency. When she hesitantly opened her mouth to his, he eased her deeper into his arms. He longed to crush her to his chest but held fast against the impatient urge. Instead, he gentled her into a closer embrace, holding her as tightly as he dared.

Saints preserve him, he needed her. But after what she'd just told him, to seduce her now would be the wrong thing to do. Both his heart and gut knew it. But his cock? Not so much.

As much as he hated to, he ended the kiss and lifted his head. But he didn't end the embrace. He kept her curves pressed against the length of him, savoring the sensation and wishing no clothing existed between them.

She settled a hand on his cheek and held his gaze. "I dinna ken if this is wise or not."

He allowed himself a smile. "I have never been accused of possessing wisdom."

She didn't smile back. Just looked sad, with the faintest frown creasing her brow. She stared off into nothingness. "Ye know nothing about me."

"I know enough." He trailed his fingertips up her long, graceful throat, then cradled her face in his palm. With the slightest shake of his head, he lowered his voice to a more intimate whisper. "But I will do nothing ye dinna wish me to do. Nor do I want ye feeling forced into anything. My protection does not hinge on ye coming to my bed. All I ask from ye is honesty and loyalty."

"Ye are such a good man." She uttered the words like a sigh, and their quietness touched him like a lover's caress. A genuine smile played across her lips this time. "I have needed a good man for a verra long time." But then her smile faded, and she dropped her gaze. With a slight shake of her head, she eased out of his arms. "I canna do this. Not yet."

"I understand." And he did. He didn't like it, but he understood. Drawing on all the control he possessed, he graced her with a kindly dip of his head. "I leave ye to yer rest, m'lady. Till morning reunites us, aye?"

"Aye," she whispered.

He turned and left, unable to bear another moment without touching her. A heavy exhale escaped him as soon as he stepped into the hallway and closed the door behind him. Perhaps it was best that the lass had stopped them. If she wielded this much power over him with nothing more than a look and kiss, what might happen if she gifted him with even more?

He increased his speed and charged into his solar. Thank the old gods, whisky waited for him here.

He filled a glass and started toward his bedchamber, then

stopped halfway. After the hearty sip he sorely needed, he backtracked to the cabinet and fetched the bottle. Whisky would warm his bed this night. He hadn't drunk himself to sleep in a long while. He was due.

After placing the bottle and glass on the bedside table, he stripped off his coat, ripped away his belt, and shed his kilt. He took another long, healthy swallow of drink before kicking off his boots and ripping away his neckcloth. He rewarded himself for not losing his balance by pouring another glass while unbuttoning his waistcoat. His shirt quickly joined the pile on the floor. Naked except for the whisky in his hand, he moved to the window and shoved it open wider. The coolness of the breeze across his heated flesh made him ache worse. It reminded him of how she had looked in that thin shift while staring out the window. The soft material had outlined everything from her nipples down to the dimples of her arse. Perhaps that was an exaggeration, but he felt sure those dimples were there, eagerly waiting for his touch.

"Bloody hell, I need more whisky."

He returned to the bedside, poured another overflowing glass, and lowered himself to the bed. Atop the covers, leaning back against the headboard, he downed the fiery nectar as fast as he could swallow it. He aimed the empty glass at the table and missed. It hit the floor with a quiet thud. He shrugged. "Glad I got that Turkish carpet," he informed the canopy overhead.

As he slid farther down into the pillows, he eyed the bottle. It was well within reach, even though the glass was not. He blew out a disgusted snort, snatched hold of it, and brought it to his lips. Why the hell shouldn't he drink from the bottle? Was he not chieftain? After a hearty swig, he propped it on his thigh and stared at the door adjoining his room with hers. One narrow wall between him and certain bliss. Bloody shame, that was. He took another long, deep drink.

Eyes still on the door, he slowly lowered the bottle. He blinked hard then squinted at it through the dimness of the room. The whisky must be toying with him. Then the latch clicked again and the door slowly swung open. Mila stood framed in the doorway, carrying a candle. Chemise untied. Neckline hanging open. One side of it slipped off, revealing her bare shoulder.

He blinked hard again, then raised the bottle in front of the candle burning at his bedside. The level of the liquid wasn't all that low. The vision couldn't be from the whisky. Perhaps it was a dream.

"I hope ye have some left," she said softly. "I would like some too." She crossed the room and set her candle next to his. "May I join ye?"

"Be this a dream?" He held out a hand. "Not that I mind, ye understand."

"This is not a dream." She ran her fingertips across his palm, sending an explosion of sensations through him.

"Are ye certain, lass?" He was still sober enough to worry about what she would think when it was all said and done. "Because once we start…"

She bent to retrieve his glass from the floor, giving him a clear view into her open neckline. "I am positive." She filled her glass and drank it all before pouring herself another. "'Tis fine whisky." She handed the bottle back to him, gathered her shift up above her knees, and climbed into the bed. Her gaze dropped as she slowly stroked a finger up his thigh. "I couldna sleep. Not after that kiss." She smoothed her hand across his stomach then up his chest. After a brief pause, she held out her glass and whispered, "More."

"More indeed." He filled her glass, took a long, hard pull on the bottle, then set it on the table. When he turned back to her, she held out the empty cup. "More, m'lady?" He reached for the bottle.

She shook her head. "No. Please set the glass on the table. For later, aye?"

"Aye." He hurried to comply, then faced her, opened his mouth to speak, and promptly forgot what he was about to say.

She tipped her head forward as if ready to hang on his every word. "Ye were about to say?"

"I dinna ken." He gently caught hold of her arms and pulled her across him. "I am glad ye changed yer mind," he rasped as he slid both hands into her hair and pulled her down for a kiss.

Without breaking the smoldering connection, she resettled her position, placing a knee on either side of him. She barely pulled back, interrupting the kiss. "I have been so lonely for so verra long," she whispered, her lips brushing across his. "It has worn me weary."

"Seek yer ease with me, m'lady. Let loneliness trouble ye no more." It alarmed him to realize more than simple lust pounded through him. But it didn't alarm him enough to make him stop.

He slid his hands up under her shift and smiled to himself. Just as he had thought. A pair of dimples waited to be kissed at the small of her back. His breath caught in his throat as she arched upright, slipped off her night rail, and tossed it to the floor. Her body glowed a tawny gold in the candlelight.

He ran both hands up her taut stomach, then cupped the pert mounds of her breasts. His mouth watered for the taste of her dusky nipples. "Perfection itself."

She responded by leaning into his touch and grazing a trail of nibbling kisses up his throat. "I am not a patient woman," she murmured after a nip of his earlobe. She sat up and smiled down at him. "At least not the first time, anyway. It has been too verra long since…" Her words trailed off, and she licked his neck. With a breathiness that threatened to undo him, she continued, "I will try to be more patient the next round, aye?"

"I await yer commands, m'lady. Tell me what ye wish."

"Oblivion." She slid down on him, mounting him with such calculating slowness that the excruciating pleasure almost killed him. And then she rode. Hard. Her intensity and speed increased with every thrust of her hips until his world exploded.

Oblivion, indeed.

Chapter Nine

W*HAT THE DEVIL was I thinking?* With the liberating effects of the whisky worn off and her dangerous yearnings sated, Mila's missing-in-action common sense came flooding back with a vengeance. It brought with it a heady dose of regret and an extra-large helping of *oh shite*.

She eased up and peered over at Teague. He lay with his face turned away, but his left arm remained curled around her. That masterful right hand of his rested on his taut stomach. Her gaze slid lower. Even at rest, *that* part of him was still impressive, too. A renewed surge of wanting cascaded through her.

"Stop it!" she hissed under her breath, then froze, fearing she had awakened him. He didn't stir. Thankfully, the man slept like the dead. She released the breath she held and eased up to a sitting position. Luckily, she had only dozed long enough to sober up and come to her senses. Time for as much damage control as she could muster.

She checked the window. Still night, but not much longer. The sky already shimmered with a lighter hue. She slid off the bed, tiptoed around it, and scooped up her shift from the floor. After another glance at the steady rise and fall of his chest, she skittered out through the connecting door back to her bedchamber.

She yanked on her shift, then patted the wall in search of the hook holding the key. Without the aid of a candle, she fumbled it off to the floor. It hit with an extraordinarily loud metallic ping. She froze and waited to see if either Teague or, even worse, Robbie heard it. Silence reigned through all the rooms, granting her the right to continue on.

She dropped to all fours and patted around until she found the key. Once the door was locked, she made her way to the cushioned bench in front of the window and collapsed. With her forehead resting in the crook of her arm, she continued her inner damning. How could she have been so stupid? So weak? So bloody irresponsible? Never had she behaved like this before. Jumping into bed with a man she hardly knew?

"I am such a fool," she whispered.

A disturbing aroma broke through her self-condemnation. She lifted her head and sniffed herself. Heaven help her, she smelled like Teague. Not only that, she reeked of their lovemaking. She hurried to the pitcher on the low cabinet across the room, sloshed some water into the bowl, and scrubbed. But no amount of washing would cleanse her irritation with herself. She scooped another handful of the soft, rose-scented soap and scrubbed some more. "After all my self-righteous lectures to Robbie about safe sex…"

That thought made her go still and mentally count the days into her current cycle.

"Lovely. Now I have yet another thing to worry about." She washed harder. "Ye are such a damned fool, Mila Loraine!"

"Mi?" A light tapping on the door followed Robbie's soft call. "Are ye up yet?"

She dropped the cloth into the bowl, took a running leap, and dove into the bed. While thrashing her way under the covers, she did her best to assume a sleepy tone. "I am awake. Come in, if ye like."

The door slowly swung open. Robbie lifted a nearly spent

candle, sweeping it back and forth like a modern-day flashlight. "I thought I heard ye talking when I walked past yer door."

"Why were ye walking past my door?" She clutched the covers higher to hide the water she had splashed all over her shift. He had refused to talk with her last night after charging into his bedroom. Said all he wanted was privacy and time to think. "Are ye all right, my handsome brat?"

"I am fine." He set the candle on the bedside table and perched on the side of the bed. "I drank all my water, so I got more from the parlor."

If he drank that much water, he probably needed to pee. She couldn't remember if she had told him about chamber pots. "Is there a chamber pot in yer room? A container to pee in?"

He eyed her as if he thought her addled, then dipped a nod. "Aye. There's this weird cabinet that opens into a chair with a hole in the seat. The chamber pot's under it. Grissa showed me." His expression settled into a troubled scowl, and he stared down at his hands. "I think I am going to have to stop wearing my trainers."

"Did someone ask where ye got the shoes?"

"Chieftain Teague." He lifted his eyes to hers. "He knows we lied about the duke and my parents."

"I know." She rubbed her forehead, trying to recall her latest tale word for word. "I had hoped ye eavesdropped and overheard the new lie."

"Ye told me eavesdropping was rude."

"And since when do ye listen to everything I tell ye?" She scooted up in the bed and leaned back against the headboard. "I told him I was the child of the duke's father's mistress. That's why I lied about being the duke's sister."

"Why would that make a difference?"

"Out-of-wedlock children are not well thought of in this era. Especially not the children of extramarital affairs. And most especially not daughters." She waited for him to sort through all that before continuing. "I also told him the duke's friends were verra attracted to yer mother and me."

"And?"

She shrugged. "I was vague after that. Mentioned something about the kill-or-be-killed theory."

He wrinkled his nose and rubbed his forehead. "So what am I supposed to say happened to my parents?"

"Same story there. Both were killed while we fought off the fictitious men who wanted yer mother and me. Then I took ye and ran." She gave a decisive nod. "I couldna verra well leave ye there with yer parents murdered."

He stared at the ceiling and blew out a heavy sigh. "It would be so much easier to tell him the truth."

"That a thunderstorm carried us back in time three hundred years?"

"Well, of course it sounds bad when ye say it like that." He hopped off the bed, went to the window seat, and plopped down on it. He propped his chin in his hand. "What are we going to do here, Mi?" He cast a despondent look back at her. "I mean, after we keep Chieftain Teague from getting killed?"

"Live, I guess. What else is there?" She offered him a teasing grin. "At least until ye figure out the quantum physics of this mess and discover how to reverse the effects of that storm."

"His journal said this is May 1722. Same day as in our time, I think." He hugged his knees. "It's like the centuries run parallel."

"So we were thrown into a different time loop?" She closed her weary eyes and rubbed them. "How do we hop back to ours?"

"I dinna ken that part yet." His sour expression hardened even more. "And dinna get yer hopes up, either. Even Einstein was still refining his theory when he died. His equations proved we could travel forward. They hadn't worked out the back-in-time part yet."

"Then we should concentrate on saving Chieftain Teague for now and worry about the rest later. Agreed?"

"Agreed. But I sure dinna want to give up my trainers. I love those shoes."

She gave a jaw-creaking yawn. "We will have to come up with a story about them, too."

He pushed up from the seat and blew out the candle. "Sun's up enough to see." He frowned. "Did ye not sleep well?"

"Am I that bad?" She pulled up her knees, folded her arms atop them, and rested her forehead on her arms. The lad never lied. At least, not about that. She could always count on him for an opinion, no matter how abrasive. "Ye could lie to save my feelings, ye ken?"

"I would rather not, and ye know it."

She lifted her head and glared at him.

A wicked grin tugged at his mouth. "Ye could pack a week's worth of clothes in those bags under yer eyes."

She pointed at the door. "Out. I am going to try for a little more sleep."

"Better try for a lot more from the look of ye." He sidled toward the door. "Can I go downstairs? I can snoop around more if not too many are up yet."

"Watch what ye say and to whom ye say it, aye?" She slid down into the bed and burrowed under the covers. "And if ye hear anyone mention Jacobites, eavesdrop like ye have never eavesdropped before. The Jacobite cause was the reason for Teague's arrest and execution."

"Aye, Mi." The door clicked, but then it clicked again and creaked back open.

She lifted her head enough to see what the lad wanted.

"Ye know I love ye, aye?" Robbie's face was a picture of worry.

"Aye, my handsome brat. I do know that. And ye know I love ye too. Even more than I loved our minibus."

His worried expression disappeared.

She smiled as he slipped back out and the door clicked shut again. The lad loved to tease, but his conscience nettled him something fierce if he thought he'd hurt her feelings. She closed her eyes, struggling to get her mind to quiet down and leave her in peace for a bit. Her thoughts refused. Instead, her worries about surviving, saving Teague, and sleeping with the infernal man after just meeting him replayed over and over. Her heart chimed in, whispering that the real reason she had gone to his bed was not only loneliness but because she liked him. More than she had ever liked anyone. Especially someone she had just met.

That revelation irked her. She huffed and smacked away a strand of hair tickling her nose. If she never found Mr. Right in her time, how silly was it to think she would find him here within a few hours of arrival? "Just shut it and go to sleep!"

She squeezed her eyes tighter shut and conjured up images of waves crashing across a beach. As they hit the rocky strand, she counted them off and forced herself to concentrate on their sound. Just as she started drifting away, a knock at the door startled her back to wakefulness.

"What?"

The hinges gave their slow, creaking whine, grating on her already raw nerves.

"I brought ye some tea and a warmed bannock, mistress," Grissa said softly. "Master Robbie said ye are feeling poorly."

Curled on her side and determined to remain buried in the pillows, Mila pulled the covers up to her nose. "Master Robbie exaggerates. I didna sleep well last night. That is all."

Moving with the stealth of a cat, Grissa eased the tray onto the bedside table while bending to peer closer. "Ye do look a mite peely-wally under there."

Mila gritted her teeth, biting back a very unkindly retort that the concerned maid didn't deserve. "I promise I am fine. Just overtired because of…things."

The lass gave an understanding nod. She went to the window and pushed the panes open wide. "Fresh air will do ye a world of good." She crossed to the window on the other side of the bed and opened it too. "I had a cousin once who fretted herself straight into the grave." She returned to the table and filled a small, handle-less cup with tea. "Sad wee thing, she was. Always worrying about something." She placed the delicate porcelain bowl on a matching saucer and held it out. "Drink it whilst it's hot, aye? It will help with yer ailing." She wrinkled her nose and lowered her voice. "Is it time for yer courses? I stocked the drawer like I said I would. I can fetch a tisane that helps with the belly pains."

Mila prayed for control to keep from strangling the well-meaning girl. She pushed up on an elbow, accepted the bowl, and sipped it. Strong and bitter. She almost laughed. Gran had once told her if she didn't let people close, she would end up like a cup of over-brewed tea: strong and bitter.

"Thank ye, Grissa. The tea is nice." She took another sip, then handed it back. "Just let me lie abed a little longer, aye? Just an hour or so." She managed a smile. "I am less ratty when I am rested."

The maid took the cup and placed it back on the tray. "I just dinna want ye angry with me." She cast a worried glance down at the meager breakfast while nervously tapping a finger on the table. "Do ye burn those black candles often?"

Mila suppressed a groan. What a bloody hypocrite she was. Warning Robbie over and over to watch his words, and what had she done in one mindless slip? Convinced this poor lass that she was a witch. She had to stanch Grissa's concerns quickly and nip that worry in the bud.

She sat upright, scrubbed a hand across her forehead, then raked her hair back from her face. "I am not a witch. I dinna cast spells, conjure spirits, or consort with demons. What I said about that black candle was meant in jest, because I am not afraid of Lizzie's snarkiness."

Grissa eyed her as if weighing her words for a grain of truth. "I wouldna mind if ye were a witch, ye ken? A good one, that is. Like a healer or a white lady with second sight. That could be helpful to the clan."

Mila lifted both hands in surrender. "Sorry. I am just me. A woman who talks when she should be listening." *And minding her tongue*, she added to herself. She flopped back down, sorted her covers, and released a heavy sigh. "And please dinna think me a lazy layabout. One more hour abed and then I will rise and tend to whatever duties I need do, aye?"

"Ye are certain it isna yer courses?" The lass gave an encouraging nod. "Ye can tell me, mistress. I am yer maid. It is for me to know and help with, ye ken?"

Eyes closed, Mila considered shoving her head under the covers to escape, then decided against it. "It is not my courses. I promise."

"Hmm."

She cracked open an eye wide enough to shoot the girl a hard glare. "Go away, Grissa, and I mean that as kindly as possible."

"Yes, mistress."

Mila closed her eyes again and waited for the click of the door closing behind the maid. It never came. She sat up and squinted against the blinding sunbeam trespassing across the bed. The maid, hands primly folded in her lap, perched on the end of a chair beside the bath chamber door.

"What are ye doing now?" Mila flinched, hating the shrillness of her tone.

"Ye asked for naught but an hour more in the bed." The lass shrugged. "By the time I reheated the water for yer washbowl, told Greta to fix ye a proper breakfast, sent the lads for more wood for yer hearths, and told Malie and Dorrie to wait a bit to tidy yer rooms, it would be past time to help ye rise and prepare for the day." She tipped her head toward the bathing chamber. "So, I pushed the kettles back over the fire and decided to wait here. I didna wish yer day to start late because of me."

The door leading in from the sitting room flew open. Teague stood framed in it. Barefooted. Clad in nothing but his léine. Long black hair loose and tumbling across his shoulders. "Mila? What is it?" He hurried to her bedside and leaned over her. "Calder came to me straight away when Robbie told him ye were ailing."

"I will be fetching yer breakfast now, mistress!" Grissa ran for the door. She slowed enough to pull it shut behind her with a quiet bang.

He pressed the backs of his fingers to her cheek, his expression tense with worry. "Praise God there is no fever."

She scooted away from his touch and pressed back against the headboard. "Robbie lied," she said. "I am not sick." She hugged her knees to her chest. Heaven help her, what a feckin' mess. "I merely wanted some sleep."

He frustrated her even more by rumbling with a low, seductive chuckle while climbing into her bed. "I see, m'lady."

"No, ye do not." She scooted again, putting more space between them. "Thanks to yer nearly naked entrance, Grissa now knows what we did."

"I chose her to be yer maid because ye can trust her," he said quietly. His understanding smile made her heart flutter. Her traitorous body hummed with readiness as he tucked an errant curl behind her ear. "She will keep all yer confidences, m'lady."

"That is not the point." Weariness, frustration, and an overwhelming mix of emotions threatened to reduce her to a sobbing mess. She covered her face with both hands. "She will think I am a...a slut. Or worse, a plotting female trying to control her chieftain with sex."

"I can think of worse ways for ye to try to control me."

She dropped her hands and glared at him. "Ye know what I mean."

"Why did ye leave my bed?" The caring in his tone touched her heart, making it swell with an aching she preferred not to address. He reached over and grazed a fingertip along the back of her hand. "When I awoke and ye werena there, I worried after ye. For what we had done and yer earlier reservations about joining me in my bed. Then when I tried our door, it was locked. Why, my precious dove? Why, after the wonderful night we shared?"

His questions caught her off guard. She stared at him, trying to think of something, anything but the truth. She couldn't tell him she had allowed herself to be seduced because she wanted to be. Or that for the first time in her life, her loneliness had overpowered her. She had already told him that much. At least, she thought she had. The alcohol she had consumed made her memory of the things she had said a bit fuzzy. However, the things they had done remained quite clear in her mind. Strange thing, alcohol.

She bowed her head, unable to face him any longer. "Last night was a mistake," she confessed. "I should never have come to ye. Ye need to go, aye?" She shook her head. "I am sorry."

"Last night was not a mistake." He scooped her hand into his and brushed kisses across her fingers. "Mila."

The way he said her name—deep, rasping, coaxing as a siren's song. She struggled against his hypnotic spell. This dear man would die in a few months if she could not change history. "Teague," she said without meeting his gaze. "Please go." A distraught gasp escaped her. Her tone lacked the conviction she needed. "Ye should go. Now."

"Are ye certain, lass?"

Ever so gently, he pulled her into his arms and cradled her close. After a tender kiss to the top of her head, he combed her hair with his fingers. The mesmerizing strokes threatened to be her undoing. She could feel herself melting into him, relaxing under his touch.

"I will leave ye be if ye truly wish it," he said softly. "But I need ye to say it with meaning." He settled more comfortably back against the headboard and pillowed her head on his chest. "Mila?"

His warmth against her cheek. The strong firmness of his chest beneath her. Their perfection together. How they fit each other like long-lost pieces of a puzzle. All this lulled her even more. Against her will, her heavy eyelids closed.

"No," she whispered. "I guess ye can stay. For now."

"Sleep, my own," he said. "Find yer rest here safe in my arms. I willna allow anyone or anything to trouble ye ever again."

Oh, how she wished that was true. She hugged him closer, panicking as tears squeezed free, rolled down her cheek, and splashed onto him.

"Lass." He gathered her up so he could look her in the face. With a touch as gentle as a whisper, he wiped the tears away. "What is it? Tell me so I can make it right." He pressed a tender kiss to her forehead, then disarmed her even more with that crooked smile. "No one will ever hurt ye again. I swear it."

She ran her fingertips through the short hairs of his neatly trimmed beard. If only she could tell him the truth. The need to protect him from what lay ahead ached within her. The urgency to save him from his fate grew stronger with each passing minute.

A soft sob escaped her. "Dinna go near Stirling the rest of this year. Nor most of next year either. Promise me, aye?"

"Why, m'lady?"

Maybe she could make him think she had the sight. Grissa had hoped for such, said it would be a boon to the clan. If she worded things just right, surely she could pull it off. "Ye will be arrested near Stirling in late November, then hanged, drawn, and quartered in December." She caught her bottom lip between her teeth, praying that her plan worked. This could go so very wrong in so many ways.

His jaw tightened and his dark brows drew together into a fierce knot. In fact, his entire body tensed beneath her. But he didn't speak. Just eyed her with an unreadable expression.

Heaven help her. Perhaps her instincts had been dead wrong. She tried to ease away.

"How do ye know this?"

"I saw it." That was not a lie. An artist's rendering in the history book depicted the terrible execution alongside the article. "But I only discovered it was about you when Grissa told me yer full name." Again. All that was true.

"And what do they charge me with?" His tone had gone cold as death.

"Treason," she whispered. "They name ye a Jacobite trying to renew the Cause." More of the article came to mind. "Ye must deny all associations with the Bishop of Rochester, the Earl of Sunderland, and, most importantly, Christopher Layer. Sunderland died in April, but the others I mentioned and even more will soon be arrested." She prayed he not only believed her, but also wouldn't throw her and Robbie into the dungeon for such outlandish tales. "Some will be exiled. Others will share yer fate."

Teague didn't speak, just stared off into space, dumbstruck by her prophecy.

After easing free of his hold, she backed off the bed, aching for him to say something. Anything. She needed to know where she stood. She regretted burning her clothes. Maybe she could've somehow disguised herself to be a man.

Her throat ached with the need to sob. Clothes were the least of her regrets right now. She didn't want to leave. Teague would be so hard to forget.

"I am not a witch," she said, deciding to put it out there. "And neither is Robbie. So I beg ye not to think ill of him."

"What?" He pivoted his trancelike stare to her.

"Dinna hurt Robbie, and I am not a witch. Neither of us is."

Her charming seducer of moments ago had disappeared. Teague rose from the bed without taking his narrow-eyed stare from her. "I would never hurt Robbie." His detached tone made her worry that his words were a lie.

Without a doubt, once again, she had made the wrong choice. Her first thoughtless act, the decision to join him in his bed, suddenly didn't seem so bad.

She backed away a few more steps, clutching the neckline of her shift. "Thank ye for yer kindness to him. I will trust ye to keep yer word."

He finally blinked and looked at her as though seeing her for the first time. "I willna hurt ye either, Mila. Ye should know that by now." He took another step toward her, turmoil churning in his dark eyes. "Can the things ye see be altered?"

"I dinna ken," she answered softly. "I hope so."

A cold scowl hardened his features. He slowly bowed his head. "Aye," he rasped, with an absent-minded nod. "I hope so as well." With a long, hurried stride, he left the room without another word.

Grissa entered, carrying the breakfast tray and walking sideways as she watched him go. "Mistress?"

Mila sank into a nearby chair and dropped her head into her hands. Teague had said she and Robbie were safe, but had the distraught man even known what he was saying? He was obviously in shock. Whether because he didn't believe her or maybe because he did, it was hard to say.

The maid set the food on a large, round table beside the far window, then pulled a chair over to it. "Come eat, mistress. Ye dinna look well at all."

Mila ignored the girl. Instead, she rose and moved to the nearest window overlooking some sort of garden. "Where is Robbie? Do ye know?" She had to warn him about what she had done.

Grissa came to her and gently guided her back to the table. "I dinna ken where the lad has gone to, but I will go and find him. Come now. Ye must eat. I fear ye will fall ill."

"I need to talk to him. As quick as possible." She stared at the elaborate spread of parritch, toasty brown bannocks, crocks of butter and honey, and small dishes of jams. Even a platter of meats and cheeses. "I canna eat until I speak with Robbie."

The concerned maid sidled toward the door while casting worried glances her way. Poor Grissa was obviously torn between leaving and staying. "Ye stay right there and enjoy yer tea whilst I fetch him myself. Ye can manage a few sips, aye? See the honey there? It's right tasty in the tea. Try it."

Mila picked up the delicate porcelain bowl of the steaming beverage and cupped it between her hands. That seemed to appease Grissa enough to make her leave. As soon as the girl closed the door, Mila set the cup back on the table and sagged back in the chair. What would become of Robbie and her? All because she had played the odds and lost.

Perhaps she should pack some things while she waited for Robbie. She chewed the corner of her lip, replaying Teague's reaction and studying it closer. He had said they both were safe, but his tone lacked conviction. Could be he was still in shock. Or could be because he was just saying it to throw her off guard until he decided on what to do with them.

That decided it. She hurried to the bed, stripped off the linens, and spread them on the floor beside the table.

During her frantic piling of items into the middle of the sheets, Robbie burst through the door. "What's wrong? Grissa said to get up here fast as I could."

"I told him." She glanced around the room, wishing she had something to store water in. If only they hadn't been forced to abandon their backpacks. Their thermoses and water bottles would have come in handy.

"Told him what?"

"When and how he dies." She wrapped the bannocks in a kerchief and packed them.

"Ye did *what*?" He grabbed hold of her arm. "Mi! Be still and talk!"

She eyed the fifteen-year-old then dropped her head in shame. He was old enough to hear it all. "After several glasses of port, I went to Teague's room. We shared quite a bit of whisky and then…more."

"What exactly do ye mean by *more*?"

She lifted her head and braced herself. "I slept with him."

The boy frowned. "Why would ye tell him how and when he dies after having sex with him? Was it that bad?"

"Robbie!"

"Well." He shrugged. "I may not be experienced in such things, but I am not a numpty. Are ye not supposed to cuddle and whisper syrupy stuff ye regret later after ye've had a good tumble?"

"I refuse to discuss lovemaking protocol—"

"Did ye use protection?" he interrupted.

She clenched her teeth. While his question made her proud that he thought of such things, now was not the time. "We may be in danger here."

"Why?"

"Because he may think I am a witch, since I told him I had seen his future."

He pulled in a deep breath and blew out a heavy sigh. "Ye messed up big, aye?"

She nodded. "I am sorry."

He gathered up the crocks, rolled them in a smaller cloth, then placed them in the middle of a larger one. "I'll pack up all this. Ye get dressed, then we will be on our way."

"I am sorry," she repeated. Robbie had fallen in love with this place as soon as they set foot in it. She had ruined that as well. Her heart ached for them both: his loss of an exciting life at Éirich Castle and her loss of Teague.

He shrugged. "Least I can wear my trainers now and not worry about coming up with another lie."

CHAPTER TEN

HANGED, DRAWN, THEN quartered. In seven months' time. According to the woman who just gave him the most incredible night of his life. Teague stormed through the keep, ignoring anyone who tried to catch his attention and stop him.

"I am not to be disturbed," he bellowed before slamming the library door shut behind him.

He crossed the room to the double doors and stared out at the garden. Teeth clenched as tight as his gut, he wrestled with the urge to punch through the glass. Nay, he would not weaken to that temptation. The glass was too dear to destroy in a fit of anger. He had not fought and scraped all his days to fritter away his clan's niceties now.

Instead of shattering the panes, he shoved the doors open wide. A deep inhale of the cool Highland morning did nothing to calm him. He slowly shook his head, still battling with Mila's prophecy. It wasn't merely her prophecy that troubled him. It was the damned mystery of the irresistible woman he couldn't oust from his thoughts. God Almighty help him. How could life have tasted so sweet last night, then turned so sour today?

The library door opened, then closed with a click of the latch and a thump.

Teague didn't turn. "I said I was not to be disturbed." The intruder better heed the order if they valued their hide.

"A messenger arrived." Calder ignored the threat. "Sunderland is dead and his papers seized. Walpole has agents searching for more evidence against the Cause. Several have already been arrested."

"So it begins." Teague went to the long mahogany cabinet covered in decanters and bottles. He selected his best whisky, filled a pair of glasses, and waved Calder over. "None of our missives to Sunderland bore any specific names or locations. I took great pains to ensure that and always wrote in code." He paused for a long, deep drink while debating whether to share all that he knew. "But if any of our other acquaintances are taken, I canna say the same for them." He hoped their allies had enough sense to observe the same precautions.

Calder frowned down at the glass of whisky while slowly rotating it between his fingers. "What did ye mean by *so it begins*?"

Teague looked up from his drink and studied Calder, still debating. The man had proven his trustworthiness many times. He couldn't recall a single incident where this chosen brother of his had ever failed him. "What would ye say if I told ye I will be arrested in November then hanged, drawn, and quartered in December?"

Calder raked off his tam and crushed it in his fist. "I would say that is a damn sorry jest indeed."

With a tip of his head toward Calder's glass, Teague smiled. "Drink yer whisky, man. I have a tale to tell ye."

"If ye dinna mind, I would rather hear it sober."

"Lady Mila came to my room last night." He topped off his glass before continuing. It might be early in the day, but this sorry business required drink, and plenty of it. "And this morning, she begged me to stay away from Stirling for a year or more. She saw my death in a vision."

Calder downed his whisky and held it out for another. He stole a glance back at the door, then leaned closer. "Ye think she be a witch, or mayhap a white lady?"

"She says she is not."

"Well, of course she says she is not," Calder said. "She doesna wish to be burned." He took another step forward and lowered his voice even more. "And what about her story of being a Roxburghe? Ye ken as well as I that Carthson is the wrong name for that line. Remember the duke? Wasn't that cheating bastard's family name Ker?"

Teague took another sip before answering. "She explained that as well. It appears she is his bastard sister."

"And he ran her off once his father died." Calder nodded. "That explains her being on the run, but what about the boy? Is he really her son?"

"No. She and Robbie's mother were set upon by several of the duke's acquaintances. The lad's mother failed to survive their escape. Mila refused to leave the boy behind." Teague admired her for that. Not every woman alone and on the run would take on the additional burden of another woman's child.

Calder crossed himself. "God bless her, then. God bless them both."

"Aye, God bless them indeed." Teague lifted his whisky as though toasting the sentiment. "But I dinna ken what to do about what she told me."

Calder placed his empty glass on the cabinet with a noncommittal shrug and waved away a refill. "Perhaps she has the sight." A leery grimace twisted his face. "Either that or she is a spy sent to us courtesy of Walpole."

"She told me about Sunderland's death before ye did. And also said I should deny any associations with him, the Bishop of Rochester, and Christopher Layer."

"She knew about Atterbury and Layer?" Calder nervously shifted his weight back and forth from one foot to the other as though preparing to run. "Ye think she worked in one of their households? Or is an agent for Walpole? That bastard would stop at nothing to end the Cause."

Teague thumped his glass back on the cabinet and slowly shook his head. "I dinna feckin' know what to believe or do anymore." Especially since whatever he decided would directly involve Mila. Not only had he promised no harm would come to her, but at some point during their pleasuring, he had come to realize that this woman was no idle tumble. Ever since he set eyes on her, she had haunted his every waking hour. And after last night's visit to his bed, she now resided in his dreams. If he were brutally honest, she had dangerously taken up residence in his heart as well.

Mounting frustration drove him back to staring out the double doors. "What would ye do, Calder?" he asked without looking back.

"I dinna ken." Calder joined him at the entrance to the garden. "I could talk to the lad. He is a damned poor liar. Evades answering by chattering nonsense about other things. Do ye wish me to speak with him?"

"Aye. Call him in from the stables. When Dorrie brought fresh water to my room this morning, she said she saw him heading that way."

Calder shook his head. "He isna there. Grissa came down and told him something that set his tail on fire. He shouted to Iagan that Lady Mila was sick, and he had to go to her. That's how I knew to tell ye of her ailing."

Teague frowned, replaying the morning in his thoughts. His abrupt departure may have upset the lass. The fearful dread with which she had looked at him came to mind. "She probably sent for him. When I left her this morning, I handled it poorly. She may have misunderstood my actions." Both insight and instinct told him Mila and Robbie planned to bolt. He felt it as surely as the whisky warming his gut. "Spread the word to watch for them. If caught trying to leave, they are to be stopped."

Calder nodded and headed toward the hallway. "I will alert Iagan and Auley. They can watch the stables."

"But be discreet," Teague ordered him. "Make up a tale about keeping them safe from the duke's family. In case I am wrong about their running. I will not have embarrassment brought down upon either of them." He didn't believe he was wrong—but still. He swung about and joined Calder. "I shall check her chambers and speak to her maid. It is my hope I am not right about this."

"I would lay odds ye are correct. Yer instincts are always dead on." Calder paused at the great hall's entrance. "So, will ye heed her warning? And about the next meeting—shall I send word that all must be delayed till things calm a bit?"

"That is a decision for later." Teague stepped into the stairwell, then looked back at his friend. "For now, Mila and Robbie are my priority." His grandmother's remarks about Lizzie came to mind. "And keep Lizzie away from Bethia, aye? Tell Duff to get a move on and convince that girl to marry him."

Calder gave a perturbed shake of his head before walking away. "I canna control any of that, and ye damn well know it." He urged Teague onward with a flip of his hand. "Lizzie willna stop until ye marry, and maybe not even then. She's as bloodthirsty as a wee midge, and ye know it. Best warn Lady Mila about that too."

"Soon as I find her, I will." Teague vaulted up the steps, taking them two at a time. As soon as he reached the third floor, he knew it was too late. Doors opening and closing along with shouts of *not here* told him that several searched everywhere for his flighty dove and the lad.

He stepped into her sitting room and waited for one of the searchers to scurry into view.

"Chieftain," Grissa squeaked as she careened to a halt after exiting the smaller bedchamber. She popped a nervous curtsy and kept her gaze lowered. An unusual posture, since all the servants always looked him in the eyes. He had made it clear long ago that they could do so without fear. "How can I be of help to ye?"

"How long ago since ye saw her last?"

The girl's face went red, crinkling with a sudden onslaught of tears. "After I sent Master Robbie to her, I went to the kitchens to fetch her a tisane to help with her ailing." The girl hitched in a pitiful, shuddering sniff and cast a disheartened look at Mila's bedchamber door. "I came back to find the linens stripped from the bed, breakfast gone—crocks included—and neither Mistress Mila nor Master Robbie anywhere to be found."

"How long?" he repeated. While her account told him they had packed and run, it did not reveal how long since they left.

"Naught but an hour or so. Mayhap two at the most."

"Ready this place for yer mistress. I want it perfect for her return." He spun about and charged from the room. An hour. Maybe two. On foot, they would not have gone far. If they took horses, the search area would require expanding. He thundered down the steps, charged across the dining hall, and burst outside.

Once he reached the stables, Iagan and Calder's looks told him their news would not please him. "How many horses did they take?"

"That's just it," Iagan said. "They took none." He turned and motioned his son forward. "Auley saw them toting bundles. Headed south, and not on the road." A sad smile twitched the man's grizzled beard as he proudly patted his lad's shoulder. "He wrote it out for me. Robbie done helped him with his writing and reading. Said Auley is a canny lad who learns quick." He ducked his head. "We need to find them, my chieftain. Robbie be a fine asset to this clan."

"They both are," Teague corrected him.

Auley stepped forward with a mournful frown, thumped his fist to his heart, then clasped his hands in supplication.

"Robbie will be back, lad," Teague reassured him, understanding the boy with no need for words.

"The horses are ready." Calder walked the mounts forward. He glanced up at the sky. "Another storm's coming. The sun's already hiding its face from us."

"It blazed bright enough earlier." Teague launched himself up into the saddle and cast a bitter look at the gathering clouds.

"Perhaps it hides from the darkness of my mood."

He urged his horse into a fast trot, more than a little concerned about the direction his precious guests reportedly took. If Mila and Robbie avoided the road, southward was not safe. Ravines and chasms riddled that part of the land, many of them hidden by overgrowth. He noted that Calder and Iagan had lashed extra coils of ropes to the saddles. They knew the land was dangerous as well, and prepared accordingly.

Distant thunder rumbled across the ridges, and the sky darkened. Rain would slow the runaways but also make their going more hazardous. Teague urged his horse to pick its way faster across the rough ground. He scanned the landscape for the slightest movement or flash of color that didn't belong. Grissa had said the bed linens were gone, and Auley had reported they carried bundles. The creamy white of the cloth, as long as it remained dry, would shine like a beacon amid the early summer colors of the mountainside.

But the Highland weather laughed at him. The clouds released their waters as though trying to wash them down the hills. The horses slowed. Teague squinted through the grayness of the deluge but saw nothing.

Calder shouted and waved to the left.

Teague leaned forward. He shielded his eyes from the downpour and gave a critical sweep of that area. At first, he spotted nothing, but knew Calder possessed a sharper eye than he. He kept searching and finally made out an oddly shaped mound that didn't fit in with the landscape. It had to be them, huddled together against the harshness of the wind and rain.

He allowed his horse to select the best route toward them. The animal knew better than he which way would be treacherous and which would not. He motioned for Calder to circle around and approach on the other side. He feared that when he flushed out his precious dove, she would be foolhardy enough to take flight and succumb to one of the mountain's snares.

The storm's intensity provided the perfect cover. Once close enough, he dismounted. Neither Mila nor the lad had looked out from under the bundles they clutched over their heads. He lunged forward, snatched hold of her arm, and yanked her up to his chest.

She unleashed a bloodcurdling scream that rivaled the tempest, thrashing and kicking like a captured animal.

Robbie fell backward while trying to scramble to his feet. Calder headed him off, caught him by the back of his tunic, and hugged an arm around his waist.

"Let us go!" She beat Teague's chest while squinting against the onslaught of weather.

He didn't speak, just let her fight and squirm until she ran out of wind and realized fighting was futile. It didn't take long until her pummeling weakened to pitiful thumps against his chest that kept time with her sobbing. He buried a hand in her hair, pulled her head back, and upturned her face to his. Then he kissed her, the same way he had kissed her last night during their strongest throes of passion. He poured everything into the connection. Every hope. Every fear. All that she made him feel, whether he wished to feel it or not. She had to realize, once and for all, that she need never fear him.

He broke the connection and scowled at her. "Ye are mine," he bellowed over the wind. Grim satisfaction filled him as she stared up at him with her luscious, kiss-reddened lips barely parted. "Do ye hear me, woman? Ye. Are. Mine."

"I hear ye," she said so softly that he read the words in the movements of her mouth rather than heard them.

"Good enough." He swept her up into his arms, trudged back to his horse, and placed her in the saddle. After a curt nod at Calder, he launched himself up and settled in behind her.

The man grinned and did the same with Robbie.

Before starting the journey back, Teague shucked his coat and wrapped it around her. He drew up the length of his great kilt, hooded it over his head, and wrapped that around them both too. The foolhardy woman risked catching her death from this lunacy, and, if she did, he would be sorely displeased with her.

His heart lifted as she huddled back against him and held tight to his arm around her. Perhaps she finally understood his intentions. It was about damn time.

Due to the fearsomeness of the weather, talking proved impossible. Just as well. He had said his piece for now, and she had heard him. He would clear away any remaining misunderstandings later.

When they reached the keep, he rode straight to the stable, dismounted, and once again swept her into his arms. Cradled against his chest, she wrapped her arms around him and hid her face in the crook of his neck. He didn't understand why she did so, and nor did he care. All he knew for certain was that before this day ended, all would be clear between them.

Even though several servants and clansmen milled throughout the keep tending to their duties, not a one spoke as he strode past them. The place fell silent as a tomb. Through the great hall and up the stairs, he kept a fast, determined pace. The sound of scurrying footfalls behind him assured him that Grissa knew the mistress of the keep had returned. That brought him a smile. Mistress of Éirich Castle. Aye, the title had a fine ring to it.

He kicked open the door to his solar, not giving a whit if he damaged the hinges or not. Grissa charged around him, rushed to the hearth, and stoked the fire. Yet another reason he had chosen the girl to look after Mila. She took care of what needed doing without being told.

After easing his rain-soaked lady down into a chair in front of the hearth, he turned to the maid. "A hot bath as fast as can be readied. Then food and drink here in my solar. After that, we are not to be disturbed unless it is the second coming of Christ Almighty Himself. Understand?"

"Aye, m'chieftain." Grissa made to rush away, then halted. "And Master Robbie? Shall I ensure he is seen to?"

"Master Robbie will spend this evening as a guest of Auley and Iagan. They will see that he is dried out, warm, and fed." He pulled a heavy woven plaid off the wooden rack beside the hearth and tucked it around Mila. "Send more food and drink to their cottage, aye? Greta's best cakes and a fine joint of meat. 'Tis my understanding Auley wishes to celebrate the safe return of his good friend."

Grissa bobbed a curtsy and ran to carry out his orders.

As the maid closed the door that had survived his kick, he focused fully on his errant lady. "Ye scared ten years off me, woman."

She didn't look up at him, just clutched the wrap tighter around her shoulders. "Ye scared me first," she finally said in a hoarse whisper.

He poured two whiskies and brought them and the decanter back to the hearth. "Here, m'lady." He placed hers between her hands, then pulled up a stool and sat next to her. Her accusation floated between them. "I know I frightened ye," he admitted. "And for that, I beg yer forgiveness." He downed his dram and poured another. "I can only claim the shock of learning the day I die as an excuse."

"Fair point." She drained her glass and held it out for another. "So, ye dinna believe I am a witch, then—right?"

That made him smile as he filled her glass with the body-warming water of life. "All women are witches. To some extent, anyway." He lifted his glass in a toast. "But if ye fear I wish to drown ye or burn ye at the stake, ye sadly misunderstand my intentions."

As she watched him over the rim of her glass, her rich, dark eyes flashed with more emotions than he could decipher. "And what are those intentions?"

"I think ye know."

"A woman likes to hear the words, my chieftain." Before he could respond, she lifted her chin to a defiant angle. "And dinna say ye love me. Ye have not known me long enough to claim such feelings."

"Aye, but I have known ye long enough to know I *could* love ye." He softly clinked his glass to hers to toast the admission. "That is...if ye choose to allow it." He held her eyes. "And if ye feel ye might someday decide to love me back."

She tore her gaze away and stared down at the wrap, idly picking at a loose thread. "I might could love ye. Someday."

"And do ye also think ye could speak with me from now on rather than running all over the Highlands trying to hide because ye fear I may or may not do something?"

She rewarded that question with a hard glare. "If I say yes, will ye accept it and let it go? I am not partial to having the past thrown in my face at every opportunity, ye ken?"

Trying not to laugh at her delightful sauciness, he refilled both their glasses, then lifted his in a toast. "Agreed, m'lady. To all that we have discussed, aye? A toast to our new accord?"

The hint of a smile curved her tempting mouth and sparkled in her eyes. "To our new accord." She clinked her glass to his and tossed back an impressive swallow of whisky. But then she grew quiet again, staring down at her drink as she idly ran a finger around its rim. "Thank ye."

Confusion filled him. He reached up and brushed her damp hair back from her face. "For what, m'lady?"

A heavy sigh escaped her as she met his gaze. "Yer kindness and patience. Ye are a good man, Teague MacDonald, in a world where good men are sometimes in short supply." She smiled again, but it was filled with sadness. "I pray we can keep ye safe. Ye will listen to me, aye? Stay away from Stirling?"

"I will do anything for ye, m'lady," he whispered. He leaned forward and sealed the vow with a tender kiss across the soft fullness of her lips. "Anything ye wish."

A light tap on the door ended the moment.

"*A mhic an Diabhail,*" he muttered.

Mila laughed. "O son of the Devil?"

"I couldha said worse." He rose to his feet and offered a gallant bow. "The presence of my lady love demanded I curb my tongue."

Her cheeks flushed with a delightful pinkness, but he didn't remark on how much that pleased him. Instead, he kissed her forehead, then crossed the room and opened the door.

Grissa, along with maids Malie and Dorrie, waited with trays piled high with food.

He directed them to the open entrance of his bedchamber with a wave of his hand. "On the table beside the window, aye?" As he watched them file in, he continued, "And how is the bath coming along?"

"Nearly ready," Grissa called out. "Mrs. Cain herself is tending to it. She gathered every lad from the kitchen to haul water already hot up from the laundress and has more heating over the fire in the bathing chamber. That way ye can add more when ye need it." She stood in the doorway, wiping her hands on her apron. "Should I ask her how much longer?"

"Ask her to hurry, lass." He tipped his head toward Mila. "M'lady and I are chilled to the bone. We are ready for a good, hot soak."

Grissa's eyes flared wide with understanding. She spun about and disappeared. Just as he calculated she would, she returned to the doorway in a matter of moments. "Mrs. Cain says 'tis ready. Me and the girls are nearly done setting the table." With a hurried bob of her head, she flew back into the room.

"*We* are ready for a good, hot soak?" Mila had risen from the chair and stood with the blanket wrapped around her like a cloak.

"Aye, m'lady." He sauntered closer. "Whisky is not the only way to toast an accord."

"We are finished, my chieftain," Grissa called out as she and the other two maids shot across the room and scurried out into the hallway. She paused right before closing the door behind them. "And all in the keep understand ye are not to be disturbed for any reason." The door clicked shut.

When he turned back to Mila, both her stance and expression made him grin.

"Proud of yerself, aren't ye?" she said.

"That I am, m'lady." He offered his arm, then leaned close and whispered, "Or shall I carry ye to our bath?"

She picked up the whisky decanter in one hand and their glasses in the other. "I shall carry myself and these while ye ensure the hall door is bolted, aye?"

"As ye wish." He did as she asked, then joined her in the bedchamber. Or he would have if she had been there. The door connecting his room with the bathing chamber stood ajar. Several muffled noises hinted she might be disrobing.

He unbelted his kilt, let everything fall to the floor, then stripped off his léine. After kicking off his boots, he eased open the door and swallowed hard.

His precious dove lay back in the large tub, head pillowed on a folded linen and eyes closed. Steam rose from the water's surface, filling the air with a delicate floral scent.

"Close the door," she said in a lazy, sultry voice. "I dinna want to lose any of this lovely warm air."

He clicked it shut, then joined her in the tub. Rather than recline back, he knelt and stretched to nibble kisses along her collarbone. "Delicious, my sweet dove. Finer than honeyed wine."

She combed her fingers through his hair and floated higher while guiding his mouth to her breasts. "As long as neither of us drowns," she said. She slid a knee along his flank, then wrapped her leg around him.

"Oh, we willna drown." He teased the tip of his tongue across her wet nipple. "I intend to bathe ye, dear one. Soap ye from stem to stern." He paused for a brief suckle that he couldn't resist. At the quickening of her breath, he moved his mouth to hers. "And when we're both slippery as eels, we'll writhe together to our passion's delight, either on the bed or in front of the hearth—"

"Or all of the above," she said. She reached under the water and treated him to a long, slow pull.

"Aye," he agreed. "Most definitely all of the above." He gave her a wicked grin. "And then I shall lay ye on the bed, dine on my favorite fruit off yer belly, and lap wine from between yer breasts."

The smile she returned was just as wicked and even more inflaming as she slid her fingers down his cock and palmed his bollocks. "I intend to do some dining myself." She licked his ear. "I have a dire craving for honey-drizzled Highlander. Reckon the maids thought to bring some?"

"If they failed to," he said as he reached for the soap and slathered it across her breasts, "I will send for it. I grant ye that." He caught her against his chest. Their mutual rubbing worked the thick lather into bubbling frothiness. "After all, I intend to satisfy yer every craving."

"I am sure ye shall," she said, then squeezed him with her thighs. "I am sure ye shall."

CHAPTER ELEVEN

ARMED WITH HER gathering basket and pruning knife, Mila took refuge in her favorite place: the peaceful herb and vegetable garden next to the kitchens. Today she needed some quiet alone time. Nothing bad had happened, but the stress of all the changes in the weeks since she and Robbie first arrived at Éirich Castle had become overwhelming. Much of it thanks to Teague announcing she shared his chambers. Everyone treated her differently now. Robbie hadn't noticed, but she had.

She pinched off some mint, crushed the pungent leaves between her fingers, and inhaled the crisp, clean scent. It helped calm her. Somehow, it cleared and enabled her to gather her scattered thoughts. She huffed a soft laugh while rubbing at the green stains the herbs left behind. Life was so very different now. Kind of like participating in a never-ending history reenactment that included a genuine love story.

She tossed away the smashed mint and cut more to add to her basket. "I should not complain," she informed the plants. "Teague spoils me." And he did. The man made her feel cherished like never before.

Even so, her status in the keep's pecking order had risen to a level she found herself ill-prepared to handle. Mrs. Cain consulted her about housekeeping issues. Greta the cook came to her regarding meals. The priest dropped constant hints about the sanctity of marriage, the value of confessing one's sins, and the benefits of leaving evil behind. Most of the clan continued a respectful friendliness, but a few eyed her as if they didn't trust her. And then there were those who made no attempt to hide their contempt or jealousy. Lizzie and her circle of friends always looked as if they were plotting Mila's murder.

As early summer aged and became late July and August, that woman's hatefulness had increased. Wee bundles of leaves, twigs, and the dry bones of small animals turned up in places to which Lizzie should not have access. Grissa usually found them while laying out Mila's clothing or restocking the bathing chamber. Ill wishes they were, curses intended to bring her bad luck. Mila recognized it as a hate campaign but wasn't sure what to do other than ignore it. At least social media didn't yet exist and give Lizzie even more means of attacking her.

A memory came to her as she knelt to harvest a stem of rosemary. Gran's grimoire and teachings came back to her word for word. Lizzie best take care. How many times had Gran and Mother both stressed *an' it harm none, do what ye will*? Along with *whatsoever ye send out returns to ye times three*?

"There ye be, mistress."

Mila looked up and smiled, grateful for the interruption. Maybe alone time had been a bad idea after all. "Aye, here I am."

Grissa hurried up the path, her sunny disposition making her face glow. As she neared, she cast a quick look all around. "Does my heart good to see ye smiling and unaffected by yet another ill wish." She stamped her foot. "If I ever catch them sneaking into yer chambers, I swear I'll snatch them up by the hair and drag them straight to himself."

"Ye dinna think Malie or Dorrie side with Lizzie, do ye?" Other than Grissa, those were the only two maids Mila knew who accessed her personal rooms.

Grissa looked appropriately shocked. "Nay, mistress. They

ken well enough that I would skin their arses if they were to do so." She gave a curt nod. "Besides that, I made sure they both knew 'twas yer idea that their straw pallets on the floor be replaced with real beds. I told them what ye said about hard workers deserving a good night's rest." Her beaming smile returned. "All the working lads and lassies know it was yerself who asked the chieftain for such a fine thing."

"Teague wouldha thought of it himself. Eventually." Mila didn't reveal Teague's surprise about the request. After all, the man believed the only thing that mattered was keeping his people safe, warm, and fed. Which was true enough, but a few basic comforts didn't hurt either.

Grissa's dubious expression showed she did not agree that her chieftain would have come up with the additional comforts on his own. "Whatever ye say, mistress. But I have thought quite a lot about the problem of the ill wishes. I know how ye could end Lizzie's foolishness."

Mila straightened and gave the maid her full attention. "How?"

"Ye could speak with the Lady MacDonald." The girl took on a self-righteous air. "She would put an end to the foolishness."

Mila busied herself by snipping more herbs. Grissa had unknowingly hit upon what bothered her most about her relationship with Teague. Not once had he ever mentioned introducing her to his grandmother. She tried telling herself it was because the woman was in poor health, but it still hurt that he never asked her to join him on his daily visits to see Lady MacDonald. "I canna visit the lady without Teague's approval. In fact, it would be rude of me to go to her without his introduction."

"Has he said ye canna see her?" Grissa's incredulous tone made Mila even more uncomfortable.

"No."

"Then why would ye think he'd be angry? Ye are his lady."

"I am his mistress. Not his wife."

"Nay, mistress—"

Mila lifted a hand. "It is what it is. I'll not listen to arguments meant to paint it into something it's not." Another sensitive topic.

She turned away and headed toward the lavender. Now would be a good time to gather that calming herb. Not that she wanted to marry. At least, not just yet. But she wasn't sure how much longer the contraceptive odds of tansy oil or vinegar-soaked wool would be in her favor, no matter what Vivyanne and her girls said. After all, all three of Vivyanne's harlots had at least one child apiece. Her highest earner, Scarlett, had four.

Mila knew pregnancy and all the dangers that came with it in this century were a real possibility. And if she remained unmarried, became pregnant, then Teague died because she couldn't change history…

She uprooted a handful of lavender and threw it in the basket. "Bugger it all straight to hell and back!"

"Mistress!" Grissa sidled in front of her with a worried frown. "I didna mean to upset ye. Beg pardon. Please."

"The facts are not yer fault." Mila squeezed the kind girl's arm, grateful to have her as a friend she could trust. "I will figure things out like always."

"Talk to himself. Have ye asked him why he doesna wish ye to meet his grandmother?"

"No."

"Well, if ye dinna mind my asking, why have ye not spoken to him?" Grissa reminded Mila of a puppy waiting for its master to throw the ball. She would not let up. "Everyone knows he is purely taken with ye. I canna imagine he would deny ye anything. He so much as said so at the feast when he announced the two of ye were one."

Mila wished she could be as positive as Grissa. The dear girl romanticized everything. "Maybe I dinna wish to know the real reason why he doesna want me to meet her."

Her relationship with Teague still both thrilled and frightened her. Even though they had only been together three months, it felt like a lifetime. In a good way. Any kind of relationship before had always been a struggle, and bonds of friendship were rare. She had never experienced what she had with Teague and didn't want to risk losing it.

"I wish I had some of my self-help books here."

"Pardon, mistress?" Grissa paused in weeding the garden and looked up at her.

"Never mind," Mila said. "Not important."

"There be my precious dove." Teague swung open the waist-high gate to the garden. He came straight to her, took her in his arms, and set her aflame with a passionate kiss. "To keep ye wanting me," he whispered while nuzzling her ear.

"As if I could ever stop." And she meant that. Every word. She eased out of his arms and recovered her basket and knife. "Such a greeting. Ye're not off to somewhere, are ye?" That was her greatest fear: that history would find a way to get him even though he had promised to steer clear of Stirling.

"Nay, m'love. Calder and I just returned from inspecting the cattle. I am headed for a visit with Grandmother. She enjoys hearing about the prosperity of the clan." He swept a proud gaze across the grounds. "I believe this is the best garden we have ever had. Ye are a boon to us, my lady love."

"I can finish gathering the herbs if ye wish to take Lady Mila with ye," Grissa said with a knowing smile. "I am sure Lady MacDonald would be more than pleased to meet her."

"Grissa!" Mila scowled at the maid, willing her to shut her mouth.

Teague nodded as though the idea had never occurred to him. "A fine suggestion, indeed. Grandmother could do with someone new to spark her energy." A somberness came over him. Something akin to dread. "Perhaps she will choose to tarry with us a bit longer then."

"I dinna wish to tire her." Mila brushed at her skirts, which were dusty and stained from her working in the garden. "And I canna see her looking like this. It would be disrespectful."

"Nonsense." He took her hand and kissed it. "Ye are loveliness itself, and Grandmother admires those who dinna fear getting a bit dirty with their labors."

Mila swung about and glared at Grissa, then shoved her basket into the maid's hands. "Greta needs as many greens as ye can find, aye?"

The lass beamed a triumphant smile and nodded. "Happily, mistress. I shall do ye proud."

Teague stepped aside so she might take the lead up the narrow garden path. "I feel certain Bethia has kept Grandmother apprised about ye. Dinna be startled if she knows more than ye thought she would."

Mila didn't know if that was good or bad. "Bethia is good to help her stay connected with the clan. Being forced to stay abed canna be a pleasant existence." She caught sight of her hands and flinched. Dirt under her nails and fingers stained green from weeding and crushing aromatic herbs. What would his grandmother think? "I must at least scrub my hands before I see her." She turned for the kitchen door.

"She willna judge ye harshly, love." Teague caught hold of her and spun her into his arms. "She knows how happy ye have made me."

The love gleaming in his dark brown eyes threatened to make her weep. She rested a hand on his cheek and smiled. "Ye have made me happy as well."

His sleek black brows drew together. "Then why, my sweetest dove, do ye look ready to cry?"

She blinked away the moisture, eased free of his hold, and hurried to the basin just inside the kitchen door. "Happy tears. Women do that, ye ken?"

"I suppose." He leaned against the door facing and watched her while she scrubbed. After shifting positions as though uncomfortable, he cleared his throat. "Ye wouldna happen to be with child, would ye?"

As she dried her hands on a rag, she studied him, trying to

decipher his expression. "I dinna think so." She shook out the cloth and returned it to its peg. "What would happen if I was?" She needed to know, even though she feared what he might say.

His grin widened into a smile, as if the answer couldn't be simpler. "We would have our first bairn."

Hands fisted against her middle, she nodded, subtly prodding him. "Aye, but the bairn's last name would be Carthson."

His smile shifted to a frown. "The hell it would. My son or daughter would be a MacDonald."

"But we are not married. I am merely yer mistress."

He expelled a huff. "In the eyes of God, my clan, and the irregular marriage laws of Scotland, we are man and wife, my precious dove." He stared at her in disbelief, obviously shocked they were having this conversation. "I announced to one and all that ye share my bed as well as my life. At supper. Weeks and weeks ago. We celebrated with a great many toasts. Did the whisky make ye forget?"

She *had* forgotten about the irregular marriage laws that weren't changed until 1940. However, if he considered them married, why hadn't he taken her to meet his grandmother sooner? "I have not forgotten, but if I am yer wife as ye say, should I have not already met yer grandmother by now?"

He hung his head and scowled at the floor. "Aye. Ye should have," he admitted quietly. "My only excuse is that every time I go to her door, I expect her to have moved on through the veil. I am a selfish man, my dove. I hoard every additional minute of her company that I am allowed." He raised his head and fixed her with a sorrowful gaze. "My father died at Glencoe. My mother died bringing me into this world on that same hellish night. Then my aunt died a year later. Grandmother raised me. She is the only close kin I have."

"But Calder?"

He smiled, took her hands, and eased her into a hug. "Adopted brother, ye might say. We dinna share the same blood, but he is as true a brother as if we did."

She hugged him tight, sorry for ever doubting him. "Forgive me," she whispered against his chest.

He set her back a bit and smiled down at her. "For what?"

An embarrassed laugh bubbled free of her. "For not realizing we were married."

"Aye, well, perhaps I wasna clear on the matter." He cupped her chin in his hand. "We two need to work on our understanding of one another. Our solicitor leaves for Edinburgh tomorrow. He can draw up the papers, and we can sign them today. The priest can record them in our kirk's records, and Ferguson can carry a copy to Edinburgh." He leaned in for a kiss, then paused and frowned.

"What?"

"Did ye want a church wedding? I forgot about a woman's penchant for such things."

"Absolutely not." The idea of being the center of attention at such an event made her stomach churn. "When the priest sees the papers, maybe he will finally agree we are not living in sin and stop threatening me with eternal damnation."

"I doubt that. Father John enjoys that topic immensely." He gifted her with the kiss he'd withheld earlier. "Now that we know where we stand, let us introduce ye to Grandmother, aye?"

She felt loads better as they strolled to the stairs leading to Lady MacDonald's private tower. Bless Grissa's heart and soul for meddling, because, once again, Mila hadn't shared her worries with Teague as she should have. She promised herself to work on that and do better. It would save her sanity.

Teague paused when they reached the door to the landing. "Grandmother is a mite…" He tilted his head and cringed. "She says whatever she thinks, whether or not ye wish to hear it."

"My grandmother was the same." She took a deep breath and nodded at the door. "I hope she likes me."

"She will. I feel sure of it." His tense smile cast significant doubt on that statement as he swung open the door.

The modest sitting room was not only immaculate but also

empty. Cut flowers filled several pitchers and vases, lending their sweet fragrance to the brightness of the room. Teague made a sweeping motion that encompassed the area. "She yearned for lots of windows, and now 'tis rare she even makes it in here." He stared off into space with a sad smile. "She threatened to skin me alive when I offered to have her carried to that window couch each day."

Mila gave his arm a reassuring squeeze. "Stubborn and independent. Sounds like someone I know."

"I suppose so." He rolled his shoulders as if fighting off the melancholy of his grandmother growing weaker. After pulling in a deep breath, he strode to the bedchamber door and softly knocked. "Grandmother?"

"'Tis about time," came the tart reply from the other side.

He lifted a brow at Mila. "Ye have been warned," he mouthed. He eased open the door while waving her forward. "I have someone I would like ye to meet, Grandmother."

"As I said—'tis about time ye brought yer wife to me."

Fighting the urge to turn tail and run, Mila adopted her best smile. She stayed close to Teague as he led her over to the side of the bed. After an awkward moment, she managed a clumsy curtsy. "Lady MacDonald. It is so good to meet ye."

While the tiny woman seemed frail, she possessed the bright, snapping eyes of a hawk. "Mila Carthson." Her wrinkled face quirked with a faint smile. "Beg pardon, I should say Mila MacDonald." With a regal nod, she held out a hand crippled with arthritis. "Step closer, child. Let me get a good look at ye."

Mila did as asked, taking the lady's hand carefully so as not to cause the elder any pain. Lady MacDonald's grip surprised her. It was—strong for one so infirm.

The white-haired matron studied her for a brief moment, then snapped her focus back to Teague. "I have a fearsome hunger for some freshly fried bread. Sizzling hot from the pan, mind ye. Slathered in butter and soaked with honey. Fetch it for me, aye?"

"Fetch it for ye?" Teague eyed her suspiciously. "What are ye playing at, sly one? I dinna fetch things. I send for them."

She released Mila's hand and shook a curled finger at him. "Ye refuse my request? Deny the woman who raised ye? The verra one who wiped yer arse and yer nose and kept ye safe and warm when all was lost?" She shook her finger again, then thumped her hand to her chest. "Shame on ye, Drummond Maclain Teague MacDonald. For shame, for shame."

Teague's jaw flexed as if he fought to avoid saying something he shouldn't. He scrubbed a hand across his face, then lifted it in surrender. "Fine! I shall fetch ye the bread."

"Hmpf! Good enough, then. Be quick about it, aye?" Lady MacDonald dismissed him with a curt dip of her pointy chin.

"Shall I help?" Mila needed to escape. She ached with the need to laugh.

"Why no, child," the matron said. "Stay here and keep an old woman company while he carries out his chores."

With a roll of his eyes, Teague spun about and charged out the door, but did not slam it. He respectfully closed it behind him without a sound.

Lady MacDonald immediately transformed into an even feistier elder. She pushed herself up in the bed, leaned back against the headboard, and patted the spot beside her. "Now we can speak freely."

"I suppose we can." Mila eased down to sit on the bed and forced a smile. "What would ye like to talk about?"

The pert matron smiled, then leaned forward with a teasing wink. "Ye dinna remember me, do ye?"

Mila wondered if dementia made the lady think they had met before. "I am afraid not, m'lady. Could ye jiggle my memory about where we met?" She didn't want to upset Teague's grandmother by yanking her back to the present with the truth. There was no harm in playing along.

"Bless me, child. Ye are Francene made over." The senior's pleased expression melted into a faraway look. "I knew ye would grow up to be just like her the moment I saw ye playing with that wooden bowl and spoon I gifted her before I left."

Mila couldn't move. Or swallow. Or breathe. Surprisingly enough, her heart continued to beat, even though the shock of what Lady MacDonald just said had locked every faculty she possessed.

"How is my dear Francene? I do so miss our chats."

"I am afraid my grandmother is gone," Mila said, forcing out the words. "Cancer took her. A little over a year ago now."

Lady MacDonald lifted a trembling hand to her mouth, and her eyes filled with tears. "Ach, no. She was my dearest sister under the moon."

"The moon," Mila whispered as the faintest memories from her childhood emerged. "We danced under the full moon with braids of flowers in our hair. I remember now. Ye are Cora Campbell. Ye visited Gran all the time."

The old lady nodded, the corners of her sad smile quivering. "Aye, lass. Although it is Cora *MacDonald* now. And we did dance. Every month, remember? The goddess always blessed us because we brought her such joy."

None of this made sense. Mila's mind spun with dizzying confusion. Her stomach churned along with it. "How can ye be here? How can ye be Teague's grandmother?"

"I came back in time to correct the heinous acts of my ancestors at Glencoe. But I always had the damnedest time with wording my spells, and I shot myself back several years too far." She smiled and pulled in a deep, satisfied breath. "Aye, but the goddess meant it to be. I met the other half of my soul, and we loved ourselves two fine sons into being, even though I was almost forty years old when I got here." Her smile faded and tears rolled down her withered cheeks. "But they all died. My husband. Our sons. Murdered by those of my blood. Just as history had told it." She closed her eyes. "My precious Teague, goddess bless him. He was born that terrible night. His mother, her sister, and I made it to a cave, and she birthed him during a howling snowstorm. It was the only shelter we could find to escape the Campbells." She sadly shook her head. "We canna save him, child. He dies this year. I know ye know this because he told me what ye said." She took Mila's hand and gave it a squeeze. "History canna be changed, child. I know this because I tried and failed. Destiny is destiny. There is nothing can be done except to love him whilst he is with us. Get with child, Mila. Quick as ye can, aye? At least that way, a bit of him will be left behind."

Mila jerked her hand out of the old one's grasp. The loss of so many loved ones overloaded her senses, smothered her with a mixture of grief and rage at the unfairness of it all. Gran. Her parents. Robbie's mother.

Furious determination filled her. She refused to lose any more. "I will save him. I will change history." She rose and stepped away from the bed. "Fate can go straight to hell. I will not allow it to take him from me."

Lady MacDonald gave another sad shake of her head. "I see ye got Francene's stubbornness as well."

"He has promised not to go near Stirling the rest of this year, and I will convince him to steer clear of it next year too." Mila eyed the tiny woman, seeing her as the bubbly, larger-than-life best friend of her grandmother's from long ago. She cast a glance back at the door, then leaned closer and lowered her voice. "And ye are telling me ye have a spell that sends ye through time?"

"I did have." The elder shuddered. "I destroyed it. My entire grimoire, in fact. I couldna risk it being found once I arrived in the 1600s."

"Dinna play games with me," Mila said. "Every good Wiccan memorizes her most powerful rituals and spells."

"Why do ye want to know?" Lady MacDonald glared at her. "Do ye wish to desert my grandson? Leave him to spend his last days miserable from the loss of his lady love?"

That halted Mila like a slap in the face. It made her think of all the things she missed from the twenty-first century.

Then she admitted the truth: she missed *things*. Conveniences. She might not have those here, but with Teague, she possessed so much more.

"I will not leave him as long as he lives." She squared her shoulders. "But if what ye say is true, I willna stay here. Nor will I keep Robbie here with the bloodiest times of Scotland's history yet to arrive."

The matron pulled a square of linen out of her sleeve and dabbed the corners of her eyes. "Once he is gone, I will give ye the spell with my blessing." She sniffed and pressed the cloth to the end of her nose. "I understand why ye wouldna wish to stay." Her dark eyes narrowed. "But if ye didna use a ritual to travel to this time, how the devil did ye get here?"

"Robbie and I were eating lunch above the Three Sisters overlook. A strange storm engulfed us, made us both dizzy and sick as could be. When the clouds lifted, we were here." Mila hugged herself. The memory of the experience still made her queasy.

Lady MacDonald nodded. "Aye, lass. Time travel is not for the faint of heart. Even with a ritual, 'tis a miserable bugger I would never repeat."

Something thumped against the bedchamber door, and muffled cursing followed. "Mila, lass! Can ye open this feckin' door?"

Lady MacDonald chuckled. "Apparently, my grandson does not possess Bethia's skill of balancing a tray so she can open a door. Ye best rescue the poor lad."

Mila hurried to open the door. Teague's dark expression as he angled his way into the room with a tray almost too wide for the entrance made her want to laugh.

"What have ye got there, boy?" Lady MacDonald called out. "Ye didna have to bring one of Greta's worktables. A tray wouldha been just fine."

He glared at her as he gingerly crossed the room without allowing the contents to slide off the tray. "Does my heart good to find ye in such high spirits, Grandmother." His tone negated the sentiment. He eased the offering down across her lap, then stepped back while brushing his hands together. "Fried bread straight off the iron. Butter. Honey. And I took the liberty of bringing the jam and some parritch with cream, too."

She gifted him with a smug tip of her head. "Thank ye, laddie. Well done, indeed."

He turned to Mila. "So the two of ye had a fine visit, then?"

Before Mila could answer, Lady MacDonald chimed in as she spread butter across the toasty brown bread. "We did at that. She is eager to get with child so I might finally hold my great-grandchild afore I cross over." She added a stern nod at Teague. "Ye best take care of that, laddie. Put yer back into it, aye?"

"I did not—" Mila's cheeks burned as if set on fire. How dare that old woman say such a thing?

Teague grinned. "I promise ye, Grandmother, there is no lack of trying." He hugged Mila to his side and kissed her flaming cheek. "Is there, my dove?"

Mila glared at him, then at his grandmother. "No. There is not. And that is all I will say on that verra private matter."

Lady MacDonald pointed at the door with her butter knife. "On yer way out, send in Bethia. I shall never eat this abundance of food." She winked at Teague. "Thank ye, laddie." Her attention shifted to Mila. "And I enjoyed meeting ye, child. I do believe ye two were destined for one another." Her expression turned somber. "And as we all know, destiny canna be changed. Ye two may go now."

"Aye, but there are stronger forces than destiny, m'lady." Mila dipped a curt nod and led the way to the door. She would prove the old Wiccan wrong and crow about it the rest of her days. "Just ye wait and see, Mistress Cora."

"Beg pardon?" Teague said.

Mila smiled. "Nothing, my love. 'Tis a wee bet between myself and Grandmother MacDonald."

CHAPTER TWELVE

"THEY REQUEST A meeting."

Teague looked up from his desk. "I thought we decided to forgo any meetings for a while?"

"We did," Calder said. "But Laird Bellingham insists there are several matters yet to settle. Especially with Walpole and his spies still combing the Highlands."

"Bellingham." Teague snorted. "The man is a fool. Bored with his wife, his mistresses, and running his estate. He as much as admitted that the only reason he joined the Cause was for the excitement."

"'Tis men like him that give Jacobites a bad name." Calder turned toward the door but didn't move to leave. "Shall I send back that we refuse?"

Teague rolled the ink-stained quill between his fingers. If he refused, it might raise questions about where his loyalties lay. "I will meet nowhere near Stirling. I promised Mila, and I willna break my word."

"But this is August," Calder said. "Did she not foretell November as the month of doom?"

"Keep yer voice down, man." Teague aimed a pointed glance at the double doors to the garden that were thrown open wide.

"She is just outside," he whispered. "Picking bugs off roses or some such thing she swore needed doing." He stretched to one side and glimpsed her skirts just beyond the bench. Upon returning his attention to Calder, he slowly shook his head. "I willna split hairs when it comes to my precious dove. I promised her I wouldna go near Stirling the rest of this year. 'Tis final, ye ken?"

Besides, if he ever hoped to convince her to stop using that tansy oil concoction and give him a bairn, she had to be able to trust him. She didn't know he knew about her precautions to keep from getting with child. And he hadn't known until Vivyanne mentioned her seeking such advice. Vivyanne couldn't keep quiet about anything. Mila should never have confided in the old harlot, no matter what promise of secrecy Vivyanne gave her. He had to show his lady love that if he said he would do something, he did it.

Then the solution came to him. "Tell Bellingham to meet us here. We will send a guide to lead them in. Next month. At the full of the moon. Tell him I have a new wife I dinna wish to leave." He couldn't resist an indulgent smile, because it was true. He enjoyed every precious moment in her presence.

"Aye, ye've got it bad, then, have ye?" Calder grinned. "Never thought I would see the day."

"Ye have no idea."

Even at this very moment, Teague could hardly wait until Calder left so he could join Mila in the garden. They had yet to try the bench along the wall. She could either sit astraddle him, or he would happily bend her over it. The choice was hers.

He shifted to give his rising the room it needed. "Next month. Full of the moon. Here, ye ken?"

"As ye wish it."

As soon as Calder left, Teague exited the library in search of his dear one. Perhaps a surprise seduction in the garden would keep her from her protections long enough for a bairn to take seed.

He eased up behind her, admiring the view of her fine backside as she took her wee pruning knife to a tangle of roses.

"Such loveliness in the garden," he commented, not wishing to startle her.

She straightened and wiped the sweat from her brow while smiling at the bush loaded with crimson blooms. "It is beautiful. Deep red roses have always been my favorite."

He took the knife out of her hand and tossed it down into her basket. "I was referring to yerself, m'love. Roses canna compare."

"Ye are up to something," she said, eyeing him with suspicion. "Out with it."

Catching her close, he cupped her fine arse in both hands and ground his hardness against her. "Feel what ye have done to me, woman. Now do ye believe I find ye an irresistible beauty?"

With her hands resting on his shoulders, she hooked a leg around him. "Ye know I am all sweaty and covered in dirt."

He licked her neck and caught her earlobe between his teeth. "I am rather fond of sweaty and dirty, ye ken?"

Her breathing shifted to that gasping shudder that assured him he had aroused her. "Ye dinna fear someone might come upon us?" She guided his mouth lower to the salty sweetness of her collarbone.

"I dinna give a damn if the entire clan watches us from the gate." He grazed his mouth across her flesh while breathing in her delicious scent of rose oil and yearning. He worked a hand up under her skirts and slipped a finger inside her hot wetness. "It doesna feel as if ye care that we are watched either, my dove."

She tightened her grip on his shoulders and swayed with a breathy moan. "How can I care when ye make me—" She cut herself off and caught her bottom lip between her teeth.

"Aye, m'love?" He nuzzled his way inside her neckline and teased the tip of her nipple with his tongue. "Ye were saying?"

She bucked as he ground the heel of his hand against the nubbin of her sex and slipped another finger in with the first. As he pumped them faster, she ran her hands up into his hair and held on tight. A long, low groan escaped her. "Take. Me. Now," she ordered him with another wee growl.

"Gladly, m'lady." With his fingers still buried deep, he hoisted her off her feet and backed her up to the wall. He pinned her there, replacing his fingers with his cock, and ground in deep. She wrapped her legs around his pumping hips and held tight to his shoulders. Then she framed his face in her hands and treated him to a fiery kiss that drove him into a frenzy.

He swallowed her cries as she reached her bliss, then pounded harder and reached his own. Buried inside her, he poured out a long, groaning bellow along with his seed.

Leaning hard against her to keep them both from falling, he partook in the sweetest kisses as their breathing returned to normal. "I believe I now love the garden as much as ye do, my dove."

Her eyes still closed and her head resting back against the wall, she smiled. "I told ye the garden was a fine sanctuary."

"As always, ye were right." He nibbled kisses along her throat, then eased her down to her feet.

Something hit the ground behind him, landing with a wet splat.

"What in the world?" Mila peered around him.

As he turned, he kept her shielded behind him. A small, wet sack that appeared to be seeping blood lay on the ground. The neck of it was cinched closed with string knotted in a bundle of stinging nettles. He sidled toward the door, still keeping himself between Mila and the item. He didn't have to examine it to know what it held. "Into the keep with ye, love. And dinna come back out until I discover who is behind this."

"That is the nastiest ill wish yet." She eyed the thing with disgust.

"Yet?" He turned and locked eyes with her. "There have been others?"

She wrinkled her nose and gave a sheepish shrug, reminding him of a child caught doing something they shouldn't. "A few.

But none as disgusting as that one."

"A few," he repeated, concern churning until it blew into protective anger. "And ye never thought to mention these *threats*?"

"I thought if I ignored them, they would eventually get bored and stop."

He gently but firmly took her by the arm, walked her inside, and closed the garden doors behind them. Before facing her, he pulled in long, slow, deep breaths to keep from bellowing his frustrations. How could she not realize the danger of keeping such things from him?

He scrubbed his face with both hands, then turned to her. "Those that do these things dinna get bored and go away. The ill wishes become more brazen and dangerous until they oust ye from the keep. Or kill ye! That is how those cowards win."

"I am sorry," she said in a small voice that convinced him she meant it. "I didna wish to worry ye over something as trivial and childish as a prank of jealousy."

He blew out a heavy sigh. "Ill wishes are no small matter. At least not here." He found her attitude about them confusing as well as concerning. "They can become a valid threat. Have ye never known people who do such things? How relentless they can be?"

She turned away, but not before he spied her frown. "I suppose I have. But with Robbie. Not me." Another vague twitch rippled across her shoulders. "I dinna fear for myself. Just him. And now you, of course. Ye have made me fear for ye as well."

"Then ye should know how I fear for ye." He eased her around to face him, leaning in to make sure she looked him in the eyes. "Who else knows of the ill wishes cast at ye?"

She clamped her lips tighter shut. Her determination not to speak flashed in her eyes.

"Grissa." Frustration exploded from him in a disgruntled huff. "I shall have words with her immediately."

"Do not scold her, ye ken? I told her not to tell ye."

"A lady's maid should bring concerns about her mistress's safety to the master of the keep immediately." His voice rose. He couldn't help it. Thoughts of Mila in any kind of danger crazed him. He paused and bowed his head. "Forgive me. I didna mean..." He pulled her into a tender embrace. "I canna bear it if anything happens to ye. Can ye not understand that?"

"I understand." And she did. He saw it in her face. "But I dinna think Grissa can tell ye anything that she has not already told me."

"Well, since neither of ye offered me the common courtesy of being included in those conversations, that remains to be seen."

Both her brows ratcheted up to her hairline with a *how dare you* look.

"Ye know I am right," he said, refusing to back down.

"Fine. I will compromise. Ye can talk with her as long as I am present. Agreed?"

"Agreed." A quick kiss between them sealed the pact but did not make him feel any better. He maintained his hold on her shoulders and lost himself in her eyes. Not only did he need to speak with Grissa, but Mila needed to be made aware of next month's meeting. Instinct warned him that she would not be pleased.

"What?" She searched his face as though trying to tap into his thoughts.

"A messenger arrived today. With a request."

Her eyes flared open wide. "Ye promised to stay away from Stirling."

He released his hold on her and eased a step back. "And I fully intend to keep that promise. However, Calder and I canna ignore the call for a meeting. To do so would bring our loyalties into question and endanger us all."

"But ye advised them to lie low for a while. Sound advice, I might add." She clasped her hands together and pressed them to her middle—a sure sign he had upset her. "Why can ye not wait until after Hogmanay to meet?" She turned away. "Or withdraw from the meetings completely. Have ye forgotten all I warned ye about?"

The visions she had shared about the coming years still pained him. He prayed she was wrong. "The Jacobite Cause canna be lost. I know ye believe it will be, but given time, I feel certain we can prevail."

She bowed her head. "And what response did ye send back with today's messenger?"

"They will meet here. Next month. At the full moon."

"Here," she repeated, lifting her head and eyeing him with a tight-jawed look. "Their names? If ye dinna mind."

She was sorely displeased. The sharpness in her tone betrayed the depths of her unhappiness.

He widened his stance and clasped his hands behind his back. "Lairds Drummond, Devon, and Bellingham. Do their names mean anything to ye?"

"No. They do not." She turned away and made her way back to the doors overlooking the garden. "How long have ye dealt with these men?" After a glance back at him, she added, "Are ye certain they can be trusted?"

"They have never crossed me before."

"I find that less than reassuring." With an abruptness that revealed her growing displeasure, she spun about and headed for the hallway door.

He caught her arm and stopped her. "I must do this, ye ken? Much hinges upon it."

She stared at him for an uncomfortable moment. "I agree that much hinges upon it. I just wish ye realized it is more than mere loyalty at stake here. It is yer life, ye ken?" Her voice broke. She quickly swiped her hand across her eyes, then pecked a kiss to his cheek. "I will see ye at supper, aye?"

"Aye." Disappointment filled him. He recognized the statement as a silent request to leave her alone for the rest of the day. If that was what she wished, he would honor it. "Dinna forget we must speak with Grissa about the ill wishes," he called after her.

"Another time." She didn't look back, just exited the room and softly closed the door behind her.

⋙⋘

TEAGUE SNORTED A frustrated huff as he donned his best neckcloth for the meeting that had proven to be a pain in his arse before it even started. Things were still not right between himself and his precious dove. He had lost count of the times he caught her weeping in the darkness when she thought he was asleep. No matter what he said, no matter what he promised, she accepted no reassurances or granted either of them any relief. She even refused to visit Grandmother again, saying the two of them had nothing left to say. When he confronted the old, sly one, she said the same. Both women refused to reveal anything about their last visit after the meeting was announced.

Maybe once the lairds had their say and departed, peace would return to the keep. He only wished he knew of a way to convince his dear one to have faith and believe in him. He knew what he was doing.

Someone tapped on his bedchamber's outer door. "A moment, aye?" He finished tying the neckcloth and went to answer it while buttoning his waistcoat.

Robbie waited on the other side, looking miserable. "Mi sent me."

"From the looks of ye, this canna be good." He ushered the boy in and pointed him toward the bench at the foot of the bed. "Is she still dressing?"

"She says to tell ye she isna coming down." The lad cringed as if bracing for an outburst.

"I see." Teague donned his best coat and tugged the ruffled cuffs of his shirt out past the edge of the coat's sleeves. "She is still angry about our conversation with Grissa?"

Robbie shrugged. "I dinna think so. She said ye were an unrelenting arse about that, but she also said she understands why." The lad made a face as if he tasted something bad. "She knows ye fear for her and gets all cow-eyed when she speaks about it." His demeanor changed as he squared his shoulders and stretched to as tall as he could stand. "It is about this meeting with those men. She fears fate will find another way to steal ye away, since she warned ye about Stirling. She is afraid to lose ye."

"I know she is afraid." Teague frowned at his reflection in the mirror while securing his colors to his shoulder with the MacDonald crest. He turned back to the boy. "And how do ye feel about my going to this meeting?"

"I am afraid of the same things as Mi." The youngling shook his head. "She is rarely wrong about such things. And Mama always said that Mi's mother and grandmother had the second sight that was never wrong. If she feels uneasy about something, ye need to listen to her."

Teague tucked an extra dagger into the sheath he wore strapped under his arm inside his coat. "That is why I agreed to stay away from Stirling and had these men come here."

"Still." The boy shrugged and backed toward the door. "She says she willna come down and be a part of yer execution."

"I will speak with her."

With his hand on the door latch, Robbie aimed a nod at the far wall covered in weaponry. "Ye best take yer shield. She's in a black mood."

"On wi' ye, then. Save yerself, aye?"

"She loves ye. That's never happened to her before. Bear that in mind, aye?" the lad said before closing the door behind him.

"Aye." Teague waved the boy away, then turned and glared at the adjoining door that connected his chambers with Mila's. It had remained open since she moved into his bed. At least, it had until three weeks ago, when the news of the meeting had closed it. Even though she still spent each night at his side, every morning, she rose before he did, went to her rooms, and closed the door behind her.

Jaw clenched, he strode to the wall, yanked down a two-handed sword, and marched back to the adjoining door. With it propped open as wide as it would go, he drove the blade all the way through and into the wall behind it. The damned thing would stay open now.

"Teague!" Mila rushed into view, her face filled with fear. As soon as their eyes met, she pressed a hand to her chest. "Ye are all right, then? What the devil was that noise?"

He didn't answer. Instead, he took hold of her hand, tugged her through the short passage, and showed her the door. "No more barriers between us, woman. Not now. Not ever. Understand?"

Her eyes narrowed into angry slits, and her chin jerked up in defiance. "Then cancel this meeting. Feed them if ye must, then send them on their way. Tell them ye want no part of their talks about what ye have decided is a lost cause." She moved closer, grabbed his hand, and squeezed it. "Lay this groundwork. Set this trap. I swear these men, or at the verra least someone with them, is setting a snare for ye. I feel it. Why else would they insist on a meeting while Walpole is still scouring the Highlands?"

"Even though yer argument holds some merit, I canna do that, Mila. I refuse to appear a coward."

"Tell them ye invited them here to discuss a new plot to vex the Campbells, nothing more. Surely ye didna mention the Cause to a messenger? While in their presence, refuse to speak of anything but the Campbells." She squeezed his hand again. "If ye will do this, I can prove I am right about these men."

"And how do ye intend to do that? Ye said ye didna know any of them."

"I know their type. Trust me. Please." She released his hand and touched his face with such caring, such pleading, how could deny her anything?

"Ye are killing me, woman."

With a sad smile, she shook her head. "No, my love. I am trying my damnedest to keep ye alive."

"If I agree to yer terms, will ye come down and sit at my side where ye belong?" He needed her there. Not only for appearance's sake, but for his own sake as well. She completed him like no other. Helped him think three steps ahead of everyone else in this dangerous game they played.

Her mouth curled with a smile that revealed just how sly she was. "I will not only sit by yer side at dinner, but also join ye in the meeting. After all, I can provide insight should ye need it."

He pondered her offer even though he knew her terms might not be negotiable. "I dinna like the idea of ye endangering yerself by sitting in whilst we discuss business."

"Either I stay at yer side at supper and the meeting both or I dinna join ye at all."

"Ye are a stubborn wee hen."

"Aye. I am."

It was then he realized she wore a gown he had never seen before, a pretty thing of the deepest blue silk that not only portrayed the fineness of her figure but perfectly displayed the temptation of her bosoms. He itched to run his fingers across the mounds of her breasts swelling above the daring neckline.

"Yer dress." That was all he could say. Her loveliness struck him mute.

"I wondered if ye were going to notice." She fluffed her mane of dark curls pinned up high at the back of her head, then left loose to tumble down her back. "Grissa wanted to tame it a bit more, but I like it like this. What do ye think?" Before he could answer, she leaned in and bared her throat to him. "And Mrs. Cain concocted this scent just for me. Do ye like it?"

He breathed in the delicate essence, then fought the urge to bury his face against her warm neck and lick her from stem to stern. "Aye, I like it," he said in a rasping whisper, then swallowed hard. "It makes me regret the fact we have guests to tend to when I would rather strip ye down and lay ye across our bed."

"I will hold ye to that later." She took his arm and hugged it close. "Are ye ready?"

It took him a moment to realize she meant to go down to supper. "Aye, my dove. I am more than ready. Let us get this affair behind us so we can address much more enjoyable endeavors."

With a graceful nod and a pleased-with-herself smile, she walked beside him. "Tell me their names again, and describe them this time. I want to get a jump on this meeting."

"*Get a jump on?*" She came out with the strangest things sometimes. In the beginning, it bothered him. Now, he accepted it as just a part of who she was. "What does that mean?"

"I want as much information as possible so I can watch them closer, ye ken? Be ahead of whatever evil they might plan."

He nodded and slowed their pace. "Laird Bellingham is the one who insisted on the meeting. As Calder says, he is a poor excuse for a Jacobite because to hear the man talk, he only joins in because he is bored. But he has money and spends it freely. For that reason, the Cause welcomes him."

"Laird Bellingham, the moneybags," she repeated. As they reached the stairwell, she released his arm and entered the passage first, since it was too narrow to walk side by side. "Next?"

"Laird Devon. Quiet man who canna handle his drink. If he is ever captured, all they need do is get him sotted. He will sob out everything he has ever done since the day he was weaned."

"Laird Devon the drunk." She descended the steps slowly, struggling with the fullness of her skirts. "Grissa insisted on extra petticoats. This is ridiculous."

"Aye, but ye look grand, m'lady." He took care to step close to the wall to keep from stepping on the short train trailing behind her. "Laird Drummond is the last of the trio, and perhaps the most intelligent and beneficial to the Cause. Cunning man, and I wouldna turn my back on him."

She halted and gave him an incredulous look. "Then why in the devil are ye meeting with him?"

"His benefits far outweigh his risks."

With a roll of her eyes and a snorting huff that left no doubt about her opinion, she resumed her descent. "Men are ridiculous."

"I heard that."

"I meant for ye to," she said without slowing. "Is anyone else attending this circus?"

"Circus? Why would ye reference a circular arena?"

She increased the speed of her descent as they passed the second landing. "Is anyone accompanying the three men ye already described?"

He could tell she gritted her teeth by the way she spoke. She needed to calm herself, but telling her so would only vex her more. "I am certain they more than likely brought solicitors, advisors, attendants. Some such lot. Why?"

She stopped so quickly that he nearly trod on her. Her worried glare back at him made him realize the foolishness of his last statement.

"Aye, I know what ye are thinking. Any of those people could work for Walpole."

"Exactly." She took his hand and fixed him with that look that always melted him. "Every stranger entering this keep, every questionable person, needs watching by people ye trust with yer life. This is not a time to be lax just because these men have come to yer home rather than lured ye somewhere else. They are even more dangerous here."

"I am not a fool, my dove." Pride a bit bruised, he tried not to take insult from her warnings. "We will find our way through these dangerous waters together, aye?" He kissed her hand, then stared deep into her eyes. "But I must also ask that ye dinna underestimate me. Trust me when I say I am not a lamb among wolves."

"I know." The torchlight at the bottom of the stairwell revealed her unshed tears. Her dark eyes glistened like pools of onyx. "Ye have made me love ye. I canna lose ye now."

He caught and held her, closing his eyes and burying his face into her silky curls. "I love ye with a fury, my precious dove.

Nothing will ever part us. I swear."

She clutched him even tighter. "I will hold ye to that," she whispered. "And remember what Robbie said about making me angry."

Unable to keep from chuckling, he drew back and kissed her forehead. "Aye, I do. My precious dove becomes a raging lioness when she loses her temper."

CHAPTER THIRTEEN

"I NOW UNDERSTAND why Commander MacDonald didna wish to leave." Laird Drummond offered a polite nod, but a predatory gleam shone in his beady eyes, adding a chilling effect to his smile. "It is a pleasure to meet ye, Lady MacDonald."

"The pleasure is mine," Mila said, fighting to hide her true feelings from the enemy. While the other two lairds had presented themselves as smarmy fools, Laird Drummond appeared to be the alpha of this dangerous trio of wolves. "I hope yer journey was pleasant. The Highlands are lovely this time of year."

"Quite," he agreed with a distracted air as he repeatedly swept his gaze across the large room.

She bit the inside of her cheek to keep from asking if he was taking inventory of valuables or measuring square footage. Thankfully, Teague took over the conversation, freeing her to observe the rest of those assembled. It was going to be a long evening with this treacherous group. She envied Robbie his place in the entry hall with Auley and a few of the other lads. They had their own secret society of sorts. Robbie had taught them all sign language, and the scamps used it to communicate with each other and leave everyone else guessing. At least they seemed to be enjoying the festivities.

Taking care to keep her surveillance as low-key as possible, she eyed the man Teague had failed to mention. Master James Cranson, Laird Drummond's solicitor. The man not only reminded her of a river rat, but also seemed entirely too familiar with Lizzie. Strange behavior for someone who supposedly had never been to Éirich Castle before.

As luck would have it, Laird Drummond's assessing eye lit on the massive liquor cabinet behind the head table. Procured from France, the mahogany treasure detailed with exquisite gold-leaf decorations on the doors appeared to pull the man across the room. He stroked its polished surface like a lover.

She caught Teague's attention and motioned for him to join her in a quiet spot away from the crowd.

He cast a watchful glance around the room, then pretended to steal a kiss. "What is it, m'love?" he whispered while nuzzling her ear.

"How long has it been since Lizzie and her father returned from Edinburgh with parts for the new forge?" She playfully pushed him away, as if telling him to behave in front of their guests.

He gave her a teasing wink and pulled her close again. "I dinna ken how long it has been. Why?"

She tapped the tip of his nose, shook a finger, and acted as if trying to pull away again. "She and Master Cranson seem awfully close for two who have just met."

"I shall warn Calder to watch her, but I am sure it is nothing." He spun her about, stole another kiss, then offered his arm. "The woman thinks marriage to a leatherworker is beneath her. Ever since Duff offered for her hand, she's been frantic to find a man of higher social standing before her father forces her to marry Duff."

Even though she wished to stress the point, she didn't. It was clear Teague thought the woman nothing more than a harmless nuisance. The only way Mila had kept Grissa from naming Lizzie as the sender of the ill wishes was by telling her that neither of them had proof.

She decided to change the subject. "Do we gather for this meeting before Laird Devon drinks himself stupid or wait till after supper and have our discussion without him?"

He patted her hand where it rested in the crook of his arm. "Is my precious dove's thirst for blood that strong?"

"No," she replied through a forced smile as Laird Bellingham approached them. "Yer lioness hungers to protect her mate."

"The others I mentioned should arrive any time, commander." The large-nosed man ran the tip of his tongue across his pale, plump lips that reminded Mila of overstuffed sausages. He gave a simpering bow while surreptitiously ogling her cleavage. "We didna expect such delightful company when the invitation came, m'lady." He rattled with a wheezing chortle at his poor attempt at humor.

Mila tried not to gag. "Nor did I expect such interesting guests." She dropped all pretenses and allowed a bit of protective sternness to creep into her tone. "Who is yet to arrive, m'lord? None of us are getting any younger."

The man's watery blue eyes widened, making the paunchy bags beneath them bulge. "Pray tell, have we put ye out by inviting extra supporters, dear lady?"

"I was not aware so many shared my husband's zeal to put the Campbells in their place." She held her breath, eager to see the fool's reaction to her bait.

"Campbells?" A frown puckered his sweaty brow as his befuddled gaze slid to Teague. Then a knowing smile curled his plump mouth. "Ahh yes. The *Campbells*. Many support the commander in his endeavors. Many indeed. But we shall try not to keep him from ye overlong. Our meeting is only needed to refine a few minor points."

"Minor points, ye say? Yet all of ye refused to postpone this meeting, considering the current witch hunt scouring the Highlands." Teague spoke quietly, but a coldness as hard as steel had crept into his tone.

Laird Bellingham nervously smacked his mouth open and closed like a fish out of water. "The Cause demanded it, sir," he hissed. "And besides, ye were the one who insisted—"

"I did not, m'lord. I no longer support the Cause." Teague didn't bother to lower his voice this time. "And neither does my clan. 'Tis an ill-fated venture that will do nothing but bring harm to my people." He cast a sly scan around the hall. "We may not be overly fond of King George, but we are loyal to him."

Mila squeezed his arm and proudly lifted her chin. "Long live King George."

"Long live King George, indeed," a snide voice echoed from just inside the entry hall. "A sentiment rarely heard in the Highlands."

A fearful coldness swept across her, making it difficult to speak. Knowing she needed to recover quickly to protect Teague, she swept toward the newcomer with her hand extended. This man was the most dangerous guest of all. She recognized him from his portraits in her history books.

"Ye grace us with yer presence, sir. Welcome to Éirich Castle."

One of Britain's first ministers, Sir Robert Walpole himself, eyed her as he took her hand and bent over it. "And how is it you know of me, m'lady? I would most certainly remember if we had met."

Mila managed a coy smile even though the off-putting smell of the man's powdered wig was about to make her gag. It reeked of lavender, sweat, and rancid oils. "I admired ye from afar during a visit to London. Please allow me to introduce ye to my husband."

"Husband," he repeated with a haughty sniff. "However so disappointing."

"Teague." She silently willed him to work harder at hiding his disgust. "Allow me to introduce ye to Sir Robert Walpole."

"Walpole." Teague curled his lip as though struggling not to bare his teeth and offered only an insulting tip of his head.

Walpole's smirk showed he reciprocated Teague's feelings. "Quite the fortress ye have here, MacDonald. Difficult to find, I might add."

"And yet ye found it."

Mila stayed close, determined to control the outcome of this unexpected confrontation. She adopted a sultry demeanor and arched her back to better display her cleavage. Or, at least, she tried. She was not an expert at these games. "I hope ye paid yer informant well, sir, because now we have to kill them."

The man rewarded her with a snorting laugh and a genuine smile. "Pray do not be so hard on them, m'lady. A castle this fine could not remain hidden forever."

"It is not a matter of whether it could or could not remain hidden," Teague said. "It is a matter of trust and loyalty—or the lack thereof." He waved down a servant and motioned for the lad to offer Walpole a glass from the tray. "An important thing, loyalty is. Do ye not agree?"

"Absolutely, Chieftain MacDonald. Or is it Commander MacDonald?" Walpole's eyes narrowed as he sipped his wine.

"Either is fine." Teague met the challenge with a narrow-eyed glare of his own. "*Commander* is a holdover from days gone by."

"Days gone by," the devil softly repeated, then offered Mila a half-smile. "I was not aware that the MacDonald had married. My congratulations to you both."

Mila granted the repulsive man a graceful nod. "Thank ye, fine sir. Ye must sit with us at the head table after we meet with Lairds Drummond, Bellingham, and Devon." She rejoiced in the shock registering on Walpole's face. "Ye appear confused. I felt sure a man as connected as yerself knew this gathering was for a meeting. Did ye not?" She thrust the question at him with an innocent batting of her lashes.

"I was aware of a meeting," he said with enough cautiousness to make her heart sing.

"Aye." She moved closer, taking care to breathe through her mouth to avoid his foul odor. "We tire of the Campbells' constant thievery and disrespect of our borders. 'Tis high time it ended."

"Clan Campbell," he repeated slowly.

Teague joined in the game, his brusque gruffness quite convincing. "Aye. The bloody bastards escaped with twenty from our finest herd. I will stomach them no more."

"Is this the registering of an official complaint?" Walpole snorted a pinch of snuff, turned aside, and sneezed so hard it was a wonder his wig didn't fly off.

Mila eyed the dusty gray curls, wondering how he attached them so securely to his head. Before pondering the mechanics further, she cleared her throat and stepped between Teague and Walpole. "Best to leave the clans to work it out between themselves, good sir. I am sure a man of yer stature wouldna wish to be seen as taking sides." She fixed him with a pointed glare. "Remember what happened to Dalrymple over the treachery at Glencoe?"

He didn't respond. Instead, he immediately turned his focus to Teague. "It appears ye have married quite an astute woman."

"I have." Teague rested his hand at the small of her back and gently pressed. "She is my precious dove as well as my fearsome lioness."

Mila noted that the trio of lairds who had insisted on the dangerous meeting were nowhere to be seen. Even Lizzie's admirer, Master Cranson, was gone. "It appears some of our guests are no longer with us." She turned to Teague. "Was their guide ready to lead them out on a moment's notice?"

"Aye," Teague said, but it sounded more like the growl of an irritated mongrel. He craned his neck, scoping out every corner and shadow of the room. "He was to be available to them whenever they wished."

"How very rude," Walpole commented, then flicked a glance back at his men waiting near the keep's entrance. Their unspoken orders received, the four exited at a fast pace. "I expected more mannerly behavior from Bellingham, Drummond, and Devon."

"Laird Devon is probably asleep under a table," Mila murmured without thinking. She clamped her lips shut tight, hoping Walpole hadn't heard.

He had, and laughed. "A fair assessment of the man, m'lady." While fiddling with his snuffbox, he studied her. "Such an intriguing woman. And what, pray tell, is your assessment of me?"

Even though Teague shot her a warning look, she couldn't help herself. "Predatory. Dangerous. Plotting. Much like a man-eating tiger terrorizing villagers as it picks them off one by one."

Unmistakable pride gleamed in the statesman's eyes as he tucked his snuff back into his pocket. "Why, thank you, m'lady. I shall treasure that compliment always."

"Ye are most welcome," she replied. "Ye will join us for dinner, aye?"

"Under normal circumstances, I would consider it an honor, Lady MacDonald." He paused long enough to cast a barbed smirk at Teague. "But I fear a matter of some urgency requires my presence elsewhere. Do forgive me for begging off."

"Why of course. If ye must go, then ye must." An ominous feeling of doom wrapped icy fingers around her heart and squeezed. The man didn't appear disappointed that his prey had escaped. Quite the contrary. Victory gleamed in his eyes.

"Good evening to you, Chieftain MacDonald." Walpole leaned a dismissive bow, then paused. "I shall be certain to relay your newfound loyalty to the king."

Teague replied with a scowling nod.

Walpole offered her a politer smile and a bow, then turned and sauntered from the room like a predator willing to bide its time for the final kill.

"Something just happened here," she said while watching him leave their midst.

"I agree." Teague cast a dark look around the room, found Calder, and summoned him with a flip of his hand. "This reeks of a trap, and I dinna ken if we stepped in it or slipped out of it."

"I was trying to break free of Duff's caterwauling to come to warn ye that Laird Devon was nay as drunk as he seemed." Calder turned and scowled at those left milling around the room waiting for the feast to be served.

Mila held up a hand before either man could utter another word. "We should not speak here. Remember, we have a traitor in our midst."

"What?" Calder looked from her to Teague.

"To the library." Teague led the way, charging from the room.

AS SOON AS Teague stepped into the library, he knew things were not right. Treachery filled the air like the stench of a rotting corpse. The doors to the garden stood partially ajar, as though whoever passed through hadn't taken the time to close them properly. He stared at them, clenching his teeth until his jaws ached. "Those doors were locked."

"Only to those trying to get in from outside," Calder said.

"Is anything missing?" Mila circled around to the back of his desk. Worry creased her brow as she bent and eyed the drawers. "This one wasna closed all the way." She pulled it open, then lifted her gaze to his. "But it doesna seem to be empty."

He joined her and stared down at the disarray inside the drawer. Without even looking, he knew the compartment hidden beneath the false bottom would be empty. The tip of his dagger triggered the mechanism and popped it open. Just as he feared. Everything was gone.

"It is empty, my dove," he quietly corrected her. "Dangerously empty."

"All of it?" Calder asked.

Teague nodded, too enraged to speak.

"All of what?" Mila looked back and forth between them. "All of what?" she repeated a little louder.

"Journals. Ledgers. Ship's logs. Damning things that pave a way straight to the gallows." He dropped into his chair, as shook as if punched in the gut. "Seal the wall," he ordered Calder. "Drop the portcullis and close the gate." He stared off into space, slowly pinching his bottom lip as he replayed everything that had happened until the lairds and Master Cranson disappeared. "One by one, I want every individual brought to me. I dinna care if it takes all feckin' night; I will speak to each servant and member of this clan who stepped inside the skirting wall since late this afternoon, ye ken?"

Calder jerked a nod and left without another word.

"After all I have done for this clan," Teague muttered. The thief's betrayal ached like a gaping wound that drove through his core.

"How many know about that drawer and the way to open it?" Mila drew closer and gave his shoulder a consoling squeeze.

He stared down at the feckin' thing that was supposed to safeguard his most secretive documents. "Only Calder." Then he eyed the garden doors. "But if someone hid among those bushes and watched long enough, they might discover my desk's secrets."

"Calder would never betray ye." She nudged between him and the desk and sat on his lap. "And besides, he was in the hall the entire evening." But she frowned down at the drawer and then back up at the garden doors.

"What? Ye might as well say whatever it is ye are thinking."

She rubbed the spot between her eyebrows as if trying to massage her thoughts away. "When did ye last see the contents of that drawer? When do ye know for certain everything was there?"

"Why?"

With a sad shake of her head, she tapped on the desk. "Both the garden doors and the drawer could have been staged to look as if the robbery happened this evening. The thief could be trying to make ye think it was one of our disappearing guests who did it." She thumped the desktop again. "Were ye in that drawer earlier today? Was everything there at that time?"

"I made a note in my journal before going upstairs to dress and speak with ye."

"And everything was here then?"

"Aye, as far as I could tell. Everything looked the same." At this point, he doubted everything.

"Were ye alone?"

He gritted his teeth, refusing to answer. What she suggested could not be possible.

A heavy sigh escaped her. "Was there anyone else here besides yerself and Calder?"

He looked aside to avoid her gaze. "Ye know me too well, my precious dove."

"I am not saying Calder is the culprit. Just because he was here, it does not mean he is guilty." She pressed a lingering kiss to his forehead. The kiss a mother would use to soothe her troubled child. "It could be someone attempting to cast doubt between the two of ye while they got away with this terrible deed." She offered him a hopeful smile. "Divide and conquer, ye ken? If they set ye against each other, that leaves them free to cause even more discord."

"He is my brother. Maybe not by blood, but by years of trust and loyalty. It canna be him."

"I never thought it was," she said. "But what concerns me more than who did this is, what do they intend to do with what they stole?" Her eyes glistened with unshed tears. "And more importantly, how long do we have before the rest of their plot unfolds?"

"And Walpole now knows the way to Éirich." He caught her hand, kissed her fingers, then pressed it to his cheek. "I am not so foolish as to think he never wouldha found us, but it wouldha been a damn site harder for him if a traitor had not shown him the way."

She rose from his lap, marched over to a large wing-back chair beside the hearth, and started wrestling it across the room.

"Woman!" He jumped up and gently but firmly set her away from it. "What are ye doing?"

She pointed at his chair behind the desk. "Put it over there beside yers."

"Why?"

"Because I intend to stay at yer side until we find out who did this." She glared at him with a fierceness that dared him to argue.

He caught her in a hug. "What would I do without ye?"

She tightened her hold on him and whispered, "I pray we never find out."

A tap on the door interrupted the moment. Teague grudgingly released her, picked up the chair, and placed it beside his own. "Time to snare a traitor. Pour us all a whisky. Calder too, aye? I am sure it is him with our first interview."

"Happily," she said without looking happy at all. "And I will bring the bottle over. I feel sure we will need more than one."

SHE WAS RIGHT. In fact, by the time the bell in the kirk tower tolled the midnight hour, they had finished the whisky and switched to water to make it through the rest of those waiting to be questioned.

As dawn pinked the horizon, Calder escorted Lizzie into the room.

Out of the corner of his eye, Teague noticed Mila became more alert and leaned forward as if ready to pounce. Grissa did the same from where she perched on a footstool beside her mistress. The maid had refused to leave Mila's side after completing an unnecessary round of questioning. That young woman was more devoted to her mistress and loyal to him than a beloved hound. Neither she nor Mila liked Lizzie, and from the lass's haughty expression, she hated them too.

"We never had to worry about loyalties till ye married her, ye ken?" Lizzie jerked her head in Mila's direction, her lip curled into a sneer.

"A thorn in yer side takes a while to fester," Mila said before Teague could comment. "And someone stupid enough to waste their time tying bundles of dried twigs and animal bones together is capable of anything."

Teague forced himself to sit back into the depths of his chair. It had been a long, trying night. He was raw-tempered, weary, and thirsty for revenge, and the slightest thing would provoke him into a blind rage. Perhaps it was best that his dear one handle this part.

"Are ye calling me stupid?" Lizzie charged forward till she almost touched the front of the desk.

Mila smiled. "So ye confess, then?"

The snarling woman's white-knuckled fists trembled at her sides. Her mouth dropped open. "I confess nothing. I have done nothing wrong."

"Then why would ye take my statement so personally?" Mila rose, rounded the desk, and slowly circled the fuming young woman. "I mentioned no names. I merely spoke of thorns, festering wounds, and people who do stupid things."

Lizzie reared back as though about to spit, but Mila stopped her by clapping her hand across her mouth and holding it shut.

"And yet again ye prove yer intelligence," she said, shoving the girl back a step. "Ye try to spit on the chieftain's wife. In front of him, even. While being questioned about yer loyalty."

Calder rose, took hold of Lizzie, and pulled her back to the hearth on the far wall. "Ye will stand here and answer himself's questions." He cast an admiring nod in Mila's direction. "Or the questions of herself. Although it appears ye have answered her already." He looked to Teague for approval.

"My wife shall decide yer punishment for the ill wishes," Teague said. He pushed up from the chair, leaned over his desk, and glared at the girl. "Ye will find her kinder, because if it were up to me, I would have yer father brand yer face with the mark of a witch."

Lizzie's blue eyes widened and filled with the fake tears she was known for. "I was trying to protect ye from her clutches. She is the witch!" She thumped a fist against her chest and held it there. "Ye were mine first."

"I was never yers!" he bellowed. "Ye have always been nothing but a malcontent ever since I've known ye. Even as a bairn ye stirred trouble wherever ye could. What else have ye done to weaken this clan?"

The downturned corners of her mouth deepened and her bottom lip quivered. "Nothing." She dropped her gaze. "I confess to the ill wishes. Those I did." With a weary shrug, she quietly added, "I have done nothing else. I swear it."

He turned to his beloved dove. "Do as ye will with her. She deserves the worst of yer ire for the worry she caused and needs to be humbled."

"She has not caused me that much worry." Mila strolled back and forth in front of Lizzie. Her expression became more thoughtful. "But I do have another question before we decide on her sentence."

Lizzie lifted her head with a sullenness tempered by defeat. She didn't speak. Just stood there. Waiting.

"How come ye to be so close to Master Cranson?" Mila asked. "Did ye meet with him while in Edinburgh with yer father?"

"More like he met me." With a huffing sigh, the woman shook her head. "He came up to us, to Da and me, whilst we ate supper in the pub. Said he overheard us talking and asked for an introduction." She flipped a hand in Teague's direction. "Claimed he had always admired our chieftain."

"And ye didna find that suspicious?" Teague asked. "Ye know as well as anyone in this clan that my business dealings are verra selective by nature." He shot Mila an apologetic smile. "Aye, m'love. Ye married a smuggler." He swung his focus back to Lizzie. "Did ye and yer father tell him how to get here?"

The wretch didn't answer. Just stared at the floor.

"I take that as a yes," Mila said.

"As do I," Teague agreed. He dropped back into his seat and bowed his head. "Fool girl. How could ye endanger this clan in such a way?"

"He swore he believed the same as we do. He knows our true monarch is King James." A hiccupping sob escaped Lizzie. "And I wanted to make ye jealous. Make ye look at me instead of her."

"What ye have done is put my neck in the noose!" He brought his fist down hard on the desk. "Did ye lead him in here as well? Help him pry open my desk and steal my papers?"

Tears streamed down Lizzie's face. She dropped to her knees. "I swear I did none of that. Please believe me."

"Lock her away until we decide what to do with her. She has doomed us all." Teague didn't dare say another word to the selfish she-devil. Not after all she had just admitted.

Calder hefted her to her feet and dragged her from the room.

"Off to yer bed, Grissa," Mila said. "Himself and I will go up soon."

"I laid yer shift on the bed, mistress." The maid gave a weary curtsy and a sad shake of her head. "I shall pray verra hard before I sleep. I swear it."

"Thank ye." As soon as the girl departed and closed the door, Mila went to him and took his hand. "Come. We need sleep to think straight."

"It is already dawn, lass."

"I dinna care." She tugged him. "Come. To bed with ye. At least for a little while. We need to rest while we can."

He allowed her to lead him up to their chambers, strip him down, then tuck him into bed like a child. She lay beside him on top of the covers, still fully clothed in her evening finery. He pushed himself upright. "Let me help ye with yer laces, aye?"

She stayed his hand. "No. Grissa can help me later. For now, I would rather remain clothed."

He frowned, knowing the answer before he ever asked it. "Why?"

"It takes me a lot longer to dress than it does for ye to sling a kilt around yer waist and strap a sword to yer side. Fully clothed, I am ready as soon as my feet hit the floor."

"Ye need sleep as much as I." He leaned back into the pillows, pulling her with him and tucking her close.

She huffed an amused snort and nestled her head in the dip of his shoulder. "As Gran always said, 'I can sleep when I am dead.'"

"Dinna speak of death," he rasped, hugging her tighter. "Not today." It was no longer his death he feared, but hers. The thought of her suffering because of him was more than he could bear.

She raised her head and soothed him with a tender kiss. "Sleep, my love. We are together and all will be well. I refuse to think otherwise."

"I hope ye are right, my dove."

"I am always right," she whispered, then started humming a softly lilting tune that seemed so familiar.

"What is that?"

"What?"

"That song."

"A lullaby my Gran always sang whenever I couldna sleep." Her soft laugh warmed him. "Even when I was grown, if I had a bad day and couldna sleep, she would sing it for me and I would drift away."

"Do ye ken the words?" He felt foolish asking, but for a reason he couldn't fathom, he needed to hear the words.

"I will guard yer wishes and dreams, my own...
I will guard the wants of yer heart...
There is nothing to fear in this world, my own...
For I will always be yer guard."

She went quiet, but kept tapping the rhythm of the song against his chest. "I canna remember the rest." Another soft laugh escaped her. "Probably because I always fell asleep before she sang it all." She lightly traced her fingers across his face. The sensation mesmerized him, making it impossible to keep his eyes open. "She would tickle my face like this as she sang," she whispered. "It was pure magic."

He didn't hear the rest.

CHAPTER FOURTEEN

MILA MINDLESSLY COUNTED his breaths while watching the slow, steady rise and fall of his chest. Teague finally slept. She eased away from him, halting every time he stirred. He might be asleep, but it was a troubled, restless slumber. She prayed she could do what needed to be done before he awakened.

With as little noise as possible, she crept from the room. The loud whine of the creaking door hinges made her cringe. Once safe on the other side, she held her breath and waited, listening for the bellowing of her name. It didn't come. She applauded herself for a successful escape.

Gathering her skirts in both hands, she flew down the hallway to the hidden stairs connecting their floor to the passage leading to Lady MacDonald's tower. After stealing a look around, she pulled aside the massive tapestry that concealed the stairwell.

"Eww." She recoiled while still holding the weave out of the way. Spiderwebs almost sealed off the entrance to the steps. She hated the nasty, sticky things and disliked spiders even more. She squatted down and stretched under it, snagging the iron loop of the lantern kept just inside the alcove. With a candle from the hall, she lit it, then batted away the webs with the tapestry. "Nasty, wicked things!"

After that minor drama, she raced up the short flight of steps and entered the narrow passage traversing the width of the keep to Grandmother MacDonald's chambers. She hurried through the sitting room, then frantically knocked on the bedchamber door.

A surprised Bethia opened it. "Lady Mila. 'Tis entirely too early for Lady MacDonald to receive guests."

"Let her in," Teague's grandmother ordered her, sounding much stronger than usual.

Mila stepped around the maid and went to the bedside. "Tell me the spell. Now."

Lady MacDonald's pale blue eyes flew wide in alarm. With an irritated huff, she made a shooing motion toward the door. "Leave us, Bethia. Lady Mila will fetch ye when our visit is finished."

"Are ye certain, m'lady?" Bethia stayed rooted to the spot. Her calm, stoic demeanor disappeared, replaced with a rare agitated air. "It is verra early, and I have yet to finish readying ye for the day."

"I am certain." Lady MacDonald, her long gray hair only partially combed and pinned, gave a firm nod. "Off wi' ye now."

Displeasure tightening her jaw, Bethia pointed at the ivory comb and hairpins on the bedside table. "Help her ladyship, aye? She doesna like feeling unfinished."

"I will." Mila picked up the comb and moved closer to the seemingly frail old woman propped upright in her nest of pillows. After the heated discussion they'd had during their last visit, Mila knew better. Lady MacDonald's body might be weak, but her spirit was strong as iron.

Mila waited until Bethia left the room, then turned back to the matron and repeated herself. "I need yer time-travel spell. Teague's life depends on it."

The scowling elder snatched the comb out of her hands and tended to her hair faster than any maid. "What for? Spit it out, girl. What happened to make ye burst in here making such an outlandish demand? I made my terms clear about sharing that spell, and I have yet to hear anything to change them." She paused while securing the last braid in a tight coil around her head. "My grandson is alive and well. As such, ye canna have the spell to desert him and break his heart."

"Listen to me, Cora." Mila sat on the edge of the bed and leaned in close. "Last night, during our rather questionable dinner meeting, someone broke into Teague's desk and stole his papers. Damning papers, I might add. And that bloody devil Robert Walpole strutted right through our front door as if he owned the place."

"Where is my laddie boy now?"

"Sleeping. At least for a bit. That is why I must make this brief. Now tell me the spell so I can get him out of here before they come and take him away."

"Get him out of here?" Lady MacDonald glowered at her. "What the devil are ye saying?"

"If I take him to the future with me and Robbie, he will be safe."

"He would be miserable. Even if ye got him to agree to it." The matron gave a firm shake of her head. "Ye truly think he would leave his clan to suffer for his sins?"

"I will convince him." Mila grabbed hold of the old woman's hand. "And ye can come with us. There is Gran's house in Edinburgh. I inherited it. Enough room for us all. Remember how grand it was?" The more she thought about it, the more excited and determined she became. "Tell me the ritual. The words. The rules. What powers it? Candles? Moon phase? Crystals?"

"I specifically worked it out to take me *back* in time." Lady MacDonald refused to look her in the eyes and held up a hand as though demanding silence.

"Surely we could change the wording?" Mila jumped to her feet. Her excitement refused to allow her to sit any longer. "Gran did that all the time. Reversed the ritual by tweaking it."

"Yer Gran was more gifted than most." Fidgeting among her

pillows, the senior still refused to maintain eye contact. "It was fate, destiny, and blind-arsed luck that brought me back here. Pure and simple." She stared down at her hands fisted in her lap. "I canna guarantee the thing would work again." After a tense moment, she lifted her gaze and locked eyes with Mila. "And if it doesna work properly, it would kill us all."

"We have to try." Mila fought the urge to grab the stubborn lady by the shoulders and shake her. "They could come for him at any moment."

Grandmother MacDonald passed a shaking hand across her eyes. "I told ye we couldna change his fate. He is destined to die." Her voice broke, and she hissed out a wheezing sigh. "If his time is up, pray ye are with child. That is all we can do."

"Like hell it is." Mila leaned across the bed and shoved her face within an inch of the old woman's nose. "Tell me that feckin' spell. Now."

"I dinna remember it," Lady MacDonald whispered. As she slowly shook her head, her thin lips quivered and her eyes filled with tears. "I swear on my beloved husband's grave. I canna bring the words or the rite to mind. I swear it."

"Ye lie." Mila yearned to rage at her, bully her into telling what she needed to know. She wished she could reach inside the witch's head and yank the information out by the roots. "Every good Wiccan memorizes her papers. We only reference them during rites as a safety measure."

"Damn ye, child! I was never a good Wiccan." The elder's voice trembled with shame. "Francene, yer precious *gran*, tried her best to teach me and help me hone my craft. Do ye not remember the many times I left her house in tears? Did ye never hear her tell me I should give up my silly dreams because I didna have the gift?"

"Ye musta learned something from her. Ye made it back here to find yer husband."

"Francene sent me back after I begged her and swore I would attempt nothing regarding the craft ever again." She threw both hands in the air, then let them fall back to her lap. "I think she wiped my memory clean whilst she was at it, because I dinna remember a feckin' word of that ritual. All I know is that it worked."

Mila cradled her head in both hands and pressed hard on her throbbing temples. Weariness and panic threatened to make her retch. "In other words, ye lied about destroying yer grimoire? About casting the spell yerself."

"Aye. I did." The senior plucked the coverlet up closer around her shoulders. "But now ye know the truth. Yer grandmother sent me back after she divined my destiny. She knew it to be the proper thing to do."

"I canna bear this." Mila turned away, frantic to figure out another means of escape. But where else could they go? And even if she found a place, could she convince Teague to come away with her? "I refuse to stand here and wait for them to come for him."

"He willna leave here. Ye know that as well as I."

"We canna hide him here at the keep. Walpole would tear the place apart a stone at a time to get his prey. I saw it in his eyes." Mila paced back and forth, catching her thumbnail between her teeth.

"Dinna bite yer nails. Yer gran hated that." Lady MacDonald fumbled around as though trying to change positions. "Help me to the window seat. There is something I wish to show ye."

"Shall I carry ye?" Mila moved closer to the bed, knowing she could tote the tiny woman like a child.

"Ye will not!" The elder scooted to the edge and lifted both arms. "Let me hold fast to yer shoulders while ye wrap an arm around me to keep me steady."

"Where are yer slippers? The floor might be cold to ye."

Lady MacDonald glared up at her. "Forget the slippers. Did ye not say time is of the essence?"

"Fair point." Mila leaned down and helped the elder slide an arm around her shoulders. "Steady now."

Teague's grandmother slid off the bed. She emitted a soft grunt with every pained step. Once they reached the cushioned window seat, she gave a relieved groan as Mila helped her settle down into the pillows. "Three years ago, I broke a hip. Never healed proper. I shouldha ordered that horse roasted for supper."

Mila grabbed a blanket off the foot of the bed and tucked it around her. "Do ye need extra pillows?"

"No, lass. No matter what I do, the pain is the same. I have borne it so long, I wouldna ken how to act without it. 'Tis like we are old friends." With a weary smile, she tapped on the window. "See that rise over there? The one that looks more blue than green because of the morning haze?"

Crouching, Mila squinted to see through the glare of the morning sun and the last of the mist burning away by its light. "That jagged one with the split down the middle?"

"Aye." Lady MacDonald leaned back and pulled the blanket up higher around her shoulders. "That split is a ravine that leads to the cave where Teague was born. Get him there quick as ye can. It is thick with trees, ferns, and heather. They willna find him there."

"Ye truly think he will go?" Mila liked the plan. Anything was better than nothing. Convincing Teague would be the problem.

"He will be close enough to feel as though he still watches over the keep. I dinna ken anything else he might come close to considering."

"All I can do is try." Mila hesitated before turning for the door. "Shall I help ye back to yer bed?"

The somber matriarch leaned against the windowpane, her gaze lifted to the sky. "No, child. I believe I shall rest here a while and enjoy the view of the Highlands."

Still uneasy about leaving the woman alone, Mila took a chair from the small desk in the corner and butted it up against the narrow window seat. She passed off the precaution with a smile. "In case ye get rambunctious. I dinna want ye spilling out into the floor."

Lady MacDonald kept her gaze locked on the clouds. "Save my grandson," she whispered. A tear rolled down her wrinkled cheek. "Make haste, aye?"

"Aye." Mila couldn't resist giving the sad elder a quick hug. "I will keep ye informed."

Blinking away her own tears, she rushed out and nearly toppled Bethia. "She is sitting at the window, but I put a chair beside it to keep her from falling."

Alarm filled the maid's face. She rushed into the bedroom and closed the door firmly behind her.

Mila blew out a heavy sigh. This visit had been a waste of time when she had none to spare. She made her way back to her chambers, retracing her steps through the passage rather than going downstairs and crossing the hall. Before passing through her rooms and returning to Teague, she checked to see if Robbie was still abed. As she anticipated, the lad had already risen, dressed, and disappeared. He was ever the early riser.

As she closed his door and crossed the sitting room to her bedchamber, Grissa entered from the hallway.

Mila shooed her away. "Ye should still be asleep. It has not been that long since ye went to bed."

The maid shook her head. "My worries wouldna leave me be. I thought to come and lay out yer clothes while ye rested."

"I understand about the worries." Mila motioned for the lass to follow her. "Help me change into something fit for chores, aye? It looks to be a busy day."

"Working in the garden often soothes the soul." The girl hurried to the wardrobe and started gathering fresh things.

"More like riding. I think it would do himself and me some good to get out into the Highlands for a few hours." She refused to share the destination with anyone. Maybe not even Calder. She hadn't decided for certain. "What do ye think?"

Grissa frowned and shook her head. "Himself just left the kitchens. Filled a sack with oatcakes and ordered one of the lads to fetch him a flask of whisky and two skins of fresh water, and bring them to him at the stable. He only does that when planning a long trip. Are ye going with him?"

"What?" Mila stared at the girl, unable to accept what she just said.

"I said—"

"I heard what ye said. I meant… Oh, never mind!" She turned and started toward the door, then realized she had stripped down to nothing but her shift. "A cloak, Grissa! Hurry!"

"Ye canna go out in yer shift!" the girl squeaked. "It wouldna be proper."

"I dinna give a rat's arse about proper right now. Either give me a cloak or I'll grab a blanket on my way through the sitting room and wear that instead."

Grissa's eyes bulged wide, then she sprang to the wardrobe for the cloak. "Himself willna be pleased," she said as she tossed it around Mila's shoulders. "What about yer shoes?"

"I dinna need shoes. I need to catch him before he leaves." She ran for the door, then paused. "Find the lad fetching his water and whisky and stall him, ye ken?"

"But himself—"

"Just do it!" Without waiting for further laments and excuses from Grissa, Mila ran as fast she could, wishing elevators or escalators existed in the eighteenth century. Right now she would even settle for a railing or banister to slide down.

By the time she burst through the front doors, Teague stood in front of the stable, glaring at the keep. His scowl shifted to a look of surprise when he spotted her. "Ye are not even dressed! I thought ye had gone to yer room to change yer gown."

She ignored the stares as she came to a halt in front of him and poked him in the chest. "And yet ye didna have the courtesy or caring to come and tell me where ye were going?" She jabbed him again. "Ye planned to leave without telling me? What the devil is wrong with ye? Ye have never treated me with such thoughtlessness. Why would ye do so now?"

After an irritated glance at the gathering onlookers, he

grabbed her hand before she could poke him again and yanked her into the stables. Once inside, he pointed at Iagan and his son. "Out! Now!"

She braced herself, determined to meet his fury head-on. "I dinna ken what ye plan, but ye must not do it alone."

"For yer information, my stubborn dove, Calder is coming with me."

"Where are ye going?" His hesitation made her mind whirl with the worst possibilities. "I have a right to know. Tell me what this is about." She clenched her teeth so hard her jaw ached. No amount of blinking or deep breaths held back the tears fueled by frustration, anger, and love. "Tell me, damn ye! I have a right to know!"

Nostrils flaring, he bared his teeth, then shot a gaze upward as if silently shouting prayers. After entirely too long for her liking, he returned his focus to her. "Calder and I go to solve the Cause's problem."

His forced calmness only worried her more. "What is that supposed to mean? Ye mean to kill the king?"

He huffed a bitter laugh and looked away again. "Nothing as grand as that, m'love. But our quest, if all goes as planned, will be almost as effective."

"Walpole. Ye are off to kill him?"

"Aye. We intend to ensure Walpole doesna leave Scotland alive."

"That will only bring more soldiers to the Highlands." She struggled not to rail at him. "To be more precise, it will bring them to our doorstep. To our people." Surely he could not be so naïve. "His partner Townshend willna stand for it. The man will use Walpole's death after his visit to Éirich to convince the king to level our home and hunt down every MacDonald in the Highlands."

The tension in his stance softened, and he smiled. "I believe this is the first time ye ever referred to Éirich and the clan as ours."

"Now is not the time for that." She clapped a hand to his chest and gently pushed. "Ye must not carry out this madness."

"What would ye have me do? Wait for the bastards to drag me off in chains?" He leaned to one side and peered out the stable doors. "Where is that boy with my feckin' supplies?"

"How can ye not realize they will blame Walpole's murder on the MacDonalds?"

His eyes narrowed with a slyness she rarely saw in him. "They will blame the man's death on the Campbells. Calder and I have worked it out." He gently but firmly set her aside and marched back outside.

"Robbie!" Teague's bellow echoed across the courtyard.

Robbie popped his head out the dovecote door. "Aye?"

"Come here, lad!" Teague fixed her with a frustrated scowl. "Why do none of them come running when I call? They stick their heads out from wherever they are and call out 'aye.'"

"They are young and think that enough," she said, joining him outside. "What do ye want with Robbie?"

"I want the lad to fetch my supplies, since the first one has gone missing." His tone softened. "And I wish to tell him to watch after ye while I am gone."

"I spoke to yer grandmother. Told her all that happened last night. She said ye need to go to the cave where ye were born and stay there for a while. 'Twould be safer."

"I dinna hide like a woman or a child." A prideful hiss of indignation spewed from him. "I am taking care of this as I did earlier."

She grabbed hold of his arm and squeezed. "This is lunacy. Please do as yer grandmother says."

A loud and long horn blast interrupted their argument.

A chilling darkness hardened Teague's expression. Mila turned and her knees went weak. Through the newly installed portcullis, she spotted them: English soldiers, a wagon among them. Lairds Drummond, Bellingham, and Devon were inside the cage it held, clutching at the bars, bruised, bleeding, and their clothes torn.

"Close the gate!" Teague's shout rumbled across the compound like thunder. The men at the gate responded immediately. He grabbed her by the shoulders, gave her a hard kiss, then fixed her with a stern gaze. "Get inside and stay there. Now, ye ken?"

She caught hold of him and kissed him even harder. "Daren't ye die! Understand?"

"I shall do my best to obey, my precious dove. Now, inside with ye. I shall send Robbie inside too."

With a quick nod, she turned and ran for the doors. Above the chaos erupting throughout the courtyard, the sound of sobbing reached her. It took her a moment to realize it was her.

Mrs. Cain clutched a fist to her mouth. "Who attacks, m'lady?"

"English," was all Mila could force out. She had to get upstairs, get dressed, do anything to help, even if it was something as ridiculous as throwing rocks from the rooftop.

Grissa met her at the sitting-room door. "I heard the horns." She hurried her into the bedchamber. "Who is it, mistress? The horns are only sounded when an enemy approaches."

"The English." Mila threw the cloak aside and waved for the maid to hurry. "They've already arrested Drummond, Devon, and Bellingham." She shook her head. Even though she didn't like the men, she hated their sorry state. "They're caged in a wagon."

The sorrowful girl threw on the stays and tied them in record time. "Did ye catch himself? Is he safe inside the wall?"

"Aye. For now."

"Thank the Almighty for that." Grissa held a skirt, ready to toss it over Mila's head.

Rapid-fire banging shook the bedchamber door. "Mi! Are ye in there?"

"Let him in while I lace my stomacher in place." Mila dreaded having to warn Robbie about what might happen. When she turned, his expression told her he already knew. Damn this world and all its troubles. Could it not grant the boy a carefree existence for a little longer? Could it not leave her alone, too?

"I heard them shout for Teague to surrender himself or they would set fire to everything outside the wall," he said. "Dwellings. Mistress Vivyanne's house. Distillery. Everything. Then they said they would shoot flaming brands at the roof of the keep."

Mila looked up while yanking on her shoes, knowing the answer before she even asked the question. "And Teague's reply?"

"I asked for time to bid my beloved wife farewell," came the answer from the doorway connecting their bedchambers.

Grissa caught hold of Robbie's sleeve and dragged him with her out into the sitting room.

Hot tears streaming down her face, heart racing so fast she couldn't breathe, Mila shook her head. "No. Ye canna go with them. Please dinna do this."

He eased forward, sorrow and weariness slumping his shoulders. "I have no choice, my love," he said.

"Everything can be rebuilt." A hiccupping sob choked off her words as she rushed into his arms. "Ye canna be replaced. Not ever. Ye are the only one I will ever love."

"Ye know as well as I that the bastards will lock everyone inside afore they light the fires." He cradled her close and kissed the top of her head. "I canna bear that thought," he said with a chilling calmness. "And I willna risk yer life. Keep me alive in yer heart and memories. My spirit will never leave yer side. I swear it."

She clutched his waistcoat in both hands and pressed her face to his chest, inhaling his scent as though frantically branding it into her memories. Harder sobs racked her body. Misery took over.

He hugged her tighter and kissed her head again. "Shh…dinna fash yerself, m'dearest one. I may yet survive. They mean to take us to trial. In London."

"They are feckin' liars! Ye willna make it to London alive, and if ye do, it willna be a fair trial. No Scot receives justice in London. Ye know that as well as I!"

His smile looked forced as he tucked a strand of hair behind her ear. "Calder will look after ye in my stead. Keep ye safe and see that Grandmother is kept as comfortable as possible. The clan will guard ye, too." His voice rasped with the agony of his words. "I love ye, my own. More than I ever thought I could love anyone or anything." He swiped his thumb through the tears soaking her cheek. "I am thankful for the time God granted me with ye. I will cherish it always."

She stared up at him, her vision blurred from crying. "I love ye with all my heart and soul."

With a tenderness that shattered her to the core, he gave her a final kiss, then whispered his last wish across her lips. "Stay here, my love. I am a weak man and canna bear the sight of yer misery as they take me away."

"I love ye," she said, her voice breaking. "Always."

He released her and charged out the door before she could stop him. She fell to her knees, hugging herself and rocking back and forth. She screamed and railed against history's determination to kill the man she loved, then dropped forward and pounded on the floor with her fists. Hands pulled at her, trying to get her to rise. Trapped in her agony, she ignored them.

"Mi! Stop it!" Robbie crouched beside her, grabbed hold of her chin, and forced her to look at him. "Ye dishonor him by acting as though he is already dead."

"He is already dead," she forced through clenched teeth. "Ye know that."

The lad pushed closer, his face red with anger. "He is not. Not like when that feckin' drunk hit Mama and Da head on. There was no hope then. We still have hope now. We have to try to rescue him."

"What hope?" She straightened to a sitting position to keep from shoving the boy away. Once again, her sweet Robbie was all she had left in the world. "There is no hope. He willna go to trial.

Odds are, they will hang him or something even worse between here and London."

Robbie stood tall and scowled down at her, disgust filling his face. "I canna believe ye let them beat ye like this. Ye are going to sit there and let history win? What happened to ye, Mi? Ye always told me to stand fast and keep pushing, and yet here ye are, belly up like a coward. I never wouldha thought ye such a hypocrite."

"I am not a hypocrite. I am realistic." How could he turn on her now? Now, when she needed him most? "There is nothing I can do."

"How do ye know that?" He snorted. "Ye've not even attempted to think of a way to save him. All ye've done is wallow in self-pity."

She glared at him, then pushed to her feet. "Dinna speak to me with such disrespect. Ye know better."

"Aye, ye are right. 'Tis better I dinna speak to ye at all." He charged from the room and slammed the door behind him. An angry act he'd never had the audacity to do before.

"Ye have no black to wear, mistress. Shall I have the ladies of the clan see what they can spare?" Grissa stood beside the wardrobe, her nose red from crying. "Should I fetch the priest?"

"No." Something inside Mila snapped. Robbie was right: how could she give up Teague without a fight? Shame and disgust with herself filled her, then a cold, calculating fury took hold. "Where is Calder?"

"I dinna ken, mistress."

"Find him. Now." She dried her face on her sleeve and sucked in a deep breath. "And get Robbie back in here. There is work to do."

CHAPTER FIFTEEN

TEAGUE STARED DOWN at the shackles on his wrists. At least the bastards had kept their word. Or it seemed they had, as near as he could tell. He had remained standing until Éirich was out of sight before claiming a corner of the cage as his own. Ever since he'd kept an eye on the sky. No sign of fire anywhere in the mountains. That knowledge gave him what little peace there was to be found. Neither his people nor his dearest love had been burned out.

His back against the bars and his arse hitting the boards with every rut, he drew up his knees, propped his arms atop them, and closed his eyes. A grave error, closing his eyes. His precious Mila's tear-stained face filled his vision. God forgive him for causing her such agony. His own suffering he could bear. Her suffering tore out his heart.

"A trial is our only hope," Laird Drummond said. "We are of noble blood. The Scottish peerage. They will treat us with the respect we deserve."

Teague couldn't resist laughing in the man's face. "Aye, m'lord. I see how well they have treated ye so far."

"This is yer fault," Bellingham shot at him. "If not for yer damnable meeting, Walpole would have captured none of us.

First, ye say keep a low profile for a bit, and then ye call a meeting. Damned fool!"

Teague cut his eyes over at the man where he sat rubbing a bruised swelling on his head. This was the second time Bellingham had accused him of such, when it was he who'd sent the message that a meeting must be held. Had they all been duped by one of Walpole's agents? Walked right into a trap? And did this cowardly idiot not realize the guards would overhear and report every word they said?

"I called the meeting to discuss war against the Campbells. Not the king. If ye didna feel my personal grievance warranted yer attention, ye should nay have attended."

"I need a drink," Devon said. Holding his head, he moaned. "Surely they willna treat us too harshly on this journey. At least some ale or some such spirit will be given to us?"

Teague tipped his cocked hat forward over his eyes and bowed his head. It would be better if all conversation between them stopped. In his current frame of mind, he could not guarantee he would not strangle one or all of them with his chains.

Instead, he replayed his last words to Calder: *keep her safe even if it means taking her away by sea*. Whether to France, Spain, or as far as the East Indies, he cared not. As long as she was safe. The clan would take care of Grandmother, and she would understand. The beloved, sly one had neither the strength nor the inclination to leave Éirich. She had told him many times she wished to die there. The rest of the clan could take refuge deeper in the mountains. The MacDonalds had risen from the ashes once. They would rise again.

The wagon lurched to a stop. He lifted his head and waited. Either their mounts needed rest or this was where they planned to kill them. Two of the soldiers, grinning like demons about to feast on their bones, unlocked the cage and opened the gate.

"You three to the back." The larger of the duo directed the lairds with the tip of his sword.

"I demand to know yer intentions, sir!" Drummond stepped forward.

The other man, stouter than the first but not as tall, rammed the dull end of his spear hard into the laird's gut and doubled him over. "To the back, Scottish dog. Next time I use the sharp end. Understand?"

Teague rose to his feet as the other three joined him at the rear of the cage.

The stout Sassenach pointed at him with the spear. "You. MacDonald. Come forward."

The short chain between the iron cuffs around Teague's ankles permitted nothing but shuffling. He took his time. If the bloody bastards wanted to kill him, he would make them wait.

They glared at him, fully aware of his stalling. But they didn't react, leaving him to wonder why.

When he reached the end of the wagon, he smiled down at them. "Gentlemen?"

Both returned a smirk before yanking him to the ground. "The Duke of Argyll is in the mood for a bit of sport before fall and winter are upon us," said one. "Sir Walpole agreed to his request."

Acting as though the shackles caused him to flounder, Teague maneuvered into a crouch, then sprang upward and wrapped the chains between his wrists around the neck of the man with the sword. The one with the spear lifted the weapon and aimed it at Laird Drummond.

Teague laughed. "Kill him. I never liked the bastard, anyway."

Then a vicious punch to his kidneys took him to his knees. "Stupid Scot. Forget about the rest of us?" came from behind him.

"As I said," stressed the man with the spear, "your favorite Campbell, the Duke of Argyll, requested a special hunt when Walpole told him of your plot against his clan." He grinned at his partner still rubbing his throat. "Them Campbells are a right cruel bunch, but you have to admire them." He jabbed the spear toward the three lairds huddled together at the back of the cart. "There be a fine tree just across Hadrian's Wall waiting for those three." He granted Teague a spiteful grin. "You, my fine, lying chieftain, get to be the Campbells' next trophy. Wonder if they will hang your hide on their walls?"

"Enough talk," said the man who had administered the kidney punch. "We shall send a messenger to notify the Campbells that their prey has been loosed from the cage."

Teague eyed them all, then held up his wrists. "A fair gamekeeper doesna hobble the animal before releasing it."

All the Sassenachs tipped their hats and smiled. "We never said the Campbells asked for a fair hunt. Now, did we?" said one. Laughing, they returned to their mounts and rode away, leaving him standing in the middle of the rutted path.

"Bastards." Teague stole a glance all around before diving into the overgrown ditch alongside the road. He wormed his way under the vines, brambles, and hedge until certain they completely hid him from view. Time to plan. He had no water. Thank the Almighty the Highlands were riddled with burns and springs. No food, either. But it was August—blueberries and blackberries were getting ripe about now. Oats, barley, and rye were ripening as well. If he came upon a garden, that would provide sustenance. Just a matter of finding food and water without getting spotted by a bloody Campbell as he made his way back to MacDonald land.

He wondered if they would hunt him at night and day. No matter the time they sought him, it served him well to travel through the most overgrown ruts, ravines, and ditches possible. It would take him forever to get home. Especially since he could not convince anyone he came upon to help him; the shackles would give him away as a criminal on the run. He debated whether to start out now or try to sleep while buried beneath the leafy vines. Weariness would cause carelessness. Something he could ill afford.

His surroundings became quiet, almost peaceful and serene, if not for his circumstances. Birds chittered. Red squirrels, or so he assumed, rustled through the leaf mold left behind from last summer's trees. A gentle breeze set the trees to whispering. He heard no sign of horses or men. The English had said they would send a messenger to alert the Campbells that the hunt was on. He assumed that meant he had a little while before the bloodthirsty clan scoured their lands for him. He dare not waste that time sleeping.

Before rising from his leafy den, he wrapped vines and leaves around his chains to muffle their rattling as much as possible. Time to move and put as much distance as possible between himself and this spot. The British would undoubtedly report where they had dropped him.

As hesitant and careful as a beast of the woods, he eased out of his leafy cover and paused. All appeared safe and clear. He climbed back out onto the road, determined to use the easy path for the little time he had until the messenger reached the Campbells. He moved along with a fast-paced, shuffling hop for a while, then looked down and laughed. "I am a damned fool. Just like Bellingham said."

The soldiers had not stripped him of his boots before shackling him. Whether because they had little sense or were rushed to complete the chore, he didn't know nor care. He plopped down on his arse in the middle of the road and fought to worm his foot out of the boot and its shackle. After struggling against both the footwear and the binding, he cursed through clenched teeth. "Hell's fire—maybe they were not the fools I thought them."

The tight cuffs of iron bit into the leather around his anklebones. He studied their make, then smiled. His weariness had made him careless and overlook an advantage his enemy had missed: these shackles were old and secured with a puzzle lock he'd had the misfortune of encountering once before. Old Ham, one of his best mentors who had already gone to his eternal rest, had shown him the secret of the locks and how to open them. Within moments, his legs were free.

He studied the cuffs on his wrists. Regrettably, he had no

advantage with them. Those required a key, and he had nothing at his disposal to pick the lock. Equalizing that defeat with the victory over the leg irons, he jumped to his feet and tossed the things into the overgrown ditch. They disappeared just as he intended. Then he set off at a steady, ground-eating jog. He would run like this as long as he could, then take to the rougher ground to hide. God willing, he would reach the safety of MacDonald lands before the Campbells reached him.

"HEARD EVERY WORD. I swear." Fury flashed in Robbie's eyes. He fisted his hands and jerked a hard nod. "Clear as I hear my voice right now."

Mila knew her laddie never lied. She looked to Calder then slowly turned and stared at Teague's chair. Painfully empty. A stark reminder of the sacrifice he had made for them all. "I dinna have time for this. There is too much to be done. The vindictive side of me says a slow death with much suffering is deserved. But since we ride within minutes, I will settle for a blade through the traitor's heart. What say ye?"

Without answering, Calder strode to the double doors thrown open wide to the warm sunny day. "Chieftain's guards!" he bellowed. "Report to me now!" Teeth bared like a snarling beast, he marched back to Mila's side.

"I want her brought forward as well," she said. Time to cleanse the clan of those who thought of no one but themselves at the cost of everyone else.

"It will be done." Calder rested his large, meaty hand on the haft of his sword. "Soon as all gather here in the hall, I will send one of them for her."

"Let me fetch her," Robbie said.

Mila sized him up for the task. While still small for his age, a recent growth spurt and training with Calder had turned the lad into a wiry force to be respected. "Aye. Fetch her. Take Auley with ye, if ye wish."

"Come on, Auley!" Robbie said. The inseparable pair shot out the door.

Bhric, Duff, Dugald, Iagan, and Willie hurried inside shortly after. Bhric led the group. "What is it? More news?"

"Ye might say that," Mila said. "Soon as our final guest arrives, all will be made clear."

The men situated themselves in a half-circle with Calder and her at the head. They shared looks between themselves. Some hopeful. Some filled with blood lust. A few scrubbed their hands together, ready for battle. Others folded their arms across their chests. The longer they stood there, the more frequently they shuffled in place and turned to see out the doors.

"There is much to be done if ye wish to leave within the hour," Duff said. "Can we not get on with it?"

"Absolutely." Mila smiled as Robbie and Auley burst into the hall with Lizzie in tow.

"All are here now." She clasped her hands to the small of her back as she had seen Teague do so many times before. When she realized she mimicked his stance, she paused in her pacing, bowed her head, and prayed for the control she needed right now. Rage at such heartless treachery pounded through her with every beat of her heart. It was all she could do to keep from snatching Calder's knife out of his belt and stabbing the two-faced liar herself.

She stepped up onto the dais and smoothed a hand across the arm of Teague's chair. "Lizzie," she said, without sparing the woman a glance. "Share with us what Duff told ye merely moments ago. While the two of ye were in the stable."

The sound of a strained cough made her turn and face her audience. It was Duff. She closed her hands into fists at her sides, clenching them tighter until her nails dug into her palms.

"Or if ye prefer to share yer own words, Duff, then by all means—do."

He jutted out his chin and stepped forward. "I told her I loved her and we needed to marry. Did I not, Lizzie?"

After darting a fearful look his way, then one back at Mila, the woman nodded. "Aye. He did say that."

"And was that all he said, Lizzie?" Mila noticed the intense interest of the other men appeared to be growing. "Did he not say more about all he had done for ye? Out of love?"

"I had nothing to do with that," Lizzie said, shaking her head while backing toward the doors. "I swear on my mother's grave."

"Nothing to do with what?" Calder asked, his tone cold and deadly.

"Shut it, Lizzie," Duff warned her. "Shut it now."

Lizzie shook her head faster. "Nay. I willna *shut it*. I willna be banished from this clan for the likes of ye." Her raised hand trembling, she pointed at him. "'Twas him that betrayed our chieftain. Said he did it to be rid of Teague because I wouldna marry him any other way." Tears that actually seemed real streamed down her cheeks. "He set up the trap with the fake messenger to convince Teague to call the meeting. And he sent a map to Walpole. To lead him here. 'Twas also him who showed the agent where to find the papers in the desk."

A hard thunk cut her off and backed her up a step. Eyes wide, Lizzie sputtered and clawed at the dagger sticking out from the base of her throat. She stumbled to the floor, flailed for a brief moment, then became still.

Muffled curses jerked Mila's focus away from the dying girl. She turned in time to witness Dugald shoving his sword deeper up under his twin brother's ribcage.

"Ye have always been a feckin' idiot, my brother," Dugald growled. "Always." He caught Duff as he crumpled and gently lowered him to the floor.

"She b-bewitched me," Duff choked out, his gruff voice wheezing into nothingness. "Was the only…"

Death ended his excuses.

Dugald yanked his sword free and, with his head bowed,

walked over to Mila. He dropped to one knee and offered her the haft of his weapon. "He was my twin, but please know, I am not my brother." He lowered his head even more. "But if ye canna stomach my bloodline, I understand. I offer my life for the horrible cost my sibling made our clan pay. I beg yer forgiveness, m'lady."

She stepped down from the dais and rested a hand on his shoulder. "Justice has already been served, my friend. Rise. Yer chieftain needs ye alive, and so do I. Help me save him, aye?"

"We will save him, m'lady. I swear it on my life." Dugald rose and charged from the room without another look back.

Mila motioned for Mrs. Cain, who stood in the shadows of an archway. The scowling housekeeper hurried across the hall to her, spitting on Duff's body as she passed it. "Aye, m'lady?"

"Have the lads bury them, then divide their things among the clan so that every last valuable can be packed for the trip. Nothing of any worth must be left at Éirich by the time we meet in Fort William with my husband. Ye will see to it, aye?"

The matron smiled. "I will, m'lady. God bless and keep ye." She turned and made the sign of the cross over the men still waiting for their mistress's orders. "God bless all of ye. Ye will be in my fiercest prayers."

"Are we ready, then?" Calder asked.

"Not yet. I must have a word with Lady MacDonald. For Teague's sake." Mila waved Robbie over. "Once again, I ask ye to stay here and oversee the packing and transfer to Fort William. Please. It will be safer."

He glared at her. "I am not a maid, Mi. I am coming with ye."

"Just because Calder taught ye to fight and use a bow doesna mean ye are invincible." She hated the thought of him in danger.

"Teague is the closest thing I have had to a da since mine went to heaven. I owe it to him to be there." He mimicked Teague's lopsided grin. It almost made her sob. "I will be outside waiting for ye, aye?"

"Aye," she whispered, then turned and marched up the stairs

to Grandmother MacDonald's chambers.

Bethia opened the sitting-room door just as she reached for the latch. "She asks for ye," she said quietly. As Mila moved past, Bethia caught hold of her arm. "Dinna stop her, aye? She is so tired of suffering. I promise I will see to her proper."

Alarmed, Mila bolted for the bedchamber and burst into the room.

"Oh, dear. And here I specifically told her not to warn ye. The lass does not listen well of late." Reclining in a mass of pillows, Lady MacDonald looked more serene than Mila had ever seen her. Including the many years ago when she visited Gran for tea and talked of spells. She held a small, clear vial between her hands that rested on her lap. "Tell him I love him fierce and will always watch over him, aye?" She lifted the tiny glass bottle and smiled. "I have outlived my husband and both my children. I cannot bear the pain of a broken heart and a useless body any longer."

Mila eased down onto the edge of the bed and sat beside her. "Ye willna be lonely once we save him. And then we will be off to France for the winter, then Nova Scotia in the spring."

The old hen shook a finger and cocked a sparse brow. "Nay, child. Do they call it Nova Scotia yet? I thought it was still *Mi'kma'ki* or the Northern Territory."

"It was named Nova Scotia in 1621. But that doesna matter now. Please come with us." Mila's heart ached at the thought of losing the cantankerous old woman, but she understood. She remembered her grandmother's last days battling cancer had caused her excruciating pain and suffering. By the time her soul broke free of her body, it was almost a relief. "What will Teague do without ye? He says ye are his conscience."

Grandmother MacDonald patted her on the leg. "Ye are his conscience now." Then she frowned and motioned for Mila to stand. "What the devil are ye wearing?"

"I refuse to fight the tangle of skirts and petticoats while I ride across the Highlands to kill my husband's captors."

The old woman shrugged and patted the blankets for Mila to

sit back down. "Fair enough, I reckon." She shifted with a deep breath but didn't sigh. Instead, she smiled. "Thank ye, child."

"For what?"

"I can die in peace now that I know he will never be alone." She removed the glass stopper from the vial and tapped it against the opening to avoid wasting a drop of the precious liquid. "Ye best go now. It is time. My mind is made up."

"No. I willna go. I willna leave ye to die alone." Mila scooted closer and took Lady MacDonald's free hand. "I will stay here until ye pass beyond the veil and I see ye dancing in the light. I promise."

The old woman's pale blue eyes filled with tears. "I will tell Francene what a fine woman ye are. She will be so proud."

Mila didn't bother to blink away her own tears. "Tell her I love her and miss her something fierce."

"I will, child." Grandmother MacDonald downed the contents of the vial, squeezed Mila's hand, then relaxed back into her pillows. "I wonder how long it…" Lips barely parted, she went quiet. As she still stared off into the distance, the rise and fall of her chest slowed, then stopped.

"I love ye too," Mila whispered. "And I will miss ye fiercely."

The wind roared and banged the shutters so hard that every pane of glass shattered. Mila smiled. The old woman's body might have been weak, but her soul possessed the power of a storm.

"Bethia," she called out while still holding Lady MacDonald's hand.

The maid appeared at the end of the bed, silent as a specter. "Aye?"

"Yer mistress has escaped her bonds." Mila leaned forward and kissed the sly one's forehead for the last time.

Bethia crossed herself. "Thank ye, m'lady."

Mila rose and pulled herself together with a deep breath. "Take care of her, aye? See that she is buried wherever she wished to be buried. I am certain she told ye." She managed a smile at the solemn young woman. "Ye served her well and made her last years bearable. Well done, Bethia. Well done, indeed."

Eyes still lowered, Bethia dipped a curtsy but didn't speak.

Mila studied the young woman, wondering what would become of her now that she had no mistress to dedicate herself to. "Ye will come with us, aye? To France. Then on to the Northern Territory?"

"No thank ye, m'lady," Bethia whispered.

"What will become of ye?" Mila almost feared the answer. The quiet maid had always struck her as somewhat odd.

"I will stay here with my mistress." Bethia smiled for the first time, and Mila found it mildly disturbing. The look of happiness seemed strange on the woman's face. "Dinna fash yerself, m'lady. It is my lot, and I accepted it long ago."

"It doesna have to be yer lot. Come with us."

Bethia reached into her pocket and withdrew a vial identical to Lady MacDonald's. "Once my lady is laid to rest in the cave where himself was born, I shall join her. It will be fine, m'lady. It is our agreement. She waits for me. I canna disappoint her."

"Bethia—"

"Save himself and take him away from the dangers of now and those dangers that are yet to come. Lady MacDonald told me all about them. I dinna wish to live through them either." She smiled again, but this time, it seemed more natural, more serene. "Save himself. Her knowing ye could protect him brought her great peace. That brought me peace as well." She took a firm hold on Mila's arm and escorted her to the door. "It is time for ye to complete yer destiny. Farewell, m'lady. It has been an honor serving my clan in this manner."

Mila knew that more than a dozen men waited below. She hated leaving, knowing that Bethia fully intended to join her mistress in death when they laid the woman to rest in the cave. Her loyal sacrifice boggled the mind. But then Mila remembered what Bethia said about Lady MacDonald warning her about the coming years. 1746 was only twenty-four years away, and the meat of the conflict started before that. The healthy young woman could easily live to witness the end of the final Jacobite uprising and all the horrors that followed. Yet another reason why Mila had to get Teague to Nova Scotia. Europe was too dangerous, and with any luck, they could avoid the wars that would erupt in a little over fifty years on the other side of the pond.

She raced down the steps and hurried outside. Robbie, Auley, Calder, and the rest of the men already sat on their horses, waiting.

"How was she?" Robbie asked as she settled in the saddle.

"Hopeful." She would not share Lady MacDonald's passing with anyone until she told Teague. He deserved to be the first to know. "Lead us, Calder. Ye know the area and the way they might take better than I."

"They said they were bound for London. Probably a lie, but I would still lay odds they are headed south. There is but one route from here, then they cross over onto Campbell lands. We will find him, m'lady. I willna leave my brother to suffer the injustice of those bastards." With a curt nod, the man urged his mount into a run and took the lead.

CHAPTER SIXTEEN

TEAGUE DRANK DEEP from the quietly gurgling spring while staying alert to every movement and sound. Predators often waited at the water to capture their prey. He had no doubt the Campbells would do the same. All remained safe and quiet this misty morning. Nothing but peacefulness filled the area as dawn's bright rays filtered down through the leaves. A slight chill rode the breeze, kissing the dew on the grasses and stones clustered at the mouth of the stream. Frost would come soon. After that, winter snows.

A twig snapped, making him crouch lower and turn. It was naught but a squirrel seeking a drink. The wee, furry beastie spotted him, then scampered up a tree. Teague turned back to the water and splashed his face. No sound could be taken for granted. Two evenings ago, barely past dusk, a pair of his murderous hunters had walked within an arm's length of where he lay hidden under a hollowed-out, rotting log. He had eavesdropped on their conversations, hoping for information. It did him no good. All they did was complain. They resented their laird's order to seek him both night and day and bemoaned the quality of their provisions. He had nearly bitten through his tongue to keep from making a sound. Let the bastards try filling their bellies with berries, raw barley, and spring water. Then they might be more thankful for the dried meat, oatcakes, and cheap ale their liege provided.

His chains held taut to keep from rattling, he resumed his endless journey. He made slower progress now, since he dared not take to the roads. The stars led him during the nights, the sun during the days. A crude staff from a sapling he had snapped off and stripped of its leaves not only steadied him, but provided a way to check for snares that would hang him by his ankles, or covered pits with wooden spikes waiting to skewer him. The bloody Campbells stopped at nothing.

Luckily, the few men he had come across did not see him before he saw them. It surprised him to discover that some seemed uncomfortable with hunting a fellow Scot based on rumors from the British. From what he gathered from their conversations, they had the good sense to realize that if the Sassenachs would do such a thing to a MacDonald, they might do the same to a Campbell. But then there were the others, those excited to track prey capable of outwitting them.

Noise up ahead slowed him. He dropped into a crouch again. Something or someone tromped heavily through the leaves. From the rhythm of the noise, he would bet his favorite dagger that it was a Campbell. Maybe even more than one. He eased closer, taking care to crawl behind anything that would conceal him.

In the center of a small clearing, a man worked with a rope, setting up a snare. No horse was tied near him. That meant he either lived nearby or a hunting camp was within walking distance. His tartan revealed him to be a Campbell.

Teague scanned the area, then grinned and sent up a prayer of thanks. The lone hunter had removed his weapons, water skin, and pack and left them leaning against a tree while he worked.

Teague eyed the things, his mouth watering. But they were still a fair distance away, and the fiend might finish his chore before he reached them. The man turned while adjusting the length of the rope and unknowingly faced Teague.

Teague weighed his choices. He hated to kill the fool because the Campbell looked to be little more than a lad. He doubted if the youngling even shaved yet. The boy's jawline still looked soft and downy as a bairn's behind. There was naught to do but render him unconscious, gag him, then leave him dangling in his own trap.

As soon as the youngling turned his back to him again, Teague charged forward, threw the chains of his shackles around his neck, and choked off his air until he went limp. Working as fast as possible, he gagged the boy with a strip of cloth ripped from his léine, placed his feet inside the snare's loop, then triggered it.

With the lad's belongings hugged to his chest, he cast a look back at the unconscious Campbell gently swinging back and forth between the trees, kilt draped down around his head and his bare arse shining. The boy's throat and pride would be bruised, but he would live. At least now, he would know to remain vigilant even on his own land.

Teague took to higher ground even though the thinner trees provided less cover. He doubted it would take those traveling with the young one long to realize something had gone awry. As much as he yearned to stop and search through the supplies for a decent oatcake, he needed to distance himself from the dangling Campbell. Either that or find a safe place to hide for a while. He had come across several caves but avoided them. The clan might know of them, and he could end up cornered. Besides, a higher elevation might tell him how many he faced if they were careless enough to make camp and build fires. He doubted the Duke of Argyll would go long without the niceties of a hot meal.

With his back against the crag, he hooded his great kilt over his head to help him blend in with the rugged landscape of heather in full bloom. The short, bushy plants grew tall enough for him to hide among them while sitting and, if need be, lie flat to disappear even more. He rooted through the Campbell lad's bag. Two smallish oatcakes, an apple, and a meager handful of smoked meat slices dried to a jaw-torturing chewiness. Further digging brought up a worn leather flask with the letters "A C" carved on the front. A sniff of the contents made him smile. It wasn't whisky, but it would do. He appreciated the cheap ale the other Campbells complained about.

Vigilant scanning of the area below, while he wolfed down half an oatcake, revealed several thin spirals of white smoke curling upward through the treetops. All were within a small circle of one another, pinpointing the enemy's encampment.

He squinted up at the sun, then frowned. Traveling across the roughest ground had slowed him more than he thought. At least he had a decent enough sword now, a skin of water, and, if carefully rationed, food for a few days. Hunger provided an excellent incentive to keep moving.

He shoved the sword into a loop of his belt, then slung the rest of his supplies over his shoulder. Time to move. They would find their youngling hanging in the woods at any time.

Dreary gray clouds blew in and blotted the sun from the sky. Rains would start soon. With any luck, it would slow the Campbells. He could not allow it to slow him, but would have to take extra care not to leave any signs of his passing. The droplets peppered down. Slow at first, then fast and furious, as though the Highlands wept for a lost love.

Keeping low as he edged down the crag into thicker trees, he realized the rain would not only slow the Campbells but also prevent him from hearing them. He did not like depending solely on sight. Not with the murkiness of the stormy woodlands. Just in case, he eased his newly gained sword free of his belt and kept it ready. The hairs tingled on the back of his neck. It felt as though the Angel of Death himself stroked a bony finger across them. He rolled his shoulders to dispel the feeling. The rain sluiced down. He squinted harder to notice any movement among the trees, their trunks soaked to a shimmering black.

Then one of them moved.

"Ye be a slippery bastard, I gi' ye that much!" The man roared as he charged.

Teague dropped just in time, but still felt the attacker's blade whisper as it passed over him. Forced to fight with both hands clutching his sword, he spun around and doled out an effective slash.

His opponent grunted, backed up a step, and slapped a hand against his ribs.

"Ye can run if ye like," Teague said. "Since I dinna ken who ye are, I canna name ye a coward." The best way to win an unfair fight was to anger the adversary into a mind-addling rage. He grinned as the man bared his teeth, gave another growl, and charged him again.

The slipperiness of the wet ground nearly fouled his sidestep, but Teague recovered quick enough to open a long, painful slice across the man's back. This needed to end. This Campbell made more noise than a howling banshee. More were sure to arrive at any moment. He arched back, held his sword like a battle-ax, then let fly and prayed the move worked. Haft over tip it spun through the air, but the arc dropped too fast. Instead of hitting the man in a killing spot, it drove through his thigh.

With a yowling bellow, the devil staggered to the side and fell. Before the fiend could yank the steel free, Teague descended on him and slit his throat with his own blade. Noise in the distance confirmed Teague's fears: more Campbells would be upon him at any moment.

Clutching the dead man's sword, he ran. With bound wrists, he could somewhat battle one man at a time. He doubted the murderous clan would grant him the courtesy of each of them waiting their turn to fight him.

Lightning flashed through the woods. Thunder followed, crashing hard as though keeping pace with the danger. He daren't look back. To do so would only slow him. An arrow whizzed past and stuck in the ground ahead of him. He wove back and forth through the trees, increased his speed, then slowed while dodging. Anything to foil the archers' aim. One missile caught him in the meaty part of his shoulder, but he didn't stop. The arrow would have to wait. He consoled himself with the thought that at least it wasn't a spear.

The rain pelted down harder as he veered toward the road. The deep, overgrown ditch on the other side might provide a wee bit of cover if he could drop into it and make it to a ravine. At least there, he would be shielded from more arrows. He maneuvered across the muddy roadway by sticking to overgrown, weedy patches and those filled with rockfall from the hillside. It slowed him some, but if he didn't take care, the quagmire would suck him in and hold fast.

His wounded shoulder burned like a fiend, but it had to wait. Movement farther down the road to the right caught his eye. The bloody bastards had herded him into a trap. With a guttural battle cry, he lifted his sword and spun about to face the enemy. They might kill him, but by all that was holy, he would take a few of the devils with him.

"Bows and spears. Be quick about it!" Calder's bellowed war cry drowned out the noise of the storm as the MacDonalds fired on the Campbells emerging from the trees.

Bleary-eyed with disbelief, Teague stood there and stared. His own horse galloped toward him, slinging mud in its wake. Its rider was slight and cloaked in black. A slender hand reached down for him. "Teague! Come on!"

"Mila!" He feared if he grabbed her hand, he would pull her down. "Give me the stirrup, love." He latched on to the saddle, put his boot in the stirrup, and launched himself up behind her. With his shackled arms looped down around her, he held tight as she turned his mount and rode behind his men holding off the Campbells. He expected her to stop, but she kept riding, urging the horse onward as fast as the muddy road allowed.

"I willna leave them to fight my battle." He tried to take the reins, but she grabbed the chains between his wrists and yanked his hands away.

"They know what to do," she shouted. "We have it all worked out." She leaned forward, pulling him with her as she veered off the road into a stand of thick pines. Once they reached a clearing among the heavy, water-soaked boughs, she twisted in the saddle and kissed him hard. As she framed his face in her hands, her red-rimmed eyes betrayed her. She spoke in a hitching sob, searching his face as if making sure it was really him. "I feared I would never see ye again. I was so, so afraid."

"I feared the same, precious one." He reveled in the love in her eyes, unable to believe he actually held her again. Heart singing, he kissed her again, unable to get enough of her. Yet he forced himself to break the bond. "We must not tarry here. The Campbells hunt me like a beast. Call the men so we might make our way back to MacDonald land."

She didn't do as he asked, just pressed a hand to his cheek and gifted him with a sad smile. "No, my love."

He blinked and barely shifted his wounded shoulder in a useless attempt to ease the aching. Perhaps his weariness and pain had damaged his hearing. "What do ye mean, *no*?"

Without answering, she turned back in the saddle, took up the reins, and urged the horse into a careful trot through the woods. "Clan Cameron's lands will provide us brief sanctuary and the time we need to see to yer shoulder. Then it's on to the port at Fort William. Calder said yer ship is there, aye?"

"Aye."

Before he could ask what she planned, she continued, "Are ye injured anywhere else?"

"No. Just my shoulder."

She leaned down as they rode, reached into the leather pouch sewn to the front of his saddle, and pulled out his flask. "Think ye can ride and enjoy a wee dram with yer hands in shackles?"

"I will figure it out." He grasped the silver container between both hands and drank while stretching over her shoulder. "God bless ye, woman, not only for saving my arse but for bringing my whisky."

"Ye said the Campbells hunted ye. How did ye escape the British?"

"The Sassenachs set me loose on Campbell lands like a gamekeeper releasing braces of birds for the hunt."

"Bastards."

He chuckled and hugged her closer. "Aye, they are at that. But I have ye back in my arms. That is all that matters."

She leaned back into his embrace and reached back over her shoulder to caress his face. "I am glad ye feel that way, because once we reach yer ship, we sail for France. Come spring, we sail for Nova Scotia."

This time he snagged the reins before she realized it and halted the mount. "I willna desert my clan and leave them to pay for my sins."

She patted his hands and wrestled the reins back from him. "Ye dinna have to. Most have decided to come with us."

HER HEART HAD risen to her throat when she spotted him standing there in the middle of that road. Rain-soaked. Covered in mud and blood that refused to wash away. An arrow stuck in his shoulder. Sword hefted to the sky between his shackled hands. Mila shuddered at the terrible scene that refused to leave her. She broke away from the circle around the fire, supported herself against a tree, and vomited. Every time she thought of how he had looked, her stomach churned as if trying to rid her body of the memory.

"My love?"

His gentle touch triggered sobs she was powerless to stop. She had almost lost him. What would she have done if she lost him?

"Mila." His crooning tone wrapped her in caring comfort. He held her hair back out of the way as she doubled over and dry-heaved more, nearly turning herself inside out. "God bless ye, my precious love." Still holding her hair, he turned and called out to the others back at the fire. "Someone bring her some water! Now!"

"No." She straightened and clutched at his arm. Her stomach clenched again, making her press the back of her hand against her mouth. This needed to stop. "I can get it myself," she rasped. "Dinna trouble them, aye? Some are hurt and still being bandaged." She pulled a square of linen from between her breasts and wiped her nose. Thank goodness she had listened to Grissa and worn the infernal stays. They came in handy when it came to tucking things inside her shirt. She forced a smile while pulling in deep, cleansing breaths. Time to change the subject and get her mind on other things. "I see Dugald took care of yer shackles. Quite the lock picker, is he not?"

"One of his many talents." He eased her into his arms and cradled her against his chest. "Are ye better now?"

"Aye. Ye were quite the sight when we found ye. Every time I think of it, it makes me ill." Without leaving the security of his embrace, she stole a glance around. The fire in the middle of camp, hissing and spitting with every drop of rain, worried her. "Calder says the Campbells willna follow us this far onto Cameron land, but they are sure to tell the British ye escaped. Is a fire wise?"

"It will take a few days for word to travel and the weather will keep the smoke close to the ground. With any luck, we will reach the port and signal the *Vengeance* before then."

Calder had assured her that the captain of Teague's ship knew how to evade the British for as long as it took. Experts at smuggling goods that couldn't be found in Ireland, France, or the Hebrides, they knew every hidden cove between Scotland and the Indies. While they waited to hear from Teague about new opportunities, they stayed busy with short runs that kept them within a day or two of Fort William. She and Calder had sent a runner on ahead to make sure the ship would be ready when they arrived.

She noticed him favoring the side with his wounded shoulder. "Is the pain terrible?"

"'Tis easing up now. Removal of the arrow and cleaning the wound is never pleasant." He pulled her close again for a lingering kiss. "The joy of being with ye once again makes me forget it."

Taking care not to cause him any pain, she tightened her arms around him, buried her face in his chest, and inhaled his familiar warmth. "I was so afraid I would never see ye again," she whispered. She clutched him harder, unreasonably afraid that if she didn't hold him tight, he might disappear. But news she needed to share niggled at her conscience. Unable to keep it from him any longer, she lifted her head and met his loving gaze. "It was Duff who betrayed us. Because he was so jealous of Lizzie's love for ye."

His mouth flattened into a tight line, then he kissed her. With a gentle firmness, he situated her at his side and walked them farther from the fire and those gathered around it. "Dugald told me. The man has apologized a dozen times at least. The weight of his brother's guilt crushes him."

"He feels responsible." She dreaded telling him about his grandmother, but he needed to know. He would look for her when they reached the port. "Teague…"

"I already know she is gone, my dove." He stared straight ahead as they walked. Sorrowful. Forlorn. He reminded her of a lost child separated from its mother. "She came to me in a dream whilst I hid from the Campbells. I heard her whispers as I lay there 'neath that rotting log. When ye said some were coming with us to France and then onward across the seas, I knew she wouldna be among them. Her mind and soul were strong as could be, but the frailness of her body would never allow it."

"It was peaceful," she said, hoping he might find some comfort in that knowledge. "I held her hand until she crossed over." After a deep breath, she continued, "Bethia refused to come with us. She is determined to join yer grandmother once she is laid to rest in the cave where ye were born."

He slowly shook his head. "A rare loyalty in that one. God bless her and keep her in perfect peace." A deep sigh shifted him against her. "I shall miss this land of my blood."

"I understand. But it is safer for everyone if we leave. Some of the bloodiest times for our beloved Scotland will soon be upon us." She could not put into words the relief she felt he believed in her visions. If he had not… A shudder stole across her.

His arm tightened around her. "I trust ye, my precious dove. I just wish ye were wrong." He slowly shook his head. "But I daren't risk not believing ye. Not when yer words proved so right this time."

"Our children will be safer in Nova Scotia."

He slowly tipped his head forward and eyed her, his smile getting wider by the second. "Ye are with child?"

She held up a hand to slow his excitement. "Not yet. But as soon as we make landfall in our new land, I promise not to use the tansy oil or vinegar anymore." She couldn't resist a scolding glare. "Vivyanne said she told ye."

"Aye, she did." His smile settled back into the lopsided grin that always made her heart beat faster. "Never tell that woman anything ye dinna wish everyone to know."

"That advice would have been handy to have sooner rather than later." But she couldn't be angry with him. After all, he had taken her and Robbie in without knowing anything about them. And then they had *clicked*. If anyone had ever told her that such a phenomenon existed, that she would meet the missing piece in her soul's puzzle three hundred years in the past, she would have laughed them off as insane. Yet here she was. Married to him within three months of meeting him. And God help her, she loved him so much it frightened her.

"What are ye thinking, my precious dove?" With a pained grunt, he lowered himself to a fallen log and pulled her down beside him.

"That time doesna seem to be a factor when it comes to loving someone." She laced her fingers through his and balanced their clasped hands on her knee. "And I never wouldha believed such a thing before I met ye."

He squeezed her hand and pressed a gentle kiss to the back of it. "I believe our destinies are woven before we are born." The faintest smile tugged at the corner of his mouth as he stared downward. "Our threads, yer soul's and mine, were chosen to make a strong tapestry that would survive the ripples of time. We are of the same cloth. We were meant to be." He lifted his gaze to hers and cocked a brow. "Did ye not sense it when we first met?"

She hated to disappoint him, but felt she needed to be honest. "I think I was too afraid. At first, anyway." She tried to console him with a smile. "I had to learn I could trust ye. Once I learned that lesson, then yes, I sensed there was an unexplainable force pulling us together." She couldn't resist laughing at her own wording. "I suppose it was magic, aye?"

He rewarded her with that rumbling laugh that warmed her soul. "Aye, I suppose it was, at that." With a pat of her hand, he leaned closer and gave her a teasing nudge. "Grandmother told me the story," he whispered.

"What story?" she playfully whispered back, but a cold sweat peppered every inch of her flesh. Surely old Cora had not betrayed her and told their secret?

With a huffing chuckle, he shook his head. "How the two of ye knew each other far into the future and traveled back in time to find yer true loves."

"My goodness." She forced herself to swallow and concentrated on breathing carefully to keep from passing out. "And how far into the future was this time we came from?"

He chuckled again, then his eyes narrowed as if he were trying to remember. "Twentieth? No. 'Twas the twenty-first century, she said." He smiled down at their clasped hands. "Said ye were witches, but she called it something else. I canna remember the word she used." He kissed her hand again and squeezed it. "But she did say ye only did good spells, and 'twas yer grandmother that sent her back to meet my grandfather."

She stifled a gag, refusing to dry-heave again and give herself away. "And how much whisky had she had when she came up with this wonderful tale?" Her tone sounded teasing to her. She hoped it sounded convincing to him.

"Quite a bit." A happy air settled across him. "She always told the verra best stories."

"We will have to write them down so we can read them to our children someday." She prayed that would change the subject. Hard swallowing would not work much longer at delaying another round of panic vomiting.

"Ye have gone pale again, m'love." He turned a bit and shouted, "Robbie!"

Before she could come up with a harmless lie, the lad bounced over to them.

Even though the boy sported a black eye and had one arm bandaged to his side, he fairly bubbled with exuberance. "Aye?"

"Are ye fit enough to fetch yer Mi a sip of cool water?" Teague gave her a concerned nod. "Look how pale she's gone."

"What is wrong, Mi? He's safe, and we'll be at the port by tomorrow. Nearly home free, we are." Rather than run for the water, the boy crouched beside her and adopted a very mature scowl. "Are ye pregnant?"

"A woman can be ill without being pregnant." She took hold of his chin and angled his face to better see his bruises. "The two most important men in my life have worried me sick. That is what ails me. Did one of them get close enough to punch ye?"

The boy dropped his head, then cast a sheepish look up at her. "I fell off my horse." His expression turned stern, and he shook a finger. "But dinna tell anyone, and dinna laugh either, ye ken?"

"Never in a million years would I shame ye." She added to his embarrassment by kissing him on the forehead. "A drink of water would be nice, if ye dinna mind."

"As long as ye dinna kiss me again," he said, then rose and trotted away.

"He said ye were like a father to him," she mused while watching him go.

"I take that as high praise." With a gentle touch to her cheek, Teague frowned. "Ye worry me, love. Are ye certain 'tis just the day's events making ye ill?"

"Positive." He had no idea all that the day had done to her—especially his revelation about Lady MacDonald's time-traveling confessions. "Our challenges of making it to yer ship concern me as well. By then, the British will know and be looking for ye."

He pulled her closer and firmly, but gently, placed her head on his shoulder. "Hush now, my wee dove. All we can do is prepare as best we can, then face the challenge. For now, let us cherish this precious moment together rather than spoil it with thoughts of what might happen. We have *now*, ye ken? And for that, I am more than a little grateful."

Even though she felt a tiny bit chided, she had to admit he was right. "I am grateful too."

Robbie returned with water and an oatcake. "I promised Grissa I would make ye eat. I know she will ask when we get to Fort William." After she took it from him, he stood there, staring at her. "Well?"

"Well, what?"

"Are ye not going to eat it?" He widened his stance, squared his narrow shoulders, then flinched and caught hold of his arm immobilized with bandages.

"Serves ye right for yer stubborn sass." She waved him away. "Teague will make sure I eat it. All right?"

The lad's glare slid to Teague. "Will ye? Dugald is fixing a stew, but it willna be ready for a while. I dinna ken the last time she ate."

"Whatever she ate, I feel sure she lost it earlier." Teague gave a solemn nod. "I swear to see that she eats."

"Good enough." The lad turned and marched away.

"I dinna think I like him being so bossy." Although it did do her heart good to see him laughing and talking with the others.

"Eat yer oatcake."

She broke it in half. "Here. I saw how ye wolfed the others down. I canna keep down a whole one just yet."

He accepted it and touched it to hers. "To our next adventure, my precious dove."

"Aye," she said. "To our next adventure and success at the port."

He winked and leaned in close to whisper, "And to no more tansy oil or vinegar, aye?"

"Once we reach Nova Scotia. Remember?"

"Agreed," he said, then kissed the tip of her nose.

CHAPTER SEVENTEEN

TEAGUE HATED HIDING in the shadows while others risked their lives to ensure all the preparations were completed for the safe loading of the ship. But Calder insisted it was the only way until the *Vengeance* docked and everyone boarded. Mila and the others, overpowering his stubbornness with their own, had agreed with Calder and stood firm.

With a worn hat pulled low over his eyes and a tattered cloak in place of his fine black coat, he leaned back against the outer wall of the pub as though tossed outside for not being able to pay.

Robbie and Auley ran wild through the streets, blending in with the rest of the youth of the village that had sprung up around Fort William. But the two only acted as though caught up in local games. In actuality, they maintained a head count of the MacDonalds arriving. No one could be left behind.

Far too many British soldiers also roamed the streets. It made him both thankful and proud that Calder and Mila had instructed everyone to wear tartans so faded and worn that the patterns and colors could not be taken for those of Clan MacDonald. While their clothing made them appear to be wharf beggars, Teague recognized the faces of his kin. It warmed his heart to see so many had joined them on this adventure, but it also concerned him. Where would they winter in France? The *Vengeance* maintained a berth at the Port de Brest. Hopefully, that area's countryside could bear them until spring. Calder had mentioned their connection at the warehouses there might be willing to help if given the added incentive of a discount on his next shipment.

"You!" A British soldier shoved him. "Move along."

Clenching his teeth to hold in his temper, Teague grunted and shuffled away until the man disappeared into the pub. "Bastard," he growled under his breath. This feckin' cowering wore his nerves raw. At least the *Vengeance* inched closer to the docks at this very minute. The mighty galleon moved carefully through the crowded harbor toward its berth. That alone kept him from dragging that bloody Sassenach out into the street and breaking him in two.

Disguised with her hair pinned up inside a servant's cap and her cheeks smudged with dirt, Mila hurried to him from across the street with a washerwoman's basket balanced on her hip. "Just a little longer," she whispered while acting as though scolding him. She ducked her head to hide her smile. "I am proud ye chose not to knock that man on his arse. Well done, you!"

"I dinna like this."

"I know it is hard. But just a little longer, aye?" She turned and shielded her eyes, squinting at the ship in the distance. "Calder assured me everything the clan owns is in that warehouse ready to be loaded as soon she docks. Everyone has finally arrived. We will get ye aboard first. Ye can pose as a dockworker loading goods."

"I hope ye paid off the harbormaster." He snorted at the thought of the troublesome man who had caused him so much trouble in the past. "He is loyal to gold and silver only. Nothing else."

Her expression hardened. "That bloodsucking leech has been well paid. Calder saw to the transaction."

He couldn't resist a grin. "I see ye like the man as much as I do."

She turned and spat on the ground before stealing another glance around. "I have noticed more soldiers. Stay vigilant, aye? I feel certain they are looking for ye. Robbie said he spotted that Cranson man who came to our meeting with the lairds. I'd lay odds it was he who stole yer papers."

He grabbed her hand and rubbed it across his clean-shaven, yet filthy face. "He knows me as a bearded chieftain. This should help fool him, aye?"

With a squeal, she pretended to kick him as she yanked her hand away. "I miss the beard. Grow it back for me, aye?"

"I will, my precious dove." He swung his head toward the warehouse. "I shall start ambling that way. Are the others alerted and ready?"

"Aye. Be careful." She threw up a hand as though shooing him away. "Stagger a bit. Act like a drunk, aye?"

He listed to one side, kept his back bent, and shuffled toward the street. "I will be fine, love. Keep yer head down. Ye might be dressed as a lowly washerwoman, but ye are still a beauty."

"Off wi' ye, ye drunkard!" She cut an alarmed glance toward the door of the pub.

"I told you to move along!" The British soldier grabbed Teague by the nape and shoved him harder than before.

Everything in him wanted to spring to life and beat the insolence out of the fool, but for Mila's sake, and the sake of their future, he stumbled, rolled into the gutter, then lay there as though passed out.

"Disgusting," the soldier said, then turned back to Mila. He removed his hat and offered a polite nod. "My apologies, mistress. I can assure you that it will not happen again. Not on my watch."

Through eyes closed to cautious slits, Teague glared at the man's broad back, envisioning a dagger between those shoulder blades. "Get away from my wife," he growled under his breath.

Head bowed in submission, Mila backed away, bobbing a frightened curtsy with every step. "Thank ye, sir."

"Wait, mistress." The soldier moved toward her. "You need not fear me."

"I must get back to my washing, sir. Thank ye again." Mila's voice hit a frightened pitch that made Teague clench his fists tighter. But he forced himself to stay put.

"Let me help you," the Englishman offered. "I can carry your load with ease."

Teague moved to a tensed crouch. If the bastard touched Mila, it would be the last mistake he made in this sorry life.

Mila sidestepped the young soldier and stayed out of reach. "It would not be proper, sir. I must go now. My *husband* will be home soon looking for his supper."

The man immediately stepped back and offered an apologetic bow. "Forgive me, mistress. I had hoped you were unattached."

After bouncing another curtsy, Mila hefted the overloaded basket higher on her hip. "No harm done, sir. Good day to ye now."

Shoulders slumped in disappointment, the soldier turned away from Mila and scowled down at Teague. "Disgusting." He spat on him and strode away.

Mila popped back around the corner and rushed to Teague. "Thank ye, m'love. I know it was hard. Now hurry to the warehouse, aye?"

"I need to kill that bastard afore we leave." Bloodlust and jealousy pounded through him as he climbed out of the ditch.

"No. Please. I need ye safe and alive. That man is not worth the risk." She tugged him to shuffle faster across the street and led him into a narrow pass between two rows of buildings. "And besides, once I told him I had a husband, he backed away. I know he is the enemy, but at least he has some morals."

He came to a halt and faced her. "Ye are mine, my precious dove. Morals or not, any man who attempts to take what is mine will pay dearly."

Robbie stepped out of an adjoining alley. Auley accompanied him. "Calder sent us to fetch ye both to the warehouse," Robbie said. Auley agreed with a wide-eyed nod and a wave to hurry and follow.

Mila grabbed Teague's arm and squeezed. "We go straight to the warehouse and our new life, aye? Nowhere else. We dinna need to ask for trouble. I beg ye. Do this for me."

He cupped her face in his hand and forced a nod. "Only for ye, my precious one. I will step away and let the man be." The relief in her eyes and her smile helped cool his ire.

She set her basket aside, grabbed his hand, and tugged. "Let's hurry and get on that ship, aye?"

They rushed down the narrow alleyway, Robbie and Auley following close behind. Just as they reached the end of the passage between the buildings, Teague jerked to a hard stop and shoved Mila behind him.

Several soldiers loitered up ahead at the end of the walkway leading to the warehouse. Among them was Master James Cranson, casting a watchful eye all around as he talked with the redcoats.

"They know the *Vengeance* is my ship," Teague whispered while backing them all into the shadows. "The stolen records contained several of the older logbooks."

"And Cranson knows what we look like," Mila said. "There has to be another way to the warehouse. If we stick to the alleys, can we not go around them?"

"I would lay odds that Cranson has every route we might take watched." Teague leaned back against the wall. "Although none of us are the same as we were the night of that meeting."

"Except for Robbie and Auley." Mila reached down, scooped up handfuls of dirt, and rubbed it on the lads' faces. "It might help. They were both clean the last time Walpole's spy saw them. If he noticed them at all."

"We can slip past him easy," Robbie said. "All we have to do is act like we're going to fish off one of the docks and ignore them."

Auley took a small spool of twine out of his baggy pocket,

held it up, and smiled.

"Ye need sticks and bait," Teague said. "We have no time for that."

"I dinna think they will stop us," Robbie insisted. "All we have to do is pretend we are scavenging the docks or something. If we ignore them, they should pay us no mind." With a flip of his hand, he adopted a self-assured smirk. "We are nothing but midges to them. Mere lads. They are looking for MacDonald men."

Teague knew Mila feared for the young ones' lives, but they couldn't hide in the shadows forever. If Calder had sent the lads to fetch them, they needed to get to the warehouse now. "Go on wi' ye. We will stay here until we see ye safe and then figure a way to join ye." He offered Mila a reassuring smile. "We have to let them try."

"I know," she said, then pulled both the younglings into a fierce hug. She held them for a long moment, then stepped back, bowed her head, and waved them on. "Be careful."

Teague hugged her to his side as the lads scampered toward the docks as if they didn't have a care in the world. Laughing and jostling each other as boys often do, they swung past Cranson and the soldiers and, as Robbie said, totally ignored them.

Mila hitched in an alarmed breath as two of the British turned and eyed the lads. She exhaled with relief when they turned back and resumed their conversations, paying the young ones no mind.

"Now our turn." Teague held tight to her shoulders and locked eyes with her. "I will go first. If they stop me, I will tell them I'm a dockworker with one of the other warehouses. Once I am well past them, come across as if trying to catch up with the lads to make them do their chores. Call them whatever names ye like—except their own, ye ken?"

"Act like their angry mother." She cast a nervous glance at the soldiers and nodded. "I didna speak with that devil for long the night of our meeting. Surely he willna recognize me."

"I pray he does not." Teague tried to see her as if he had just met her. Even dressed as a grubby washerwoman, her beauty shone through. Even that soldier had been drawn to her. Hopefully, Cranson would be too obsessed with capturing him to realize who she was. He caught her up and kissed her, pouring all his hopes and fears into the embrace. "God be with us," he whispered, then kissed her again.

She pulled away and pressed the back of her hand to her mouth, her eyes glistening with tears. "Go now," she whispered. "Before I cry."

He hitched up his cloak around his neck, pulled his hat lower, and gimped across the street with his back bent. When he reached the group of men, he didn't spare them a glance, just ambled along at a steady pace, minding his own business.

"Sober already?"

Teague ignored the comment and kept walking while damning himself for not recognizing the young soldier from earlier. Trouble was, their uniforms, wigs, and hats made them all so similar that it was hard to tell them apart.

"You there!"

Teague didn't pause or turn until a hand grabbed his shoulder and spun him about. With one eye squinted shut, he cowered as though expecting a beating. "Aye, sir?" he rasped, keeping his gaze locked on the ground.

The young redcoat stepped closer and sniffed. "You reek of filth, but not ale or whisky. Perhaps I am mistaken. I have never seen so many drunks and beggars in my life. State your business here."

"Work in the warehouse, sir," Teague said with an apologetic bob of his head. Everything in him raged to beat these men senseless and fight for his freedom rather than cower. But he held fast and played the game. For Mila's sake. As he had promised.

"Which warehouse?" Cranson asked, circling him like a raven about to land on carrion.

Teague pointed out the warehouse at the end of the wharf,

the one next to the building housing the people of his clan and their possessions. "Mr. Fitch's there on the end. He promised me sixpence for every six rats I kill."

Cranson studied the place, then turned back and squinted at him for a long, heart-stopping moment. "A rat killer, ye say?"

"Aye."

The man stepped back and waved him on. "Good hunting to ye."

"Thank ye, sir." Teague bobbed another apologetic bow, then shuffled onward, hoping Mila hadn't fainted dead away. He daren't sneak a look at her. Not yet. Instead, he headed for the warehouse in case the men watched him. Once he reached the Fitch warehouse and stood with his hand on the door, he stole a covert glance at the soldiers. When they appeared to be looking the other way, he shot between the buildings and spied on them from around the corner. "Come to me, m'love," he whispered while crossing himself. "And may God keep ye safe."

After what felt like forever, he spotted a lone soul ambling toward the wharf's narrow boardwalk. But that couldn't possibly be Mila. This woman appeared to be quite aged. Thick in the middle with a slight hump between her shoulders, the elderly crone clutched her shawl tight under her chin. What he could see of her face that wasn't shadowed by the shawl up over her head revealed she might not be in the best of health. With skin as gray as ash, she appeared to be near death. Perhaps she was a relation that one of the clan had invited to come along. The way she looked, he doubted she would survive the journey to France.

He stretched and scanned the area behind her, trying to see into the shadows of the alley. It was too far. Where the hell was Mila?

The soldiers and Cranson ignored the old woman, not even offering her a polite tip of their heads. Rude bastards. The elderly deserved to be respected. As she shuffled along the boardwalk and neared the MacDonald warehouse, he noticed she occasionally clutched at her middle, grabbing at her clothes as if they irritated her. Then he detected a short trail of linen dangling down between her feet. When she shoved her hand down the front of her dress and yanked it back up, he slapped a hand across his mouth to keep from laughing out loud. His precious dove had chosen a different way to outwit the soldiers.

She wisely toddled along until she reached the Fitch warehouse as well, and even went so far as to open the door. Then she peeped around it, looked back at the soldiers, ran between the buildings, and joined him. With both hands clasped to her chest, she gasped as though out of breath. "I canna believe I made it."

He hugged her tight. "Well done, m'love. Well done, indeed."

"Into the warehouse now, aye?" She offered a quivering smile.

"Aye, dear one. We are nearly *home free*, as Master Robbie would say." He shared her feelings: hope, fear, excitement, and anxiousness. Never had so many emotions churned within him. But also never had so much been at stake.

They hurried into a side door of the warehouse, then halted. Teague stared all around, struck speechless. To the back of the cavernous building were the animals. As near as he could tell, only horses and the dogs that always roamed around the keep. No other livestock waited to board the ship. No fowl or any of the cattle the MacDonald clan had always protected so fiercely. There had been neither enough time nor space on the ship for everything the clan possessed. To the front of the warehouse, wagonloads of possessions stood ready to be loaded. And then there were his people. More than he had ever imagined would follow them in this.

"How many?" he asked, as Calder joined them.

"Forty families." Calder swelled with a deep intake of air, then shook his head. "The *Vengeance* will be bursting at the seams. But I didna have the heart to refuse any who wished to join us." With a somber expression, he tipped his head toward Mila. "She shared her visions of what is to come. Bethia told us Lady

MacDonald confirmed them. As we see it, this is the best way to see that our clan survives."

"God willing," Teague added.

"Aye," Calder agreed. "God willing."

"When I passed, the ship was almost docked," Mila said. "When can we start loading? I feel certain Master Cranson and his henchman will be watching our every move."

"Soon as they set the gangway, we start." Calder waved Bhric and Iagan over. "Get them organized to load. Goods and animals with a few people scattered among them. We dinna wish it to appear as though we are moving our entire clan."

Both men nodded and hurried away.

Mila took hold of his arm and tugged as she moved closer to Calder. "I want Teague on that ship first, ye ken? We need him safe."

With a gentle firmness, Teague removed her hand and shook his head. "Nay, m'love. I will board last, after I have seen everyone safe. It is my duty and I willna cede on this, understand?"

While she did not seem pleased, she gave an understanding nod. "Where are the boys? Robbie and Auley?"

Teague nodded toward the front of the warehouse. "Looks as though they are already helping gather the first load of goods." He threw off the ratty cloak and hat. "Time for me to join them. I am not a chieftain who watches while everyone else works."

Mila tossed her shawl in the corner and started pulling rags out of her dress. "As soon as I lose this extra weight, I will join ye."

Spirits lifting, Teague joined the lads and helped sort and lash items together. Nothing like a good, hearty chore to clear the mind. Dugald stood watch at the narrow door, waiting to open the wide double doors as soon as the crew gave the signal.

Notice finally came, and they walked the great doors open and tied them back. With the help of the *Vengeance*'s crew and every able-bodied MacDonald, possessions, animals, and families went aboard. At the point where he almost felt it safe to breathe easy, a flash of red warned him trouble had arrived.

Calder stepped in front of him, then backed him behind a stack of barrels just as Cranson and six British soldiers strode forward, bearing the new muskets Teague had heard so much about.

"I would see yer papers, sir," Master Cranson said to Calder.

"The inventories are yet to be finished," Calder said. "Ye canna verra well record everything loaded until it is loaded." He spat on the ground, barely missing the toe of Cranson's boot. "Besides, this is the *Vengeance*'s berth, and all has been properly filed and cleared through the harbormaster."

"In other words, ye paid the man off." Cranson craned his neck, squinting as he eyed the nearly empty warehouse.

Teague's heart nearly stopped as Mila stepped into view and took her place beside Calder. "Master Cranson, have ye not tormented my family and my people enough?"

Cranson gave her an evil smile. "Yer husband brought this sorrow on yerself and yer people. Not I." He lifted his chin as though daring her to punch it. "Where is he?"

She snorted a disgusted huff. "Halfway to London by now, unless those cutthroat guards of yers have already made me a widow." She jerked a cloth from her sleeve and pressed it to the corners of her eyes. "I know I will be soon, anyway." Her voice quivered. "I know my beloved husband willna receive any justice in England." She hitched out a soft, pitiful sob and buried her face in the crumpled square of linen. "For the love of God, leave us in peace. Can ye not see ye have already forced us from Scotland?"

The fiend shook his head and laughed. "I did no such thing. Ye couldha stayed in yer keep." He gave her a lewd up-and-down look. "I feel sure a woman such as yerself couldha had another to warm yer bed in no time at all."

Calder grabbed Cranson by the chest and shook him. "Ye will not speak to Lady MacDonald in such a fashion."

The soldiers lifted their muskets and shoved the bayonets into

Calder's face.

With another wicked chuckle, Cranson lifted his hand, and the redcoats stepped back. "My apologies," he said, not sounding apologetic at all. "And to show ye I offer no ill, once I search that ship and this warehouse, I shall leave ye in peace, aye?"

Mila responded with a teary-eyed sneer. "What the devil are ye searching for? Ye already stole my husband."

Cranson just smiled, then flipped a hand at the soldiers. "Find him."

Two of the soldiers trotted up the gangway to the ship while the others scattered into the warehouse and started scouring the shadows.

"Who?" Mila clutched her fists to her chest while backing up against the barrels that hid Teague.

He held his breath, praying Cranson would not see through her act.

The man swaggered forward with a suggestive leer. "Ye know who I am looking for." He reached out and cupped her chin in his hand. "However, I might be persuaded to look the other way." Without releasing her, he jerked his head toward a pile of hay at the back of the warehouse. "For yer people, aye? I feel sure they wouldna mind waiting while ye paid for their freedom with one last tumble."

"Get yer hands off my wife, ye bastard," bellowed a familiar voice from behind Cranson.

Ready to lunge around the barrels himself, Teague halted, unable to believe his ears. He peered through the slit between the stacks to make sure he had heard right.

And there he was: Dugald, dressed in Teague's favorite black coat with the wide cuffs, and his best cocked hat. He held the tip of his sword in the middle of Cranson's back.

"Kill him!" Cranson shouted.

Musket fire echoed through the nearly empty warehouse.

Dugald shoved the blade through the man, then held him upright and slit his throat with a dagger. But as Cranson sagged, so did Dugald. Blood stained the ground in an ever-widening puddle.

The soldiers rushed in from the ship, joining those in the warehouse as they surrounded them. Mila shoved through them and dropped to her knees at Dugald's side.

"No," she sobbed, shaking her head. "Ye canna die."

"To make amends," he rasped loud enough for Teague to hear. "Forgive me. Forgive us."

"Ye have always been forgiven." She cradled his head in her lap, tears streaming down her face.

"We must take him with us, ma'am," one of the soldiers said.

"Can ye not at least let the man die with those who love him?" she shouted. "Get the hell away from him. I will tell ye when ye may take him, ye heartless bastards. Now, get out!"

The redcoats eyed each other, then eased a few paces back.

"I said get the hell out of here! Get outside with ye," she screamed. "Grant me privacy to share our last words."

The men tipped their hats and nodded. The youngest of the four bowed. "We will wait at the end of the boardwalk, ma'am. But please understand, we must take his body with us to show the matter closed."

"Get out!" She threw a handful of dirt at them while still holding tight to Dugald.

The redcoats rushed away.

"They are gone, m'love," she called to Teague.

He charged around the barrels, dropped to his knees, and worked his arm under Dugald's shoulders to hold him. "Damn ye, Dugald. How can we conquer Nova Scotia without ye?"

Dugald managed a faint smile. "Forgive me, my chieftain. I had to pay for my brother's treachery."

"There is nothing to forgive, but go in peace and enjoy yer eternal rest, aye? I could not ask for a more loyal clansman. Ye will be sorely missed, old friend." Teague ached to roar out his sorrow but didn't. Not after the sacrifice Dugald had just given so that they all might live.

"I thank ye, my chieftain." Dugald went still, frozen in time with his eyes wide open.

Hand shaking, Teague closed the man's eyes and pressed his forehead to his. "To heaven with ye, my brother. May yer rest be sweet." He lowered him to the ground and bowed his head. A strong hand squeezed his shoulder.

"Hie to the ship, my brother," Calder said quietly. "Dinna let his sacrifice be in vain."

"Both of ye go," Mila said. "I must stay here and call out to the soldiers."

Teeth clenched with grief and fury at the unjustness of it all, Teague clapped his beggar's hat back on his head and shrugged the cloak around his shoulders. Calder walked with him up the gangway as though helping an aged man.

Once aboard, Teague stood at the railing, his gaze locked on the front of the warehouse.

Mila emerged and waved her kerchief in the air.

The soldiers waiting at the far end of the wharf hurried to meet her, then removed their hats. One of them offered her a polite bow. She shook her fist at the man, shouting something Teague could not hear. From the fury in her stance and the redness of her face, he could not imagine what she said. Then she turned away and stormed up the gangway.

The redcoats signaled for the man waiting with the two-wheeled wagon, then loaded Dugald's body and carted away one of the most loyal men Teague had ever known.

Mila took her place at his side and squeezed his arm. "I told them if they didna bury him on holy ground, his ghost would haunt them all their days and I would curse them to die alone with no sons or daughters to mourn them."

"Thank ye," he said, his gaze still locked on the cart in the distance.

"I pray he is at peace now. A good man such as him deserves it."

"I pray so too, m'love. He does indeed deserve peace."

CHAPTER EIGHTEEN

UNABLE TO KEEP from cringing, Mila washed Teague's wounded shoulder as gently as possible and applied a clean bandage. "It bled more. Ye are sure to have a terrible scar."

"Aye," he agreed quietly. "But at least I am alive and with those I love."

She carried the basin to the bucket near the door and dumped it. After setting it on the table in the center of Captain Bartholomew's cabin, she filled it with fresh water, stripped down to her shift, and scrubbed the filth from her face and arms. "It was kind of the captain to give up his quarters for us."

With a heavy sigh, Teague leaned back into the pillows lining the bunk and stared upward. He held out his hand. "I need to hold ye, my precious dove. Will ye come to me?"

She dropped the rag into the bowl and climbed up beside him. "Always," she promised quietly. She wished there was a way to ease his mourning for Dugald, chase away the pain, the unreasonable guilt. Her heart was heavy too, but she knew it didn't compare to Teague's sorrow. She nestled her head into the dip of his shoulder and hugged his chest. "He would want us to thrive, ye ken?"

"That he would, dear one." He rumbled against her with a

sad chuckle. "He always said he would never marry because he knew he wouldna live long enough to be a proper husband." He kissed the top of her head and held her closer. "Somehow, he knew."

For his sake, she needed to turn his thoughts to brighter days ahead. "How long for us to reach France?"

He hummed as though it helped him calculate. "This time of year? A few weeks, I would say. 'Tis not as though we sailed from England."

Something suddenly occurred to her. "Robbie will have to translate for me until I learn the language. I dinna speak a word of French."

He didn't respond, just inhaled a deep breath and blew it out.

"Calder seemed to think we wouldna have any trouble wintering there," she continued. "Something about yer smuggling person helping us. Although, at the time, I dinna think he realized there would be so many."

He idly tickled her arm. "It makes me proud that so many joined us."

She pushed up on her elbow, grabbed hold of his chin, and made him look her in the eyes. "They love their chieftain. As do I."

For the first time since they boarded, he smiled. "I love ye more than ye could ever imagine, my precious dove."

"Well, good. In that case, I will share the news I was saving."

"And what news is that?"

"Remember how I promised to stop using the tansy oil and vinegar once we reached Nova Scotia?"

He cocked a dark brow. "Aye."

"I willna have to wait until then to stop Vivyanne's remedy to avoid getting with a bairn."

A hint of joy sparkled in his dark eyes. "And why is that, my love?"

"Well…as it turns out, I apparently overestimated the effectiveness of both." She waited for his reaction. Apparently, pregnancy had contributed to her ease in vomiting after all. "As near as I can figure, our wee one will arrive at around the time we are ready to depart for Nova Scotia."

"Merely days ago ye assured me ye were not with child." He reminded her of a bairn trying not to explode with excitement on Christmas morn. "But ye are certain now?"

She wrinkled her nose, trying not to sound as foolish as she felt. "It appears Grissa keeps better track of my courses than I do. When we rejoined her here and I informed her I still had no need of her arsenal of womanly supplies, she proclaimed me a mother-to-be. After a bit more thought and backward counting of days, I realized she was right."

He rumbled with a happy chuckle, rolled to his side, and pulled her into his arms. "A new land, a new home, and a fine new bairn."

"Our cup runneth over." She smiled up at him, then combed her fingers deep into his dark hair and pulled him down for a kiss. "I love ye," she whispered against his mouth. "Forever and a day."

"Not nearly long enough, m'love. Not nearly long enough at all compared to my love for ye."

EPILOGUE

Nova Scotia
September 1724

"DINNA PEEK. ROBBIE and I worked verra hard on this surprise." Barely able to contain his excitement, Teague led Mila across the large center room of their home among the evergreens of Nova Scotia.

"Ye added more shelves to the back wall of the pantry?"

Inwardly, he flinched. She, Mrs. Cain, and Greta had been nattering on about the need for more shelving since last summer. He guided her around the wooden toys scattered in front of the largest stone hearth he and the stonemasons had ever built. "No shelves, but I promise ye will like it."

"I am watching ye, Mi," Robbie said. "Dinna be cheating."

"Marella—what are Da and Robbie up to?"

Teague shook his head and mouthed *no-no* to his sixteen-month-old daughter perched on his precious dove's hip.

The lively bairn bounced, stretched for him to take her, then angrily clapped when he didn't respond fast enough to suit her. "Da! Da!"

"Ye better take her." Mila stopped and waited for him to take the child, but obediently kept her eyes squinted shut. "I know what it is! Ye routed the new drains on the back of the house to the inner well house tank Robbie invented. Now, we willna have to worry about the water freezing as long as we keep the firepits going."

"No."

"Ye dinna have to be short about it." A frown puckered her brow. "Can I open my eyes now? 'Tis baking day, and I promised Greta I would help."

"I didna mean to sound short. Marella is yanking my—beard." He untangled his daughter's chubby fingers from his whiskers, then tickled her neck with squeaky kisses before handing her over to Robbie. "Torture yer brother for a while, ye wee beastie."

The tot crowed with glee, grabbed the lad's hat off his head, and threw it on the floor. "Robbeeee," she said while pointing at the hat.

"I hate this game." Robbie held her upside down so she could grab hold of the hat, then righted her so she could throw it on the floor again.

"Give me the wee one," Grissa said as she rushed in from a side hallway. The massively sprawling home housed most of the MacDonalds who had survived the crossing from France to Nova Scotia. Eventually, they would all have dwellings of their own, but getting in supplies and building the structures with available materials took time. In a sense, this place was Éirich Castle's replacement, but constructed of wood and not stone. "Keep yer eyes shut, mistress. 'Tis worth it," she called out as she disappeared down another hallway with Marella on her hip.

Robbie waved his hand in front of Mila's face. "What do ye see?"

"Nothing." She wrinkled her nose. "But ye need to wash yer hands. Ye've been digging wild onions again, haven't ye?"

Teague grinned as Robbie rolled his eyes. He tugged her along then stopped at the crude flight of wooden stairs still under construction. He pondered the barrier, not wishing her to fall. "Ye can open yer eyes until I tell ye to close them again, aye?"

She opened them, looked around to see where she was, then fixed him with an impatient glare. "I must help with the bread making."

"The bread making is taken care of." Still holding her hand, he led her up the steps to the next floor. At their bedchamber doorway, he stood behind her and covered her eyes with his hand. "Are ye ready?" He kissed the tender spot behind her ear, finding the opportunity too tempting to resist.

"Keep kissing me like that and I shall be more than ready," she warned him.

"I am still here," Robbie announced with a groan.

Teague laughed as he reached around her and opened the door. "Ye can look now, my precious dove."

It took her a moment to spot it, but when she did, she squealed. "Ye got one! How?" She ran past their bed to the impressively large copper bathtub on a newly constructed platform next to the hearth. As she ran her hand along the gleaming, rolled edge of the tub, the delight in her face thrilled him. "The cost must have been dear. How did ye get it here and installed without my knowing?"

Robbie beamed with a proud smile and pointed at the window not too far from the tub. "I rigged a stronger pulley system than the one we used for the furniture. Not only did it bring up the bathtub and supplies with ease, but ye can also use it for bringing up the water instead of climbing the stairs. Grissa loves it, and half the bairns want a ride in the buckets." He joined her at the shining new fixture and drew her attention to the other end. "And look here. See this ceramic piping? Captain Bartholomew found it for us in Italy. When ye finish bathing, all ye have to do is open the drain, and the water sluices out through this pipe and empties into a wooden barrel outside so it doesna get all muddy." He pointed at the wall where the pipe exited. "I punched wee holes in the barrel so the water would gradually seep into the ground." He made a face. "Probably freeze come winter, but I'm still working that part out."

"Ye are a genius, my dear lad." She hugged him, then turned back to the gleaming copper tub. "It is so perfect," she whispered while dipping her hand in the steaming water. "I have missed hot baths so verra much."

Teague clapped a hand on Robbie's shoulder and whispered, "Well done. Now out wi' ye and tell everyone I dinna wish to be disturbed unless it is Christ's second coming, ye ken?"

Robbie expressed his distaste by wrinkling his nose, then hurried from the room and closed the door behind him.

"I know ye wished to help with the baking, but I had a word with Greta. She understands and gives her blessing." Teague sauntered closer, untying his neckcloth and unbuttoning his waistcoat as he walked.

"Oh, did ye now?" She rose to her feet and started unlacing her jacket. "I had no idea about any of this." She tossed her stomacher and jacket onto a nearby chair, untied her outer skirt, and stepped out of it. "How on earth…?"

"Mrs. Gillicutty helped," he confessed. "Why do ye think she kept ye at her bedside all these days for something as simple as a turned ankle?"

"And how someone told me we couldna sleep in our own room until the craftsman repaired a leak in the eaves? I canna believe I fell for that poorly contrived story." She slipped off her shoes and stockings.

Fully rid of his clothes, he pulled her into his arms. As he untied the neckline of her shift, he nibbled across her collarbone while pushing the garment off her shoulders and down into a pile at her feet. "Oft times we believe what we wish to believe."

She hummed her agreement while lacing her fingers in his hair and guiding his mouth lower. "Aye, m'love. And when we believe in the best of things, they tend to become real."

He swept her up into his arms, stepped into the tub, and lowered them both into the deliciously warm water. "I love ye, my own," he said with a husky softness as she straddled him.

She stretched forward and brushed teasing kisses across his mouth. "I love ye more than I ever believed I could love anyone."

He slid his hands down her back and cupped her bottom in his hands. "Through this life and the next, aye?"

"Aye, m'love," she whispered. "And all the lives thereafter."

About the Author

If you enjoyed SAVING HER HIGHLAND TRAITOR, please consider leaving a review on the site where you purchased your copy, or a reader site such as Goodreads, or BookBub.

If you'd like to receive my newsletter, here's the link to sign up:
maevegreyson.com/contact.html#newsletter

I love to hear from readers! Drop me a line at
maevegreyson@gmail.com

Or visit me on Facebook:
facebook.com/AuthorMaeveGreyson

Join my Facebook Group – Maeve's Corner:
facebook.com/groups/MaevesCorner

I'm also on Instagram:
maevegreyson

My website:
https://maevegreyson.com

Feel free to ask questions or leave some Reader Buzz on
bingebooks.com/author/maeve-greyson

Goodreads:
goodreads.com/maevegreyson

Follow me on these sites to get notifications about new releases, sales, and special deals:

Amazon:
amazon.com/Maeve-Greyson/e/B004PE9T9U

BookBub:
bookbub.com/authors/maeve-greyson

Many thanks and may your life always be filled with good books!
Maeve

9 781958 098974

Lightning Source UK Ltd.
Milton Keynes UK
UKHW020642040123
414815UK00012B/505